LORD ARES

Lords of the Masquerade
Book Three

Jade Lee

ARE YOU SIGNED UP FOR DRAGONBLADE'S BLOG?

You'll get the latest news and information on exclusive giveaways, exclusive excerpts, coming releases, sales, free books, cover reveals and more.

Check out our complete list of authors, too!

No spam, no junk. That's a promise!

Sign Up Here

www.dragonbladepublishing.com

Dearest Reader;

Thank you for your support of a small press. At Dragonblade Publishing, we strive to bring you the highest quality Historical Romance from some of the best authors in the business. Without your support, there is no 'us', so we sincerely hope you adore these stories and find some new favorite authors along the way.

Happy Reading!

CEO, Dragonblade Publishing

Additional Dragonblade books by Author Jade Lee

Lords of the Masquerade Series
Lord Lucifer (Book 1)
Lord Satyr (Book 2)
Lord Ares (Book 3)
Lord Scot (Book 4)
Lady Scot (Book 5)
Almost a Scot (Book 6)

The Lyon's Den Series
Into the Lyon's Den
Lyon Hearted

CHAPTER ONE

ONE YEAR AGO

ONE WOULD THINK that a man in a Roman Centurion's helmet and an armored skirt would look ridiculous. Lilah Rees studied the gentleman very closely and determined that that conclusion would be both right and wrong.

The man had the physique to play Lord Ares at tonight's masquerade. Broad shoulders, thick arms, and a barrel chest beneath the breastplate armor. He held a spear that he routinely banged upon the ground as he issued some commandment much to the amusement of the audience.

But though he looked handsome in his costumed attire, he did not have the demeanor of a true showman. He did not prance, and he certainly didn't entertain for long. He merely stood to the side of the dance area and seemed uncomfortable in a helmet that pinched his temples. Or so Lilah assumed given the way he kept frowning and adjusting the headgear.

And yet she found him handsome, alluring, and completely out of her reach. Though he was playing the role of Lord Ares at tonight's masquerade, he was in fact her brother-in-law's friend Aaron, Lord Chambers. A future earl, a wealthy man, and the picture of robust, perhaps even lusty health.

Lilah watched him from afar and imagined him as her hero in a fairytale story that filled her romantic heart to overflowing.

Then she tucked away her romantic heart and focused on the practical. She was a by-blow—a bastard—and Lord Chambers was as far above her as Ares was above mere mortals.

She needed to get started on her plan to catch a husband. Tonight was a rare opportunity for her to meet such a man. She attended a masquerade that allowed a by-blow like her to mix freely with the *haut ton*. She had dressed with care, applied her cosmetics to perfection, and had even practiced flirting to the best of her limited ability. She could only hope it served because bastards didn't get many opportunities to snare a husband.

First step: dancing. Since this was a masquerade, the usual dance cards were ignored. The dance floor was more of an unformed free-for-all where partners matched willy-nilly and one could snare a donkey or a fairy prince. With a quick wave to her family, she headed into the exuberant mix of costumed partygoers.

She charmed a man in a dark domino who was sadly much too young for her. She spun about the room with a belching baron who was already married and on the hunt for a mistress. She promenaded with a dandy who spent the time criticizing the stitching and fabric of her green fairy costume. And the whole time, she wondered if this were the full range of gentlemen for her. If so, she was in for a lonely, single life.

She also couldn't help her attention from wandering to Lord Ares where his bright helmet and thick staff towered over the guests. Indeed, her imagination made him ten feet tall as he inspected every newcomer and pronounced them worthy of attending his revels.

She turned a sigh of longing into a pretend whisper of delight. Her current partner was another man too young for her tastes, but perhaps she could mold him into an appropriate husband. His conversation was stilted, and he had an unfortunate tendency to blush, but he might grow into some confidence. He would never be a Lord Ares, but it was unfair to compare him to their host. And beggars couldn't be choosers, but surely there had to be someone better out here than a stuttering youth.

There wasn't. At least none that she could find, even with her sister Diana's help. The eligible suitors guessed her identity as a bastard and stayed away. The ones ignorant of her parentage were on the hunt for a mistress or a faster tumble as a night's entertainment.

She was an excellent catch, damn it. She could organize a household, discipline unruly servants, and even manage pets. She would cherish her husband and educate her children. But that was the painful curse of being a bastard raised as a gentlewoman. She was by definition *improper*.

Nevertheless, she smiled and persisted.

Until she couldn't take it anymore and headed alone to the buffet. But once there, a female performer caught her eye. The woman stood in the shadows of a tree, well beyond the dance floor at the edge of the green where acrobats, knife throwers, and the like performed. She appeared to be scanning the crowd for someone, and Lilah was drawn to her merely out of curiosity. Or perhaps nostalgia because her mother's acting troupe had performers such as these.

Or perhaps it was memory, since a closer inspection revealed one of her oldest friends as the woman threw up her arms in relief upon spying Lilah.

Was it really her friend? It wasn't possible. And yet Lilah moved quickly around and past the buffet, ducked behind the dancing arena, then headed into the shadows between the elite and the performers.

"Margarite, is that you?" Lilah asked.

The young girl of her memory was now older, slimmer, and considerably more muscular than the nine-year-old she remembered. It was only the particular curve of her cheek and a mole set above her right eyebrow that gave away her true identity. And the fact that she'd always loved bright pink tutus, which is what she wore.

"Me?" Margarite gasped. "Is it you?" She stepped back and

looked Lilah up and down. "Cor, but you're all grown up and dressing fancy."

Lilah didn't say that this gown was a cast-off from her half-sister Diana. Or that she had altered it herself. She merely smiled and gestured to her childhood companion. "What are you doing here? You're dressed like—"

"A rope dancer?" She cocked her head back toward the juggler's area and sure enough, there was a rope strung between two trees. "I started dancing 'ere a couple weeks ago. It's good pay if'n I can keep the men off."

Lilah nodded, reminded once again that as difficult as her life was—caught between respectability and not—she still had a full belly and a safe place to sleep. Margarite didn't, and it was only a quirk of fate that had taken Lilah's life on a path different from Margarite's. "Who is protecting you tonight? Are you safe?"

Her friend dimpled. "I got a couple friends watching me back. But I've been looking for you. Figured it'd be at a nob party like tonight."

"You've been looking for me?"

"You ain't never come by since the day you left." There was accusation in her voice and Lilah flushed.

"I wasn't allowed," she said.

"I guessed as much. But you an' me, we were the best, right?"

They'd been inseparable. Two girls of nearly the same age raised in an acting troupe. They'd played dolls together, learned their letters together thanks to Lilah's mother, and even slept in the same bed. Until Lilah's father had taken her away to a better life.

"I've missed you every day," she said.

"Margarite!" a man's voice called. Both women turned to see a large man in juggler's dress looking all around him.

"Who's that?"

"It's Jamis. He's in charge of the troupe now since his dad died."

"Jamis?" She remembered him as an older boy with a penchant for knives.

Margarite nodded. "He's the reason I wanted to talk to you."

"Jamis? Why?"

"Yer mother got a letter. Twice now."

"My mother?"

"And I told Jamis that the letter rightly belongs to you, but he just rips 'em up. Says yer mom is dead and you are too, seeing as how you forgot us."

"I never forgot—"

"It doesn't matter. He gets mean and rips 'em up."

"Margarite!" Jamis' voice cut through their hurried conversation.

"I gotta go back," Margarite said. Then she winked. "Come watch me act. It's a good one!"

"Of course, I will."

Margarite rushed away, first by running, then by doing flips as she made it to the rope strung between two trees. Lilah followed, merging into the audience as she watched her friend leap upon the rope and perform an amazing dance to music played by a man on his violin. She might have known the man years ago. She certainly remembered Jamis, who was working the crowd for coins. But mostly she watched, and she wondered at how different her life was now from theirs.

She didn't think long about the letters. Jamis had destroyed them, and she'd long since given up thinking about what she couldn't change. She simply enjoyed the show while her mind wandered through memories of her childhood with Margarite.

She lingered too long. Her family was likely looking for her, and it was inappropriate for her to be standing alone even at a *ton* party. Especially at a *ton* party where unwed girls were normally watched by their mothers. But she was feeling at loose ends tonight, a woman caught between the actress life she'd been born into and the semi-respectable one with her father's family. So she stood alone and watched. And when the show was over, she remained there thinking like a bewildered idiot.

She should have been more careful. She certainly knew better, but she was lost in her thoughts and had forgotten how easily drunk men could corner a woman. Especially a lone woman in a pleasure garden.

"Lookee here, I found a pretty bird."

"Not a bird. A fairy!"

"Dance with me, pretty fairy!"

Three men, all dandies by the look of them. Not dangerous, at least not yet, but certainly in a mood to play with her.

"Excuse me, I must get back to my mother," she said loudly. Her gaze darted to where Margarite and her protectors had been. But they'd already moved on to a new spot on the lawn as Jamis threw knives at Margarite where she stood against a tree. No help there and none from the crowd that was looking at the entertainment.

"Don't fly away," one of the dandies coaxed. "Dance with me."

She smiled warmly at him. "Of course, I will. The set is forming over there." She tried to duck past him, but his friend caught her wing and then her arm to hold her fast. "Let me go. Please!"

"We want a dance!" he said, then he swung her around while one of the others started humming a waltz.

She stumbled as he pulled her around. She twisted in his arms, but his hands were hard where they held her in place. And even as she squirmed, she could see no help beyond the three men. Panic started to beat hard and fast in her throat. What an idiot she'd been! She tried to twist free again and nearly succeeded, but the next man grabbed her.

"Let me go! I'm Lady Byrn's daughter." If ever she needed a title to protect her, it was now. But it didn't work.

"Did you hear? She's a Lady Bird!"

"No, please!"

"Damnation!" a loud voice cut through. It was deep and booming, and it did absolutely nothing to distract anyone. Nothing, that is, until one of the men was abruptly hauled back.

And then a moment later, the second one went sprawling. Lilah didn't fully register it. She was busy trying to fight the one who held her. But that quickly ended as a large hand grabbed the back of the man's neck and squeezed until he yelped. Finally, she wrested herself free, scrambling backwards while her gaze shot to her rescuer.

Lord Ares.

He looked like a gladiator from old, from the tip of his plumed helmet through to his broad shoulders, and the spear butt he used to trip up the two men trying to regain their feet.

"Are you idiots?" he demanded in a harsh voice. "There are willing women throughout London. Find one of them!"

"It were just a bit of fun," the nearest said.

"And what if her mother had seen? You would have to marry her. Is that what you want?"

"What?"

"Wot?"

"Wat?"

Apparently willingness made no difference to them. Marriage, however, did. Lord Ares harrumphed in true disgust.

"Get out. All three of you. And you can be sure I will remember your names from now on."

He stood there, his legs spread with his spear planted firmly in the ground. And when the two on the ground were slow to get up, he clapped them with the butt of it.

They protested, each one of them, but he would hear none of it. And soon the three drunks were rushing toward the exit. Which left her there shaking while Lord Ares turned to look at her.

"Are you all right?" he asked, his tone gentle.

She stared at him, her tongue unaccountably tied. She managed to nod, though, and soon she was able to straighten her clothing. Nothing serious. One wing was ripped, and the shoulder of her gown had been pulled askew. It was quickly righted, as was her mask which had somehow tilted across her eye. Her hands shook, her heart beat painfully fast, but she was able to set herself to order. If only she could find her tongue.

"Thank you," she finally managed. When the words came out breathless, she said it again more firmly. "Thank you, my lord. I shouldn't have wandered away, but I was watching the rope dancer."

"It's my fault for allowing those blighters to be invited. They're idiots, all three of them, but they'll be in the House of Commons soon and I thought they'd take advantage of this opportunity to learn a few things."

"At a masquerade party?"

He arched a brow at her. "I invited every one of the members of Parliament. It's always good to have some social time one and all. Gives a chance for more casual discussions." He shrugged. "But you can lead an idiot to water—"

"But you can't make him discuss politics?"

He smiled. "The country is in a deplorable state when a debutante understands the situation better than the men supposedly running it."

"I make no claims to understanding it. Merely that calling something a party and hoping that young men won't drink is an odd sort of logic." Not to mention that she had never been and never would be a debutante. That was reserved for the legitimate daughters of the *ton*.

"I'm ever hopeful that people will rise to the occasion," he said as he extended his arm. "I am sorry that you became the victim of my optimism. Are you feeling better?"

"I am," she said, as she set her fingers to his forearm. This close, she could see he wore linen beneath his breastplate, but the sleeves had been torn away such that his arms were bare. Nothing was between her hand and the warmth of his skin, the wiry touch of his hair, and the pulse of the thick muscles there. It was just a man's arm, but the feel of it made her cheeks warm with delight.

"Shall I return you to your family?"

He should. It was the proper thing to do. But by an unexpected quirk of fate, the most interesting man at the masquerade was by her side. She'd be a fool to let this opportunity slide without trying to make the most of it. "I'd prefer a walk around the garden," she said. "If you are agreeable?"

He arched his brows. "I see now how you came to be by yourself. Are you prone to wandering?"

"I suppose I am, but I prefer doing it with company." She was being bold, but how else was she to talk with the man?

"Then shall we see what mischief is brewing beyond the knife thrower? I believe there is an equestrian display."

"I should like that above all things."

They set off, but herein she faced her usual problem. She had no idea what to say to entice a gentleman in the space of five minutes. Commenting on the displays seemed mundane, asking about his horses or dogs ended up with boring discussions of animal breeds, and no other topics popped into her head. Fortunately, he saved her in that regard only to land her into another quandary.

"Are you enjoying the evening?"

To lie or not to lie? She opted for the truth. "Not so far, though I am hopeful for the rest of the night."

"Has the entertainment been so poor?" There was shock in his tone.

"I'm sure the entertainment has been exceptional for most people, my lord, but I am a lady on the hunt for a husband. All events no matter how grand are judged upon that measure alone."

"Ah," he said as he dipped his chin. "None worthy of your hand?"

"None looking for a hand."

He nodded. "A masquerade is not the usual place for such things. You'd have better luck at Almack's."

She might if she were allowed in, but a by-blow would never cross that august threshold. "Could it be that you don't know who I am?"

"It's a masquerade. I'm not supposed to know." His gaze lingered on her face, clearly trying to imagine what lay beneath her mask.

He really didn't know her, and that sent a thrill of delight down her spine. He was an eligible bachelor, and he wasn't dismissing her out of hand merely because of the conditions of her birth. "I shall not enlighten you until the unmasking."

"Perhaps I should try to guess."

"Perhaps we should discuss by what measure you judge this party."

"Me?" he said with a chuckle. "I'm afraid I'm not hunting for a wife."

"A pity."

"I was hunting for votes for my resolution."

"Were you successful?"

"Not in the least. The gentleman who needed persuading refused to listen. I'm afraid I lack the necessary oratory skills."

She doubted that. "Perhaps the fault lies in the nature of the resolution. What is it exactly?"

"I want the country to spend money on our veterans. Too many are damaged in mind and in body from the war. We barely patch them up and then send them off to live as best they can, and it's not a good life. Not a good one at all." He frowned as his gaze grew distant. "These are England's sons, and we ignore their suffering as if their service meant nothing."

"I am persuaded," she said. "Your oratory skills lack for nothing."

He flashed her a genuine smile. "If only my compatriots were so easy, but I'm afraid finding the money for the things I plan is not easy. The country is tired of taxes for the war. Now that it's over, they don't want to keep spending."

"What persuaded you?"

"Have you not seen the beggars, the thieves, and the damaged souls throughout London?" He squeezed her hand where she held his forearm. "Forgive me, of course you haven't. You're a gently reared lady."

"On the contrary, I've seen them, but so have your compatriots. What has brought this so forcefully to your attention?"

He didn't look like he would answer. His face tightened and he looked unhappy, but in the end he spoke. Though his tone was casual, she knew from his earlier expression that it was nothing of the sort for him.

"Several tenants from my family seat had a son go to war. One had two sons enlist. These are boys I played with as a child, now grown into men. They returned broken and bitter, if they came back at all. I grew up with them and now…" He shook his head. "They are shells of the men I remember. They need help, and they will not take it from me."

"If they will not take it from you, then why do you think they will take it from the government?"

His shoulder hitched. "Because they *need* it. Because their families might starve without it. Because if everyone receives it as their due for fighting, then it is not charity. It is their just deserts."

She did not disagree, but she also knew that such a resolution would be expensive. He must have read the thought from her expression because he sighed.

"I am tilting at windmills."

"You have friends you wish to help. That is not wrong."

"I know the cost to the families on my estate. How many more are there that I don't know?"

"Thousands, I imagine."

He turned to her and she saw the passion on his face. He wanted to heal friends and country alike, and she admired it.

"Don't you have a childhood friend who has been hurt by the war?" he asked. "Someone lost, someone broken?"

"And some stronger for their time at war."

He nodded, admitting her point. Meanwhile Lilah thought not of the men, but the women left behind. Margarite's father, for example, was a soldier who died on the battlefield. While Lilah had been able to play upon her father's tender emotions and become adopted into his home, Margarite had no father to turn to.

"I spent my childhood in London," she said. "I have a friend—a woman now—who I would dearly like to help."

"Does she have food?"

She nodded. "She has a trade." An unusual one to be sure, but rope dancing likely paid her bills for now. "But she is a woman without a powerful family to protect her. She is vulnerable to so many ills."

"And what would you do to help her?" he asked.

She sighed. "I am an unmarried woman. I saved my pin money for months to buy walking boots that fit my feet and were not cast offs from my relations. What can I do to help her?"

He patted her hand where it rested on his arm. "I am sure you are a great comfort to her."

How little he understood. Until tonight she hadn't seen Margarite since leaving the theater at the age of nine. "An unwed woman is powerless." In truth, a married one was powerless as well, except through her husband.

"Do you seek power?"

She shook her head. "Only a good husband." And legitimate children. No child of hers would ever suffer the label she carried.

"I am sure you will find one soon." His voice was non-committal, his expression polite. It told her without words that she had not ensnared him even though his gaze continued to linger on her face. She interested him, but not enough, and now she had run out of time. They arrived at the equestrian display. The opportunity for private talk was dwindling, especially as a few of the guests noticed him and headed their way.

She had to do something to enchant him, but what? She had no idea what conversation he liked and, truth be told, she was still rattled by her experience with the drunken dandies. Her thoughts were slow and not turned toward romance. Her only hope was with a cold recitation of her facts. For all that he was an idealist, surely he'd appreciate someone who could handle the practicalities.

"My lord, before your friends join us, I have something to say."

He arched his brows as he turned his full attention onto her. It wasn't until that moment that she realized the full force of his attention. As much power as was in his body was there in his gaze a hundredfold. Dark eyes, furrowed brow, and a complete focus on her. It was enough to make her freeze for a second in surprise.

"Is something wrong?" he asked.

She swallowed and forced herself to give her best. "My lord," she said, trying not to rush her words. "I am a faithful woman. I have run a household since I was ten. I can manage a staff, organize a ball, and watch the funds to prevent overspending. I would be an asset to any man who would have me."

His brows rose in surprise. "I'm sure you would," he began, but she kept speaking rather than hear his denial.

"I don't need pretty phrases or expensive gifts. I need a man who will stand by me. You can be that man, my lord. I would be a faithful wife and an asset to your home."

"Well," he said with a gentleness that gave her reason to hope. "That's putting it on the line."

It was and she lifted her chin hoping that he was a man of logic.

"I don't even know your name," he said.

"Lilah."

"A pretty name for a beautiful woman." The way he said the words told her that he wasn't interested in her proposal. And—if logic were the only consideration—he would need to know that she was a bastard before marrying her. A wedding would make her instantly legitimate, but it would damage his reputation.

"I don't need flattery," she began, but it was too late.

They were interrupted by newcomers who bellowed, "Lord Ares! By Jove you do look like a God!"

His head shot up and a banal smile crossed his features before he spoke. "I certainly do compared to your sad offering."

The gentleman and his lady were both dressed in a simple domino and a mask that they each carried in their hands rather than on their faces. The pair laughed at the greeting, and the conversation continued. The gentleman turned to evaluate the horseflesh that was part of the equine show. The lady gasped at the rider's antics on the animal's back. It was all very civilized while Lilah stood by and wanted to tear their hearts out for interrupting.

But in the end, it didn't matter. She knew the truth even if he hadn't had a chance to speak it. Lord Ares would not be her husband. She had failed to attract even the slightest bit of interest from him.

And then he did something unexpected.

CHAPTER TWO

O F ALL THE extraordinary things! Never had he met a female who approached the business of marriage so logically. Certainly, the daughters of the most elite knew that marriage was a business transaction, but even they wanted the trappings of courtship and romance. Obviously, this woman was not from the *haut ton*. If this green fairy of a woman were of those exalted ranks, her father and her brother would be here defending the asset that was her hand in marriage.

Clearly, she had none of those. First off, he would know her if she did. And second, she would not have been allowed to wander alone during a masquerade. Vauxhall had too many dark corners, too many chances for something to go amiss, like the attack of those drunken dandies.

Who was she? And why did she have to go to such extraordinary measures to find a husband? He combed his memory for a woman named Lilah and found none.

The equestrian demonstration went on as the onlookers cheered. Their little group had grown to seven, and the mysterious Green Fairy as he called her was now chatting with a young Mr. Hallstead. A decent option for a lady without protectors. He was a second son with an acceptable inheritance, assuming his dabbling with gambling didn't become an obsession. But the more the lady charmed the gentleman, the more Aaron disliked the liaison. Mr. Hallstead had no ambition, which was a disastrous failing in a man without a title.

As the demonstration ended, Aaron moved through the crowd to return to the lady's side. He ducked past Lord Dankworth, who wanted to talk about the Corn Laws again, and arrived just as Mr. Hallstead asked her if she wanted to dance. There was one set left before the fireworks and the midnight unmasking. If he allowed her to say yes to Mr. Hallstead, he'd never find out her true identity. She'd be lost amid the hubbub of the evening's finale.

So he did something entirely unusual to his nature. He lied.

"I'm so sorry, but I'm afraid the Green Fairy has promised the next set to me."

She looked up at him, surprise on her face. She really was extraordinarily pretty with the moonlight highlighting the perfection of her skin. Then she recovered enough for her cheeks to pink.

"You give me hope, my lord. I feared you'd forgotten me."

"Never that," he returned, though inside his heart sank. She was a mystery, to be sure, wrapped in a beautiful package. But he was the son of an earl. Just because she intrigued him didn't mean he would marry her. And yet that was clearly her hope, and he was a cad for encouraging her misperception.

And yet he could not stop himself. She intrigued him.

He extended his arm to her, and she took it with a light touch and a beautiful smile. Then they began to walk. It would take a bit to reach the pavilion, and they would likely be stopped several times as they went. Everyone would see him with this lady, and her hopes for marriage would soar.

It happened just as he feared. With the equestrian display over, their group swelled to a dozen souls all meandering back to the central pavilion. Several people wandered close to speak with him, and many gave her a curious look. As far as he could tell, all of them wondered at her identity.

She was charming with everyone, smooth as she guided them to discuss their interests without giving away anything of herself.

It was impressive. She was adept at being charming without giving offense. He had to find out her secret. There had to be some reason she was not yet wed, and he was determined to discover it.

He managed to have a private moment just before they arrived at the pavilion. He used the time to lean in and whisper into her ear.

"You must tell me," he said.

"What?"

"The secret. The reason you are not yet wed."

She stiffened at his words and he knew he was on the right track.

"I'll find it out soon enough by asking Sayres. I assume he's the one who invited you. He knows all the best women." Lord Sayres was one of the three hosts of the masquerade and one of his closest friends. Indeed, he was rather dismayed that the man hadn't told him about her beforehand.

"It's not a secret..." she began, but then her voice trailed away as she turned her gaze to the dancers. "Do you really wish to dance with me?"

There was such yearning in her voice that he was startled. "I have said so, haven't I?"

"Mr. Hallstead said you never dance. Not ever."

"That's not true. It's just that I'm a large man and a crowded dance floor does not make for easy movement. I'm constantly afraid I'll bash some young debutante, and that would be disastrous for everyone."

She nodded. "I understand. We can just watch."

Such a wealth of experience in those words. It was as though she was used to being denied. Was she someone who usually stood on the outside watching while others enjoyed their lives? Not this time, he decided. He would dance with her and use the time to discover her secret. Then he would take his departure without encouraging her matrimonial hopes.

"Maestro," he called the moment the music ended, "a waltz if you please."

The conductor heard him and nodded. Aaron set his hand to his Green Fairy's waist and swept her onto the floor.

"There are some dances," he said to her startled expression, "that are made for me." Then he smiled. "Relax. I love waltzing."

If she had a response, there wasn't time for her to say it. The first strains of the music began, and he began guiding her into the steps. She wasn't a tiny woman, which he appreciated. Her body had muscles and strength beneath the soft fabric of her dress, and better yet, she adjusted quickly to his guidance.

The waltz was an adequate dance with a timid partner. One could move about the floor at a moderate pace with some modicum of enjoyment. His green fairy, however, relaxed into his hold. She let him guide her while still matching his pace. Very soon she was arching into his hold, letting him take some of her upper body weight while he whirled her about the room. Her eyes sparkled up at him and her lips spread with obvious delight.

She would look like that during lovemaking, he thought, and his body tightened at the sight. It made him move her faster about the room and draw her closer to his body. A proper chaperone would be scandalized by their intimacy, but he couldn't stop himself. She was all but flying in his arms, and he felt like a God himself in the way he spun them through the music. His cock swelled, his attention was captivated, and his heart thrummed with hunger for the woman in his arms.

How primal it all felt. He could imagine tossing her over his shoulder as he carried her back to his cave home. He felt an internal drumbeat of desire that continued even after the music stopped. A pulse of hunger as he slowed their steps while keeping his gaze locked with hers.

"I have never felt so safe in my life," she whispered.

"You dance divinely," he said.

"It was thrilling."

It had been for him too. "Shall we find a good spot to view the fireworks?"

So much for taking his leave immediately following their dance. His offer was spoken before he'd thought about it. He shouldn't stay in her presence any longer. It would give her unfortunate ideas. Plus, he was a host of this party and should have a care that all was going as it ought. But for the first time in many long years, he cared not a whit about his responsibilities. She felt divine in his arms and he had no wish to release her. Not yet. Not until she gave up his secret to him.

The crowd was moving into viewing position. As a large man and the host, he could have easily made their way to the front. He had no such interest. Instead, he tucked her into the shadows near the back. The tree limbs blocked some of their view, but the privacy it afforded was worth it to him.

"You must tell me what the problem is," he said as they slipped into the shadows. "Is there insanity in your family? Are you impoverished?" Her clothing was of excellent quality, so it could not be that. "Are you descended from Jacobites?" She had red in her hair and the fair complexion of a Scotswoman.

"None of that," she said. "At least I don't think so."

A woman who didn't know her family's history? He felt his shoulders drop. "An orphan," he said. That made sense. She was likely someone's poor relation brought here in a desperate hope to find a husband.

"Yes," she said, and her eyes clouded. "But it's worse than that."

He shook his head. He didn't need to know more. "Is Sayres helping you? Is he the one who got you into the masquerade?"

She smiled up at him, but her expression was wistful. "How can you not know me?"

The first firework went off with a bang. He didn't look away from her, but she jumped at the sound. And then her eyes widened as she looked to the sky. Her mouth dropped open in surprise and she craned her neck to see better.

"Have you never seen fireworks before?"

"Never," she whispered, her eyes on the sky.

Now he regretted not taking her into the center of the viewing area. He pulled her forward, out from beneath the branches, and soon the colors were lighting up her face. In truth, as gorgeous as the displays were, they were even more beautiful reflected in her eyes. He saw her delight with every explosion as if magic were appearing right above their heads. Never had he seen someone look so purely delighted before, and the sight was one he knew he'd remember for the rest of his life.

She stood breathless throughout the display, and he was equally mesmerized by her delight. And when the fireworks were done, the unmasking began. So while she clapped her appreciation of the show, he touched her cheek. Her gaze immediately shot to his, all wide eyes and rosy cheeked happiness.

"It's time to take this off," he said, his voice husky. He meant her mask, but his lust thought he meant other things, other forms of disrobing.

She nodded silently as his hands slipped to the tie behind her head. Then he pulled on the laces as slowly as if he were unwrapping the most precious of presents. She remained still in the circle of his arms as he worked, and when he at last pulled the mask free, he saw blue-green eyes in a strong face. He saw the same tempting lips he'd seen before, but now they beckoned him. He didn't know her any better now without her mask than he had five minutes before, and yet she seemed exposed to him. Revealed in all her tempting beauty.

"Lilah," he whispered.

"Yes."

The word settled into his blood and burned there. The heat it caused had him tightening his arms. One hand cupped her head while the other rolled down her spine to draw her closer to him. And then there in full view of the *ton*, he dipped his head and kissed her.

Her mouth tasted like spice that set his body aflame. Heedless of the risk, he plunged into her and played with her fire. Their tongues dueled, their bodies pressed close, and he reveled in the passion that roared between them.

She was the one who stopped the kiss. Her hands were tight on his shoulders and she pushed back to breathe. He was panting as well, his mind dazed. At that moment, if they'd been alone, he would have taken her to bed without thought to the consequence. So wonderful was the blaze between them.

But they were in the middle of a party with half the *ton* around them. He couldn't bed a woman here, and he couldn't damn well be kissing one either!

He ran a hand over his face and tried to calm the riot in his blood. She was flushed a bright red as she stepped back as well. But she didn't go far. Indeed her hand slid to his wrist and gripped him there.

"Could you consider it, my lord?" she asked, her words breathless.

"What?"

"Marrying a bastard."

He didn't answer. The words didn't make sense through the fog of his lust. But then she explained.

"I'm Lilah Rees, my lord. Lady Byrn's adopted daughter."

His eyes widened as the reality set in. Now it all made sense. She was a by-blow raised as if she were legitimate. Of course, she would have all the skills of a gently reared young lady. Of course, she would know how to run a household and be an asset to a family despite the circumstances of her birth. After all, she'd been doing it since she was a child.

"Lilah Rees," he echoed. "I should have known."

She didn't answer, but there was such desperate hope in her eyes that he ached to reassure her.

"I'm a future earl," he said. "You know my marriage is a transaction of money and power. My mother spends most of her time picking out potential brides for me."

She nodded, and her gaze slid away. "I understand," she whispered, and again those two words shot pain through his heart.

"There's only one thing that would induce me to ignore such customs and overrule the dictates of generations of earls."

Her head shot up as she looked into his eyes. "What?"

"Love, Miss Rees. I would do it for love."

Her mouth opened in surprise, and no wonder. It sounded odd to himself that he had such a romantic streak.

"Our kiss," she said as she pressed her fingers to her lips. "It was special, wasn't it?"

"It was," he admitted. "But that's not love, Miss Rees. I'm sorry," he said as he stepped back from her. "It's not love."

"Yet," she stressed as she took a step forward. "It's not love *yet*."

He answered with a shrug. For all that she intrigued him, it was a large step from lust to love. Then their moment was lost. Friends found him and started speaking. The masquerade was over, but the business of leaving would take a while. He meant to keep watch over her. For all that he was mobbed by his guests, he meant to return her to her people. The Rees family must be here somewhere. But when he finally got a chance to look back for her, the shadows were empty.

She was gone.

CHAPTER THREE

ONE YEAR LATER

L ILAH STEPPED OFF the boat and headed into the Vauxhall pleasure garden. What a difference a year had made. Her half-sister Gwen had married her true love just this morning. A year ago, Gwen had been a reclusive bluestocking. Now she was the toast of the *ton* thanks to her new husband Lord Sayres. Beside her, Diana, their other half-sister was bursting with joy and, Lilah thought, was perhaps in an interesting condition thanks to her loving husband Lucas. The only pair missing were Elliott and Amber, who had attended the wedding, of course, but were now at home caring for their healthy newborn son.

Family bliss all around. Lilah was happy for them all—downright jubilant—except for that tiny part of her that wanted to be married, too. She craved a bright future with a man who adored her. It wasn't fair that she'd been doomed before she was even born, but that was the curse of being a bastard. It did no good to dwell on it.

She put on her typical smile and walked with her family into the Vauxhall masquerade. This year she'd made a different costume for herself, one more appropriate to her mood. Instead of the hopeful green fairy of last year, she wore a simple domino and the mask of an owl. She'd put a great deal of time and care into making herself appear like a wizened owl perched on a tree as she watched the world go by.

"I wish you'd picked something more colorful," said Diana as they entered the gardens. "Something to make you stand out more for all the men to see."

"Bright colors would make no difference. Every man worth considering knows who I am already and has made his opinion clear."

That was the sad truth of the last year. Thanks to Gwen's popularity, Lilah had made the round of *ton* parties—at least those that would bend enough to allow a by-blow into their midst. She had danced and flirted. She'd been as charming as she knew how, and several gentlemen had been interested in her as a less-than-legal paramour, but none had offered marriage despite her admittedly modest dowry.

"There's a new crop of gentlemen every year," Diana said. "You mustn't lose hope."

"I haven't," she said. "I've simply become realistic. I will not find a husband among the respectable *ton*. I have no idea why Papa insisted that I try."

That was the mystery of her childhood. Her father had decreed that she be raised as a blueblood. That she be educated as one, taught the manners of one, and find a husband among them. He'd even told her that her actress mother had been titled as well, but she'd never seen any proof of it. Still, he spoke of it as if having two aristocratic parents overcame the fact that she'd been born out of wedlock.

It didn't. And since her father had died years ago, she could content herself with a different path. "I intend to seek employment," she said.

"What?" Diana gasped. "Why?"

"How else am I to make my way in the world? I will not find a life among the *ton*. That much is clear. I could travel to the colonies where my parentage would not be so black a mark—"

"All the way there? But we'd never see you."

"And I'd miss you dreadfully." She would.

"You can't—"

"Do you know anyone in America? Someone who might sponsor me there?"

Diana shook her head. "I thought you and Mama rubbed along very well. That you were happy."

What Diana meant was that everyone assumed she would become the spinster aunt caring for Mama. That she would be content with such a future if no husband presented himself. But such a lackluster future held no appeal. She wanted a family of her own. And if she could not find one among the elite, then she would look among the less-than-elite. And the best way to do that was to work among them as one of their own.

"I can be an excellent housekeeper or a companion."

"But you are more than that!"

Was she? The upper crust looked down upon her and the lower orders didn't dare speak to her. And with her sisters now blissfully wed, she felt lonelier than ever. "It is time for a change," she said.

Diana squeezed her hand. "Not yet. Be merry tonight. You never know what will happen. Gwen told me you kissed someone last year at this very masquerade."

"That was nothing," she lied as she looked away. In truth, it had been everything to her.

Lord Chambers had never led her on, but her hopes had soared nonetheless. Several times that night he had made her the focus of his undivided attention and their waltz had lived nightly in her dreams. As for their kiss, nothing in her life compared to that experience. It was beyond anything she'd ever imagined.

And best—or worst—of all, he had given her hope at the end that he might overlook her parentage if he loved her. She'd immediately begun planning ways for them to meet, to spend time together, to dance and kiss again, but he'd disappeared from the *ton* the very next day. He'd gone home to his suddenly ill father and hadn't returned to the social whirl again. And though she'd waited, praying he'd return, she soon learned that his mother had fallen ill as well. Then two months ago, his father finally passed, and Lord Chambers—now Lord Kittrel—was steeped in mourning. His mother had recovered, thank God, but she was still sickly and he had remained at his family seat with her.

Lilah heard when he returned to Town for political affairs. He had to release his seat in the House of Commons and was soon set to take his place in the House of Lords. And though he never attended any society party, he was certainly the center of a great deal of gossip. An eligible Earl was the hope of every unwed lady. When he finally returned to society, he would have his choice of the cream of society.

Which meant her chance with him was gone. She could not compete with all those fresh faced, legitimate debutantes. Lilah bundled up all those sweet memories and tucked them away…again. Just as she had every one of the thousands of times before when he'd entered her thoughts.

Fortunately, they'd arrived at their box and were settling in. The dancing would soon begin now that her two brothers-in-law were here to open the festivities. While Lilah watched from the sidelines, Lord Lucifer and Lord Satyr welcomed one and all to the masquerade then led their wives onto the dance floor.

The revelry started soon afterwards. Lilah was escorted to the dance floor several times, but her heart wasn't in it. She knew these men and knew what they wanted. It wasn't her as a wife. She danced because it was polite, but eventually she slipped away into the shadows. Perhaps she could find Margarite again.

Unfortunately, the jugglers were performing, not the rope dancers, and she couldn't find her former friend anywhere. What she did notice was a woman dressed all in black trying—very badly—to be inconspicuous. She was leaning in tight to the shrubbery as if listening to someone on the other side of the path. And every so often she would scurry down and lean in again.

It was extraordinarily odd, and Lilah couldn't resist stepping closer to watch. To the side, several other people noticed her, but then moved on. She wasn't particularly interesting as a figure in black trying to sink into the shrubbery. But Lilah had nothing else to occupy her thoughts, and so she followed the woman as she moved further along the path.

Lilah was about to get bored when the lady's cloak caught on a branch. Right when the woman rushed forward, the cloak abruptly hauled her backwards. Then when she twisted to untangle herself, another branch caught her hair. Before long, she was hopelessly enmeshed, and Lilah moved in to help.

The first thing she heard were curse words. Colorful ones that she hadn't heard since she was a child. And since every one was spoken in the cultured accent of an aristocrat, the sounds made her smile.

"Slow down. Let me help," she said.

The lady jolted at the sound of Lilah's voice as she shrunk back into her domino. "No, no," she said in a false high tone. "I'm fine."

"You are definitely not fine unless you mean to rip out half your hair and tear your domino at the same time. Stay still. I'll have you free in a moment."

She could tell that the woman in black didn't want to oblige, but another minute of struggle proved the futility of her efforts. Every time she twisted, she ensnared something else.

"Oh damnation!" she finally huffed.

"Stay still," Lilah said as she began the work of disentangling the lady.

To her surprise the woman did. She stilled as if listening intently to something. Lilah had no idea what it was. She could hear the orchestra clearly as well as a cheer from the audience around the jugglers. Then as Lilah broke the last offending branch, she heard the woman moan.

"And now I've lost him. I'll never find him again in this crush."

Crush? This was the emptiest Vauxhall had ever been. It was the one day of the year where the entire park was reserved for the elite party hosted by the Lords of the Masquerade. But rather than comment, she decided to help.

"Whom were you looking for?" Lilah asked. "Perhaps we can find him together."

"Lord Loughton," the lady said with a moan. "He was with his friends on the other side of this hedge."

"And you wish to speak with him?"

The woman actively shuddered. "Heavens no."

Well, that wasn't what she expected to hear. "You were following him though."

"He's up to something nefarious. I'm sure of it and I need to find out what."

"Nefarious? Are you sure you mean Lord Loughton?" The Scottish lord had come to London in the middle of last Season. He was accounted as genial, established of a modest fortune, and a jolly good fellow among his friends. There had been nothing even hinting at nefariousness.

"Well, I hope he's up to something nefarious. He means to marry me and if I don't do something drastic soon, then I shall be shipped off to Scotland never to be heard from again."

"Scotland is said to be quite beautiful."

The lady lifted her chin and scowled fiercely. "I don't care if it's heaven on Earth. My life is in London. My friends are in London. My books are in London. I will not be forcibly wed and sent off somewhere that is not London!"

"Well, I can certainly understand that." Lilah frowned as she looked about her, searching for a nearby servant. "So you are looking for the truth about Lord Loughton?"

"Yes. I want to know what he says to his friends."

"About you?"

"About anything! Everything. I have the cleverest idea to dissuade him from me, but I can't accomplish it without more information."

That certainly piqued Lilah's curiosity. "There is a better way to do this, you know, than skulking about in the shrubbery."

"I cannot imagine what."

"Bribe one of the servants to remain close and report everything Lord Loughton says to you. Pay him only for whatever information you need."

"That's true," the lady said with a nod. "Servants hear everything. But won't whomever I hire lie and tell me what I want to hear?"

"Perhaps. But you can make it clear you won't pay for lies."

The lady looked unconvinced at first, but in the end, she gave a sad nod. "It's better than what I've been doing. I hadn't realized how terribly difficult it is to overhear things. Very well, will you help me find a servant to bribe?"

That didn't take long at all. The staff at Vauxhall were used to handling a much larger crowd, and so discovering an idle one interested in making a little extra money was simple. Telling them who to report to was a little harder. There were several women in all black dominoes.

"We can return to my box," Lilah offered. "After wandering around a bit." She'd already determined that this woman was the most interesting person here. She smiled at the servant. "We'll be in Lord Byrn's box."

"Oh my! You're a guest of Lord Byrn."

Lilah smiled, not wanting to lose their budding friendship by revealing that she was Elliott's bastard sister. Fortunately, the lady rambled on heedless of Lilah's silence.

"My brother is usually a host as well. He plays Lord Ares, but he couldn't come this year. I wouldn't have either except I needed to learn something scandalous about Lord Loughton."

Lilah felt her mouth go dry. "You're Lord Chamber—er, Lord Kittrel's sister? Lady Clara?"

The woman shrugged. "I'm not supposed to tell you, am I? It's a masquerade after all, but I suppose I've given it up anyway."

So many thoughts, so many questions crowded into Lilah's mind. She wanted to know about Aaron, how he was faring, what he was doing. She wanted to imagine him going about his day even though she knew she was simply torturing herself as she did it. But those questions were impertinent, and she had just as many questions about his odd sister, so she started with those.

"I am pleased to make your acquaintance, Lady Clara. And my condolences on the loss of your father."

"Thank you," she said, her tone wistful. "I miss him terribly. He was bookish like me, and we got along well. But it has been harder on my brother, of course. Quite a lot to do to take the reins of the earldom."

"I imagine so," she said, though she had no earthly idea what it entailed. "And how is he faring? Will we see him back in London soon?"

"Oh, he'll be back soon enough to see me bound for the altar." She sniffed in true horror at the one future that Lilah so longed for.

"Surely he can't force you if you don't want to marry."

"Mama has convinced him that it's past time for both of us to wed. He's told me that Lord Loughton applied to Papa and seems like a very amiable fellow. Pah!" She rolled her eyes. "He makes it sound like I'd be marrying a dog." She lifted her chin. "That is specifically why I returned to London now to learn the truth about the man. I shall scare him away, and he won't bother me again."

"How?"

"I have a most ingenious plan," she said smugly and refused to explain.

Lilah didn't press. She had the feeling that the lady enjoyed talking and would soon give details. It only took fifteen minutes of wandering through the maze for her to finally spill the secret. They had been talking about Lady Clara's love of the occult when she finally whispered her plan.

"I am going to host a séance."

"A what?"

"I'm going to contact the ghost of his dead ancestor and tell him that I'm the wrong person to marry."

Lilah stared at her, her mind whited out in confusion. "I'm

terribly sorry. What?"

"It's all a ruse, you see," Lady Clara said. "I've gone to several fake séances. I know all the tricks. They make the table shake with their knees. They speak in a scary voice. It's terribly frightening to those who don't know how it's done. I had nightmares for a week after my first one."

"I would imagine so. Whyever would you go back?"

"I love to be frightened. I went back as soon as I could. But after a time, I began to see how it was done."

"So your plan is to…what?"

"Frighten him. I'll invite him to the house for an evening's séance, tell him something about himself that I've learned tonight. That's very important to establish belief. And then I'll have his great-grandmother or someone tell him I'm not the lady for him and he'll go away."

"That seems like a lot of effort to say no."

The lady's eyes sparkled. "But I've already told him no, and he keeps coming back. Besides, I think this will be fun." Then her eyes widened. "Would you like to come?"

"What? Me?"

"Of course, you. I've figured out who you are, you see. You're Lord Byrn's by-blow sister, aren't you?" She said it as if it were the greatest thing to be labeled a bastard. "You're scandalous enough to come to something like this."

"What?"

The lady stopped short before exiting the maze. "You're not offended, are you? Everyone's too proper to enjoy the same things I do. I thought perhaps that you'd enjoy a bit of fun and you wouldn't have to worry too much about your reputation."

Well, that was putting a different spin on being a bastard. One that she'd never thought of before. "I'm not offended. I just never thought being disreputable was a good thing."

"Goodness, but there's a great deal of fun to be had in losing one's reputation. No one bothers you and you can do what you want."

"Except when Scottish lords insist on plaguing you."

"That is true," Lady Clara said with a kind of moan. Fortunately, the woman didn't seem to stay in the doldrums for long. She was soon smiling and chattering as if they were the best of friends. And that was a novelty for Lilah.

This stranger didn't see her parentage as a deficit. It was like taking a breath of fresh air after leaving the fish market. Her spirits lightened immediately. She was going to do everything in her power to become fast friends with Lady Clara.

"Tell me exactly what your plans are for the séance. Do you really think you can pull off the charade? Enough to make it believable?"

The lady pursed her lips. "I don't think I could be as good as some of the people I've seen. But it can't be that hard, can it? To moan about in a convincing manner?"

"I think it would be. Try it right now. Imagine yourself acting before Lord Loughton."

"Right here? Out loud?"

They were in a shadowed part of the park past the jugglers. There weren't too many people around who would be disturbed, but still, Lilah could see the doubt on the lady's face. Which was exactly the point.

"Try it—"

"I can't."

"Then pretend in your mind."

Lady Clara frowned and closed her eyes. As expected, it didn't last long. Very quickly, her lips were quivering, and her face had heated up to a frightful blush. Then she abruptly blew out her breath and looked balefully at Lilah.

"You're right. I can't do it."

Then Lilah chanced to see the rope being pulled taut between two trees. Very soon, Margarite would come out to perform.

"No matter," Lilah said. "I have an idea." She leaned forward. "But it will cost money."

Lady Clara waved a hand in the air. "Money is not a problem." She grinned. "Tell me what you have in mind."

Chapter Four

HOME.

Aaron toyed with the word in his mind as he rode the last few miles through London to make it to his residence there. It had been Aaron's home for over a decade while the country estate had been his parents' place. But now it was all his. He was the new earl. He'd thought both places would become his home, but it felt the exact opposite. Nowhere seemed to fit and he felt adrift. Everything in his old life was gone, and he had yet to refashion it into anything familiar.

Thankfully, after a year away, he was returning to London where he could create the rest of his life to his liking. It began with being officially recognized as the Earl of Kittrel. After a massive party that he dreaded, he would begin in the House of Lords and continue the business of running the country.

He carefully avoided thinking about all those things his mother had emphasized. That he needed to set up his nursery. That he needed to see his sister set up hers. According to his mother, everyone needed to be wedded and bedded in the swiftest possible manner because that was the way of the peerage.

Those were problems for tomorrow. Tonight was for brandy in a quiet house, then bed. Which made it all the more irksome that no one answered the door when he banged on it. He was coming in from the back, having settled his horse in the mews himself. It was early evening yet, much too soon for everyone to be abed. He was grumbling when he pulled out his key and opened the back kitchen door on his own. He was the earl, damn it. He employed a butler and a household staff. Why the hell was he opening…

His nose twitched the moment he entered the empty kitchen. There was a strange smell to the house like old Christmas dinners set burning on the stove. There was sweetness in the scent, but also a distinctly unpleasant smell as well. And then he heard a low moan.

Alarmed, he dropped his bag and rushed into the house. He headed straight up the stairs only to be stopped short by the laundress and a kitchen maid who were huddled together there peering out through a crack in the door.

"What's amiss?" he demanded. "Who is hurt?"

Both women squeaked in alarm as they spun around. Their fright was real, and he had to steady them both lest they tumble down the stairs.

"Milord!" the nearest one gasped. Her name was Sally and she trembled where she stood leaning hard against the wall.

"You near scared the life out of me, my lord," said the laundry woman, Mrs. Owens. What was she doing here?

"Who is hurt?" he repeated after making sure that both ladies looked hale.

"Wot?" Sally said.

"Nothing's amiss," said Mrs. Owens.

But then he heard it again. A low moan coming from beyond the doorway. "Who's that?" He meant to push forward, but the women stepped clearly into his path.

"That's nothing but a bit of playacting from Lady Clara," Mrs. Owens said. Then she tapped his arm. "How about I make you a nice pot of tea to welcome you home? You can have a rest down here until she's done."

Aaron felt his gut sink down to his toes. His sister was an eccentric woman, to be sure, but she normally kept her exploits to evenings with her friends from the lending library and the occasional odd visitor. Whatever this was marked a stark increase in his sister's oddity.

"Step aside, ladies," he said firmly. And when they did not comply, he bodily lifted Mrs. Owens up and set her down below him on the stairs. The younger Sally was agile enough to scramble out of the way as he pushed through the doorway. But two steps onto the main floor had him frowning in confusion.

"You were me favorite wee bairn. A bonny boy you were."

It was a strange woman's voice spoken in a brogue that came and went as if to suggest a Scottish origin but still make the words clear.

"Nana?" a man's voice said. "Is that you?" Now that voice he recognized…but he couldn't remember from where.

"Well o'course it's me, ye bonny lad. I've come with a message fer you."

"But how do I know it's really you?" The man sounded breathless or on the edge of a laughing fit. It was hard to tell.

"I'll bump the table to show I'm real."

Now *that* sounded more Cockney than Scottish. Truly confused, Aaron stepped around the corner to look into the dining room. The room was filled with cheap candles that smoked, placed haphazardly about the room and table. Sitting in place were seven souls. He recognized his sister and her maid, placed as though they were guests. Another woman with her back to him, plus a footman, were also seated like guests. At the head of the table was a woman dressed in colorful robes, her face and hair obscured by a hood. Before her smoked a brazier that was no doubt the source of the strange fruity-foul scent that permeated the room. And at the base of the table was a gentleman by the looks of him. The one who'd spoken before, but whom he couldn't quite remember.

"Ohhhhhhahhhhheeee."

A weird moan came from hooded woman. It was a loud sound punctuated by a groaning gasp—very theatrical and wholly ridiculous. Though when the table abruptly jumped, he was startled enough to take a step backwards. Not because he was frightened, but because he wanted to see who was under the table making such a ruckus with his furniture.

He couldn't see. The room was too dark. Besides he was distracted by the way his sister squeaked in alarm. Her and another lady.

"Never fear, Lady Clara," said the gentleman at the base of the table. "I shall protect you."

It would have sounded most gallant if there hadn't been an undercurrent of humor in the words. Meanwhile, a person approached him from the side. He saw the man coming and recognized his butler.

"If you would come away, my lord," the man whispered. "I can explain."

He didn't need the explanation. He knew his sister too well. This was one of her spiritual gatherings that had nothing to do with religion but a great deal to do with tomfoolery. Though he had no idea how she roped in his own staff to participate. There was only one thing he wanted to know, and so he leaned over to whisper in his butler's ear.

"Who is the gentleman at the end of the table?"

"Lord Loughton."

His sister's suitor! Of course. But before he could say more, the man in question started speaking.

"That tells me you're real, spirit from beyond, but not that you're my Nana."

"I am," the hooded woman said in a definite London accent. "I be your granny, the mother of yer da Seamus."

Now the woman was turning Irish, and Aaron started to smile. It was like watching a bad play in his own home.

"I held yer bonny body in me own arms when you were born."

"But how can I know it's you?" Lord Loughton pressed. "Tell me something only you would know."

"You were a lusty boy as a child. Strong legs and a way with the lasses. I remember how you kissed them lassies, full on the mouth before ye—"

"Oh my!" interrupted the woman who had his back to him. "I don't think we need to hear that."

Aaron straightened of the wall, his heart thumping hard in his chest. He knew that voice. It sounded like Lilah Rees, but it couldn't possibly be true. There was no reason for her to be in his dining room. And yet he couldn't shake the feeling that it was really her. Unfortunately, she spoke no more as Lord Loughton cut in.

"Tell me something else, Nana."

"Ye were in the Vauxhall Gardens last week. I saw ye from the heavens and heard your plans, you naughty boy."

Really? Now that was sounding more interesting. Apparently, Lord Loughton thought the same.

"What plans, Nana?"

"Aieeee! Oooooh!"

The woman let out a bloodcurdling scream that was echoed by the women in the room. He was sure the table rattled again too, though it was hard to tell as even the footman gasped out, "Blimey!"

"Nana," Lord Loughton asked. "What's the matter?"

"It's wrong, bonny boy! She's all wrong for you! You canna marry her!"

"Who? Who mustn't I marry?"

There was definitely a tremor of laughter beneath the questions, but the hooded woman went on as if everyone was terrified.

"Lady Clara is no' fer you! Doom! Toil! Blood! Boil!"

Was she trying to quote Macbeth?

"Me?" cried his sister in what was clearly a staged voice. "He can't marry me?"

"No! It will be the end of everything if he does! Aaiiiieeeee! Oooooooo!" The woman continued wailing as she thrashed in her seat. The table jumped and bounced until Aaron feared for the floor. But it wasn't until a knife sailed through the air to land with a heavy thunk on his table that Aaron had enough. Lord Loughton, too, as it landed right in front of him.

The man leaped back with a gasp and no wonder. Someone could have lost a hand! A cleaver was now embedded several inches deep into the table.

"That is enough!" Aaron shouted as he stepped into the room.

The reaction was instantaneous. His sister leaped to her feet with a gasp as did the maid and footman. The other lady—the one he didn't want to face yet—pressed her hands to her mouth in a squeak of alarm.

He went past them to the far windows which he hauled open. He wanted that horrible smoke out of the room. Unfortunately, the hooded lady was trying to hold on to her performance. She was still moaning and thrashing in her seat.

"Ye can't marry! No' her!" she cried.

"I shouldn't think he'd want to," Aaron snapped as he grabbed the brazier and tossed the contents out the window. *Bloody hell, that was hot.* Thankfully, he'd used his handkerchief to shield his fingers, but even so, he dropped the thing back on the table as soon as possible.

"Binner!" he snapped at his butler. "Bring in some good candles. And who in the hell thought it would be a good idea to throw knives in my dining room?"

"You mustn't blame them," his sister cried. "It was the spirit of his lordship's grandmother who did that."

"Oh yes," Lord Loughton said with a chuckle. "My Nana was most adamant on that, I can see." He touched the shaft of the cleaver and pulled it out of the table with a quick yank. "It's most like her to throw cleavers, too," he said.

"Really?" Clara said with a pleased gasp.

"Oh quite. She was always throwing them at people's head. Carried a satchel of them with her everywhere she went."

And when everyone just stared at him, he burst out laughing.

"Good lord, you will believe any nonsense at all, won't you?

As long as it's about a Scot." Then he crossed over and clasped Clara's hands. "Thank you, my lady, for the most entertaining evening I've had all year. This has been truly delightful."

"Delightful?" Clara echoed, obviously confused. "But the ghost of your Nana just told you we can't marry."

"Yes, well, she was always a terribly busybody in life. I didn't listen to her then, so I can't see as how I'd listen to her now."

"But…but…we can't! You've had a message from beyond the grave!"

He lifted her listless hands up to his mouth and pressed kisses onto her hands. "Come riding with me in Hyde Park tomorrow morning."

"What? No!"

"We can walk in the afternoon at the fashionable hour."

Clara actually shuddered. Aaron knew his sister hated the fashionable hour. "I cannot do that."

"Then dance with me at a ball. What do you attend? I shall gain an invitation even if it is at the palace itself."

"The palace?" She sounded even more repulsed than she had at the mention of Hyde Park. "I do not dance, my lord."

The man tweaked her chin in a fond gesture. "I'll bet my castle that you do."

"You'd lose!" Clara said, obviously not guessing that the man meant a decidedly more carnal type of dance. And that was Aaron's cue to put a stop to things.

"I think this evening is done, Lord Loughton. Perhaps you could try again with an afternoon visit."

"Yes," the man said as he smiled at Aaron. "You may be right." Then he bowed to the room in general. "A capital evening, one and all. A capital evening." Then as he grabbed his cloak from the butler, he glanced back at Aaron. "Sorry about your table, though. That's a bloody big gash in it."

"Yes," Aaron said mournfully. "So I surmised." Then he waved his hand and the man departed. Would that the rest of the people in the room could disappear so easily. All but one in particular…

CHAPTER FIVE

I N THE YEAR plus a week since she'd last seen Lord Chambers, Lilah had imagined all sorts of ways that they might meet again. Never in her wildest imagination did she think he'd walk into their fake séance. But there he was, storming into the room and throwing open the window enough to let out that cloying smoke. If only she could take a deep breath of fresh air, but her chest was tight as she looked at his towering form.

Despite her embarrassment, she drank in the sight of him. She'd wondered if his Lord Ares costume had made him look more handsome. Who could resist muscular arms as they gripped a spear? Tonight, she realized that his shoulders were just as broad as she remembered, and now they were encased in riding clothes that emphasized his narrow waist. His neckcloth was askew, and his hair was disordered enough to make her want to smooth it down with her fingers. But what she saw most was the way he looked around the room with the air of one too tired to make sense of his surroundings.

Fair enough, she thought as she looked at Margarite in her hooded cloak. Jamis was coming out from behind the door to pick up his cleaver. And Lady Clara's servants were scrambling to curtsy and bow their way out of the room. If only she could flee as well, but she wouldn't abandon Clara who was twisting her fingers together as she looked everywhere but at her brother.

"Thank you for your work, Margarite, Jamis," said Lilah. Best get them out of here, too.

Margarite threw her hood back and grinned. "Cor, it were ever so much fun."

But Jamis, ever suspicious, thrust out his chin. "We were promised two shillings each."

Lord Kittrel's head shot up. "Four shillings!"

It was an exorbitant amount, but she'd made the mistake of letting Lady Clara handle the financial negotiation. Meanwhile, the lady was fumbling in her pocket for the money. She pulled out the coins, but Lilah intervened, taking them from her hand before handing them over.

Jamis held out his hand while the other made a fist. "I'll take that," he growled.

"And you've already received half," Lilah said firmly as she tossed Margarite a single shilling. Her friend grabbed it out of the air with a grin. Lilah held back Jamis' share with a hard stare. "I expect all of my mother's mail to be sent to me immediately from now on. I'll even pay for the missives. But if I ever hear that you burned them again—"

"I don't know wot yer talking about!" Jamis bellowed.

"Then now you do," she said sternly. "Send my mother's mail to me." Then she held out the shilling.

He snatched the coin from her fingers then jerked his head at Margarite who was gathering up the brazier. She blew a kiss to Lilah and winked at Lady Clara before trailing in Jamis' wake. Just before the door, she turned and called back. "Sorry about the table, gov!" Then with a final impudent kiss, she left the house.

That left her, Lady Clara, and Lord Kittrel alone in the dining room since the servants had all disappeared. Silence built between them to an uncomfortable degree. Enough that Lilah finally touched her friend's hand.

"Perhaps I should leave as well—"

Lord Kittrel interrupted. "Please remain a moment, if you would, Miss Rees."

She swallowed and nodded. At least he remembered who she

was. Though, given the circumstances, she wasn't entirely sure that was a good thing. Meanwhile, his lordship turned to his sister.

"Clara, can you explain this please?"

"I don't want to marry Lord Loughton."

"So you had someone throw knives at him?" Lord Kittrel stepped closer to his sister. The table stood between them, but she still seemed to cringe back from him.

"It was only one knife. I was trying to dissuade him from me." She lifted her chin, though not enough to fully face him. "You asked me to see him."

"At a party! At a walk on Hyde Park. Not at...at... what the devil was this anyway?"

Lady Clara turned mulish then, pressing her lips together into a tight frown. In the end, his lordship turned to Lilah.

"Miss Rees, can you explain, please?"

She squeezed Clara's arm to give the lady encouragement to answer, but when that didn't work, Lilah framed it in the best light possible. "It was a bit of fun. We were pretending to have a séance, my lord."

"A séance!"

"Yes, my lord. A summoning of the dead to, um, persuade Lord Loughton that he and Lady Clara would not suit."

"And you hired performers, enlisted the staff, and put a three-inch gash in my table to do that?"

"Er, yes, my lord."

He held up his hands. "Clara, couldn't you have gone on a walk with him?"

His sister sniffed. "Walking is not to my tastes."

"But throwing knives at gentlemen is?" In his defense, his tone was more exasperated than angry. Still, Lilah felt compelled to soften the implied risk.

"Jamis has many faults, my lord, but he does not miss with his knives. We were all very safe."

"Yes," Lady Clara spoke up. "He even practiced several times before the actual séance."

Lilah winced. That perhaps was not the best thing to say as his Lordship hastily pulled up the tablecloth to reveal five gashes rather than the one.

"Good lord," he grumbled.

"You said you didn't like the table anyway," Lady Clara pressed.

Lord Kittrel flipped the tablecloth back in place. "That's not the point, Clara," he huffed.

"Well then what is it?" his sister asked.

He rubbed a hand over his face in frustration. "I had thought that giving you freedom away from Mother would help you settle into yourself. That you would find happiness—"

"I am happy!"

"With your lending library friends doing ghost hunts and fake séances? Surely this cannot be how you mean to go on for the rest of your life. Surely you would like some meaningful task."

Lady Clara gripped the back of her chair. "I am studying things! Learning things! It is meaningful to me. What is not meaningful is becoming shackled to a man, bearing his children, and cleaning their noses for the rest of my life."

She slammed the chair into the table with the force of a gale wind. Truly, Lilah did not think the lady had the strength to do it, but the resulting crash startled them all. Especially as she topped it off with a loud pronouncement.

"I will not marry Lord Loughton!"

Then she spun on her heel and left the room. And with the lady leaving, it was past time for Lilah to make her exit as well. Instead, she tried one last time to help Lady Clara.

"Truly, my lord, it was meant to look theatrical. There was no real danger. I made sure of it."

His eyes narrowed as he looked at her. "Those play actors were your idea?"

"I thought it better than having one of the footmen throw cutlery. Best to have an expert than an accidental skewering."

His lordship snorted, humor coming into his tone. "On that we agree." He looked back at where his sister had disappeared.

"She wanted to use the footmen?"

"She had other ideas as well. Several would have set the house on fire. A few would have required experiments in chemistry. But we talked them through, and she realized this was the best approach."

"You talked it through," he said. It was not phrased as a question. "I suspect that you talked her out of her wilder notions."

Lilah thought it best not to confirm such a thing though he was correct. "Your sister and I became acquainted a week ago." She bit her lip. "I like her a great deal and would like to continue our friendship."

He nodded, but didn't respond and Lilah was left to wonder what he meant by that. Would he bar the door to her? Would he allow Lady Clara to still call upon her? When the clock ticked on with no further response from him, Lilah decided it was time to take the conversation in another direction. Though propriety dictated that she depart immediately, she chose instead to remain for a moment more.

"I am sorry for your loss, my lord. I understand that your father had a difficult time of it."

He nodded his head sadly. "It's a terrible thing to watch one's sire fade away. He was a man who filled a room, but in the end..." His voice trailed away as he looked past her shoulder at nothing in particular.

"My mother died in much the same way," she said. "It took a year, but the illness destroyed her nonetheless."

His gaze returned to her face and his expression softened. "I am sorry."

She wondered for a moment if there were more to his words. Sorry he could not marry her like she'd asked a year ago. Sorry he disappeared for a year. Or was it simple politeness at her loss? Either way, her response was equally vague.

"Thank you," she said. Then she asked the question that had been burning on her lips since she first realized he'd walked into the room. "Are you back in London then? Do you take up your place in the House of Lords?"

He nodded. "Yes, that's my plan. I should be in town for a few months at least." He looked down at his ruined tablecloth. "I was surprised by the magnitude of the work involved in taking the reins of an earldom, but I'm working my way through it."

Of course, he was. She couldn't imagine him shirking any responsibility, and that warmed her heart to him. It wasn't what most women considered dashing, but she lived on the fringes of society. She had a great appreciation for people who didn't try to weasel out of their promises.

"Your people are lucky to have you," she said, meaning his servants, his tenants, and especially his family. Unfortunately, the very moment she had the most respect for him was the same moment she recognized the futility of her dreams. A new earl could not marry a by-blow. The very idea was preposterous. So she gave him a wistful smile. "I shall take my leave now, my lord. Pray don't be so hard on your sister. I believe she is so smart that she is bored with the usual fare in life. My sister Gwen is much like her."

He nodded. "I missed Lady Gwen's wedding. I hope it was everything she wanted."

"Her husband and their shared industry is what she wanted, and she is ecstatically happy." With that she curtseyed and took her leave. Or so she thought. As she was handed her cloak by the butler, his lordship joined her in the front hallway.

"Is your carriage here already?" he asked.

She felt her eyebrows rise. Did he think that she had her own conveyance? Her mother had command of that. "I shall walk, my lord. It is not that far."

"It's far enough," he said with a frown. "You shouldn't be out alone after dark. Come, come. I'll walk you home."

"It's not any more respectable for me to walk with a gentleman—" she began.

"But it is a good deal safer," he interrupted. "I insist."

He held out his arm to her. What could she do except take it and relish the time they had together? She doubted she would ever have another chance to walk on the arm of an earl.

CHAPTER SIX

T HEY WALKED IN silence for a time as they settled into the rhythm of the night. It wasn't late. Indeed, she doubted her mother would be home from any of the parties that helped launch the beginning of the Season. And then he spoke, and his words surprised her for their total honesty.

"I have thought about you often after last year's masquerade. Sayres told me that you helped Lady Gwen throughout last season. Did you enjoy yourself?"

She'd been accosted by the least savory members of the *ton*, sneered at by the society ladies, and generally relegated to a serving maid despite everything Gwen did to bring her forward. It had been a humiliating year. "It was a pleasure to watch Gwen blossom into the beauty she is."

He cast her a sidelong glance. "Do you always choose your words with such care?"

"Yes," she answered honestly. "Society prefers life to be pleasant. Why challenge that to no purpose?"

"Because I should like the honest truth."

He seemed to mean it, so she complied. She didn't mean to tell such an angry anecdote, but the words tumbled out anyway.

"I attended the coming out party of a young lady. I was very excited, you understand, because it was the most popular ball I had been invited to all Season. I thought perhaps I was becoming more accepted because of Gwen and Lord Sayre's patronage. I wore my best dress and resolved to charm any soul—man, woman, or young lady—who chose to come my way. I would show them that I was a delight, and they would want to have me in their company."

"Having experienced your charm firsthand, I expect you took gloriously."

Of course, he would. "I soon learned that the only reason I was there was to entertain the girl's drunken, wastrel uncle. Being family, he had to be invited to the come out, but no one wished for him to shower his attention on a proper woman. He and I were shoved together into a back room."

"The devil you say."

"I don't know what they expected me to do. Entertain him in the most lewd manner, I suppose. I did not."

"Did you cry out? Did you call them to account for such abominable behavior?"

"I was locked in a back room, my lord. And they specifically distracted Gwen so she could not come find me, though I am told she and Lord Sayres looked."

She could feel the tension in his arm. He was clearly angry on her behalf, and she was grateful that at least someone beyond her immediate family could feel outrage for her.

"What happened?" His voice was a low growl of fury that shivered along her skin.

"I broke a vase over his head, and he howled for a doctor." She smiled in memory. "He was bleeding quite profusely."

"I would prefer you had knocked him unconscious," he grumbled.

"I did try. I escaped when a servant opened the door. Then I left the ball."

"Whose ball was it?" he asked.

She turned to him. "Would you beat the man again?"

"I would." She believed him, and it made her smile.

"Then you must beat every man who makes free with a woman of lesser status. There is quite a long list."

"I'm aware," he said, and his grumpy voice rumbled into her heart. "I have been trying, you know. I have thrashed more than one idiot boy in my life."

She didn't doubt it, especially as he had done that to three drunken dandies on the night they first met. She squeezed his arm in thanks. "It is done."

"Was your entire Season like that?"

"No," she admitted. "There were evening musicales and a couple nights at the theater. Lord Sayres was very generous in bringing me around. His attention was predominantly fixed on Gwen, of course, but he was kind to me, and I am grateful."

"I would be filled with anger, were I you. Outrage and venom."

"Really?" she asked. "They why do you perpetuate the very problem that created me?" It was a bold statement, but she was tired of hiding her true thoughts. She was a lot smarter than she pretended, and he did ask for her honest opinion.

"I beg your pardon!" There was outrage in his face as he quickly spun her to face him.

She remained firm despite his expression. "Society believes that parentage is the measure of a person. I am less because I was unfortunate in my parents. You are more because you were lucky to be born to an earl."

"I don't see you as less."

"Of course, you do. You don't value skills. A man is not measured by his ability. He is measured first and foremost by his parents."

He looked at her hard and his jaw tightened. "You do not know what I value, Miss Rees."

That was true enough, but her anger was spilling out. Perhaps it was because he listened. Or more likely, it was because she knew he would never marry her simply because she was a bastard. She'd spent a year longing for him only to realize that she had missed her chance with him. Why? Because of her ill-fated parentage. It infuriated her, and now that she was alone with him, she couldn't guard her tongue. She wanted him. He was an admirable man, and he was beyond her grasp. That made her furious.

"Do you know that I have a gift for organization? No matter the task, no matter the disaster, I can have it sorted out into a logical system."

He looked at her for a moment and nodded. "Would it surprise you to know that England's army could not function without a legion of hardy women who help set up the camps, who run the laundries and other services, who make sure our men are cared for in every way possible?"

She had not known that. "I am impressed."

"They are impressive women."

"No, my lord. I am impressed that you would admit such a thing." In her experience, men never acknowledged a woman's efforts unless pressed.

His expression darkened. "You know so little of me."

Which was entirely his fault. If he had been in London this year, she would have moved heaven and earth to know him better. But that thought was unworthy of her. His father had been ill. He'd had no choice but to care for his parent.

"I beg your pardon," she finally said, as she tried to grab hold of her temper. It didn't work because she kept speaking. "But I still believe you are part of a system that values birth over ability. How can you say that a skilled workman is worth less than a wastrel of a lord who's only purpose in life is to chase skirts and drink away his days?"

"I would never say such a thing." He spoke so vehemently that she wanted to believe him.

"And yet you will only socialize with those of equal birth. You spend your days among the moneyed elite, and your evenings with their daughters."

"I have spent my evenings with my mother," he groused, "and my days with the cowherds." He turned her back to their walk, stepping carefully through the debris on the London street.

"I submit to you, Miss Rees, that you are equally biased."

"I am not! I cannot be!"

"On the contrary, you can. You have looked for a husband only among the elite. You have tried to marry into the exact problem you claim to abhor."

"I merely wish to marry respectably. That is no crime."

"Of course not. But were you to truly honor the skills of a man above his birth, then why have you not searched among the workmen of London? There are many worthy gentlemen there."

He had her there. When she'd been younger, she had flirted with the footmen, at least a little. She had also tested her feminine wiles upon a man who sold fabric and another who baked the most amazing tarts. "Lady Rees once caught me spending time with a tradesman. Several times the gentleman walked with me to the market, and she spied us returning together."

He turned to look at her. "Just returning together?" he pressed.

She colored. "She caught us kissing."

"Hmmm." The sound was half growl, half question.

"She locked me in my bedroom on bread and water for a week. She only let me out because she needed me to set the meals for the family."

"Why?" he seemed genuinely perplexed. "Was the man a blackguard?"

"I don't think so."

"Then what was her reasoning?"

That was a question that had plagued her for much of her life. Why had Lady Rees brought her—her husband's bastard—into the home to be raised as if she were a true daughter? "She said I was a blueblood, and I would act that way." She huffed out a breath. "But I'm only half-blue, and no amount of polish will change that simple fact of my birth."

"It was your mother then," he said, his voice low. "How very curious."

"It was Lady Rees," she corrected. "My mother was an actress and Lord Rees' mistress." She had not meant to sound so bitter, but Lord Kittrel made her emotions roil. Her feelings pressed her in his presence, with desire and fury being the hardest to control. She knew it was normal among the elite that a man should have a mistress, but no accommodation was made for the children of such a union. What future did she have as a bastard woman? And why had her father doomed her to this half-life?

"I am sorry that their mistakes have fallen upon you," he said, his voice kind. "That is an inadequate statement, I know, but I cannot do more."

Of course, he couldn't. He was an earl now and would never consider her as a potential wife. However, his words had given her an idea. Or perhaps he had prompted her to push for something she had been considering for some time.

"You are right, my lord. I have been allowing Lady Rees to dictate my actions for far too long. It is time I looked elsewhere."

"For a husband?"

"For employment. I believe I could be an excellent house-keeper. I have the skills to set a house running like a well-oiled clock. Someone should value that."

"Indeed. I would value that," he said.

She jolted, her heart leaping into her throat. He couldn't possibly mean to hire her, could he? From what she'd seen of his servants, they needed a firm hand. And she'd be near him, though in an entirely different capacity. The thought was unsettling and intriguing.

"Do you mean to offer me a position, my lord?"

"What? Oh! Goodness no. At least not like you're thinking."

Her heart sank. Of course, he didn't mean a place with him. It was all well and good for someone *else* to hire a bastard. But before she could frame an adequate retort, he continued speaking.

"Clara is the one who runs my household. I don't know if you've noticed, but she is singularly bad at it."

She had noticed, but it would be rude of her to agree. "Your sister is highly intelligent, my lord. But the management of servants is a special skill."

"One that you claim to have mastered."

She shrugged. "We all have our talents."

"But if my sister is so highly intelligent, do you think you could teach her? We cannot continue to live as we have. I have tried to give her instructions, but she won't hear it from me."

"It is hard to hear criticism from a brother."

"Do you think you could teach her a system, perhaps? Some way to make my home less chaotic? As a new earl, I'll have visitors, political guests—"

"Marriage-hungry misses and their mamas—"

He shot her a look akin to dread. "Whomever the guests, I'm afraid it will be too much for Clara to manage. I have suggested she hire a housekeeper to help, but the last seven have been disastrous."

"Seven?"

"Seven. All of whom had to be sacked without reference. I don't know where she finds them, but every one has been an unmitigated disaster."

The very thought boggled the mind. "You have left this all in her hands?"

"She insists on it, and I have no desire to curb her independence. It is her way of thanking me for letting her live with me rather than forcing her back to my parents. She and Mother never got along well, and she loves London." He sighed. "I just wish she was better at it."

"And you think I could help?"

"Do you think she will listen to you?"

Lilah bit her lip. She had managed difficult women before, but Lady Clara was her friend. "If you will permit me to visit often, I shall be happy to help your sister in any way possible."

"Permit you to visit? Clara is of age. I can no more stop her friends from visiting than I can prevent a séance in my own dining room."

She smiled, knowing that wasn't exactly the truth. Many men exercised drastic measures over the women in their lives. That he allowed Clara her freedom was a measure of restraint. "You wouldn't have allowed the séance if you'd been here," she said.

"I would have tried to prevent it," he said. "But she would have found another location to do it. Or made sure I was out of the house, which is what she did this time." His hand waved in irritation. "I daily persuade the leaders of England to my way of thinking, and yet my sister does what she wants willy-nilly."

Given how much Lady Rees and Gwen had fought, Lilah thought he had taken the better tack of trying to persuade without too much restriction. "As her friend, I should be happy to help her, but she needs to ask me for it. I will not start telling her what to do." She turned to him. "And I will not take money for such a thing. She is my friend."

He nodded as if he expected as much. "Just help her hire a housekeeper. Someone who doesn't get drunk on my wine then vomit on the laundry."

"No!" Lilah gasped, appalled.

"Oh yes."

"Oh dear," she said with a chuckle. "You have had a terrible time of it, haven't you?"

He sighed. "It's still better than the violent rows she and my mother had. The two have never understood one another." He looked up at the sky and his tone turned wistful. "I had hoped she and Lord Loughton might get along."

Given his reaction to tonight's debacle, Lilah had begun to wonder the same thing. Loughton had been amused rather than appalled and still determined to pursue Clara. "I shouldn't count him out yet."

"I count on nothing these days," he returned. "One year ago, my father was outside lifting stones to rebuild a fence. He was strong as an ox."

And now he was gone. "I'm sorry," Lilah said. There wasn't much else she could say except that, especially as they were now nearing her home.

"So am I," he said sadly. Then he looked up. "This is your home, isn't it?"

"Yes. Thank you for walking me here. It was very kind of you."

He nodded as he looked at her. His expression was in shadow, his eyes even more so, and yet she felt the intensity of his regard nonetheless.

"I would welcome you at any time to my house," he said. "You are a good friend to Clara."

He had no true way of knowing that, but she accepted the statement because it was true. "I enjoy her company very much."

He was silent, and though it made her heart speed up, she did not move an inch. His attention was too sweet.

"I am sorry for how abysmally you were treated last Season," he said.

She smiled. "My lord, we have been apologizing to one another the entire walk. Your loss and my unfortunate parentage are matters of fact." She searched the shadows for the particulars of his expression. "There are surely more fruitful ways we can spend our time."

His head tilted slightly. "I spend most of my time trying to change the world, Miss Rees. It has been enjoyable to merely talk with you about it."

She smiled and she waited. She wasn't even sure for what. She felt his eyes on her face and the tension in his arm where she still rested her hand. She would have moved it away, but he gripped it with his free hand even as he looked at her.

Was he thinking of kissing her? Because she was certainly remembering their last kiss. She'd nightly relived the press of his mouth on hers, the feel of his body supporting hers, and the thrust of his tongue. As always, her breath caught at the memory, and she heated inside. Her belly went liquid, her breasts became heavy and tight. And it was made all the more intense because he was looking at her, leaning toward her, and yet he held himself back.

Her lips parted, desperate to feel his touch again. She heard his breath catch, and then he spoke with a gravelly voice that rubbed along her spine in the most delicious ways.

"You are my sister's friend," he said.

"Yes," she whispered.

"Only a cad would abuse that trust."

He *was* thinking of kissing her! She was sure of it. She felt the yearning in them both, here in the shadows of the street where no one could see them.

"I understand that you won't marry me," she whispered. "But I wouldn't mind another kiss. I wouldn't mind it at all."

He lifted his hand and stroked her cheek. His touch was electric, leaving a trail of tingles in his wake. Then he rolled his thumb gently across her lower lip, and she felt it swell against him, especially as he dipped inside. Just for a moment. And her breath caught on a gasp.

"I cannot damn another for abusing you," he said, "and then trifle with you myself."

"Even if I allow it?" Even if she *asked* for it?

His fingers continued to skate across her face. Not just her lips, but her cheeks and even the tip of her nose. It was as though he were memorizing the shape of her, and the feel of it was more intimate than any kiss could be. She stood breathless as he touched her, while her heart beat so fast.

Was this how he made love? she wondered. With slow touches that burned in a delicious kind of agony?

He kept at it. He caressed the curve of her ear and slid down to the slope of her neck. She tilted her head to feel more, and she dared herself to step into his arms. She could take the kiss from him. And yet she was frozen where she stood, feeling every inch that he touched as if it were newly alive.

She didn't know how long they stood there like that, with him touching her and her reveling in every caress. At some point they both heard the clop of horses' hooves coming quickly down the lane. His hand fell away as she looked down the street, only to mew in dismay.

The Rees carriage was rolling toward them. Lady Rees had returned from whatever amusements this night had offered. It would be best if Lilah were not caught outside with a gentleman.

"I need to go inside," she said.

"I will walk you to the door," he said.

Lord, no. Everyone would know that Lord Kittrel had been alone with her. There would be too many questions from that, and she could answer none of them. "I'll go in the back through the kitchen," she said as she took a quick step back. "Thank you for a lovely walk."

"Please visit Clara soon. She'll be hurting from tonight's disaster."

"I will." Then she turned on her heel and fled to the house.

CHAPTER SEVEN

ARON TOOK TWICE as long to walk back home as he should have. He needed the time to let his embarrassing condition fade before seeing his sister. Bloody hell, if lust were the measure of a woman to marry, he would have dropped to one knee before Miss Rees right then and there. It had taken all his willpower to not kiss her and even so, he had touched her in an incredibly intimate way. He caressed only her face and neck, but the throbbing in his loins told him it had been much more than a proper touch. A kiss *might* have been less of a seduction, though remembering their last kiss, probably not.

Damnation, but he enjoyed her spunk. Imagine a woman challenging his beliefs straight to his face!

Why do you perpetuate the very problem that created me?

She had no idea what he perpetuated and what he didn't, and yet she had struck a true hit. He was expected to choose a wife from among the daughters of the elite. There were obligations to his title not to mention his position in politics, or so his mother had told him ad nauseum throughout the past year. And yet for all that, he had not been able to forget the very intriguing Miss Rees.

He made it home eventually, grumbling when he was the one who had to close the dining room windows. His servants were nowhere to be seen, and he would have been angry about that if he weren't so appreciative of the solitude. Fortunately, his valet had made it here along with his luggage. The man greeted Aaron in the master bedroom with a hot bath nearly ready.

"Fernsby, you are a wonder," he said gratefully.

"The water is still heating, my lord. If you would be patient for a few more minutes, I shall have it ready for you soon."

"Plenty of time," he said. "I need to speak with my sister first anyway." He needed to discuss her responsibilities in the coming months. And that tonight's disaster could not be repeated.

"I believe she is in her sitting room."

Aaron nodded and headed down the hall. He knocked and was bid to enter, mentally bracing himself for the disaster that was his sister's sitting room. Normally she had books, plants, rocks, and lord knew what else in a chaotic display throughout the room. She never allowed anyone to clean it, and the dust was often as bad as the clutter.

But instead of the disarray he usually saw, there was a clear organization to the room. The books were placed in a bookcase, the rocks in a box, the plants near the window, and a pathway had opened up through the room such that one could move freely through it rather than step on islands of open space.

It was a wonder.

His sister was seated on the settee, her feet curled up under her, as she read a thick book. But she looked up as he entered and so he was able to see her face as he exclaimed over the state of her parlor.

"The room looks lovely," he said. "Much easier to move about now."

Clara gave a distracted nod. "Lilah said the dust made her sneeze. Since we had to plan the séance, she helped me sort through everything and then stood by while the maids cleaned it."

"Did she now?"

"She was very good with the new maids." Clara wrinkled her nose. "Did you know there is a proper way to dust? You don't just wave the duster around. There's a method to it."

"I did not," he said as he moved a volume on astronomy to the bookcase such that he could sit on the settee. "I gather Lilah taught it to you?"

Clara pursed her lips. "Well, she taught the maids, and I listened."

"And you didn't mind that she took charge of the servants?"

His sister shrugged. "I didn't want her to sneeze and she offered to help. I didn't think you'd care."

"I don't care." He smiled as he tried to encourage his sister. "But if she knows ways to manage the staff, I think it's capital that she would share them with you."

He waited for her to respond, but as was typical when Clara felt insecure, she said absolutely nothing. The book in her lap rose as a kind of defense, and she ducked her chin as if she were reading. Knowing her, she probably was.

"Clara," he said, "we must talk about what must happen this Season."

Clara let out a heavy sigh. "You're going to lecture me about responsibilities."

"We are adults, Clara. I'm an earl now and you—"

"About Lilah," she interrupted. "What do you think of her?"

It was a clear distraction tactic. She didn't want to talk about the coming Season, so she was changing the topic. Unfortunately, it worked. At the mere mention of Miss Rees' name, his gut tightened, and words failed him. He felt lust, admiration, fascination, and so many more things in a complicated mass that clogged his throat and fogged his brain. He couldn't admit that to anyone, much less his mercurial sister, so he said something noncommittal.

"I am pleased she is your friend. Now back to the Season. I will be confirmed in the House of Lords in a few weeks—"

"That's not an answer!" Clara huffed. "I want to know what you really think of her."

He straightened in his seat and put on his most stern look. He had made men quiver with this stare and he had used it to great effect on the floor of the House of Commons. "After the confirmation, we must throw a ball."

"You walked her home, didn't you? That's a great deal of time for conversation. What do you think of her as a marriage prospect?"

His throat closed down. What he thought wasn't for his sister's ears because all he thought about were ways to bed Lilah. He wanted to possess her in the most carnal of ways.

He cleared his throat and used the time to focus his thoughts. "I know I have left the management of the staff to you," he said. Actually, Clara had "given" that to him as a Christmas present every year, elegantly written in a letter under the tree. *I will take care of your house.* It made it impossible for him to hire someone competent without hurting her feelings. "But I think this might be too much for you."

"Don't be silly. I've already been thinking about throwing more parties."

"A ball is an enormous undertaking."

Clara nodded. "I think Lilah will make someone an excellent wife."

"Maybe Lilah could help you plan the ball? I'm sure she'd have some excellent ideas."

His sister stared at him. "Of course, she has excellent ideas. That's why she'd be an excellent wife."

"Will you let her help organize the ball? It's too much for one person to handle."

"I have much grander plans than that."

He blinked. "Grander? Clara, I don't need anything grand."

"Not you, silly. Lilah. I'm going to make sure she gets married this year."

He touched his sister's hand. "She told me she did a full Season last year with Sayre's help, but most hostesses won't accept her. Last year—"

"I don't mean the *ton*! They're much too blind to see her worth. I'm going to introduce her to barristers, tradesmen, and gentlemen of industry. Your ball is the perfect place to do that."

His heart froze in horror. "No, Clara, you can't. You can't go about directing a person's life like that. It's interfering where you've no business—"

"Isn't that what *you* do every day? You play with tariffs to get people to buy our corn. You direct the canals and give money to hospitals and the like."

"That's the business of government!"

"And what is that but interfering in people's lives?"

"It's not trying to get them to marry a barrister!"

"Just restrict their choices in goods by making one more expensive than another."

Damnation, when had she started paying attention to politics? "The Corn Laws are complicated." And he didn't support them anyway.

"Well, this isn't complicated. I'm going to throw small evening parties to introduce Lilah to eligible gentlemen. Then, when she's narrowed her choices down to a few select possibilities, I'll invite them to your ball. She can make her final choice there."

"My ball is not supposed to be a matchmaking affair. Clara—"

"All balls are matchmaking affairs. Even I know that." She patted his hand. "Don't worry. I have it all under control. Now go take your bath. You smell like you've been on a horse all day."

"I have been on a horse all day."

"Exactly."

He could see that she wouldn't hear reason tonight, so he stood up and headed toward the door. "This isn't over yet, Clara. We'll talk at breakfast tomorrow. I have some—"

"We can't," she interrupted. "The cook quit."

"What?"

She waved a hand in dismissal. "Said she wouldn't be in a house that had a séance. Called it ungodly and some other nonsense."

He rubbed a hand over his face. "She's the third cook to quit like that. We need—"

"The fourth will be better. I'm sure of it. Anyway, you should break your fast at your club tomorrow. Goodnight!" She grabbed her book and immediately focused her entire attention on that.

Aaron didn't leave. He stood in the door to her sitting room and pondered his options. He had no threat to use against her. She knew he wouldn't beat her, keep her from food, or even send her back home to fight with their mother. He had tried several times to declare how things would be in his home, but whenever he became autocratic, the results had been disastrous. She became wilder with her declarations and her friends, went out of her way to destroy his peace, and even risked her life by sneaking out of their home to wander London at night on one pretext or another.

In the end, he landed on the only option that worked with her.

"I love you Clara, and I mean to do whatever I can to ensure your happiness."

She lifted her head, tilting it to one side as she looked at him.

"But," he continued, "you must see that I cannot live like this any longer. The servants are in chaos, you paid someone to throw knives in the dining room—"

"That was just one time," she began.

"The house smells of smoke, and that was just tonight." He paused as she looked down at her hands. "If we are to live with each other, then we must live in some kind of harmony."

"But that's just the thing," she said softly. "You want me to marry and harry off to Scotland." When she looked up, her eyes were bright with unshed tears. "I don't want to leave London. I like it here."

Was that the base of this latest wildness? That she didn't want to leave London? "You know I would never force you to marry anyone you didn't want."

"You know that I am trying my hardest with the servants. I don't know why they aren't working as they ought."

He took a step forward. "Miss Rees is a genius with servants.

Will you ask her for help? I am sure she will give it. And then we can start to set this household to rights."

Clara bit her lip, her expression thoughtful. Eventually, she nodded. "I will ask her. I promise. And in return for her generosity, I shall introduce her to every worthy man I can." She beamed up at him. "You'll see. It will all work out just as it ought."

CHAPTER EIGHT

L ILAH DREAMT OF midnight kisses and lingering caresses. She woke flustered and achy. It didn't delay her morning tasks—reviewing the bills, planning the week's meals, and disciplining a lazy footman—but it did make the morning difficult for her. Especially since she wanted to stare out a window and dream about him. Lord Kittrel.

A restlessness claimed her. When Clara's note arrived inviting her over for a comfortable chat, she knew she would push through her chores in order to visit her friend as soon as possible. But first, she needed to ask her adoptive mother the one question that had been on her mind since the first day she entered this home. She hadn't been brave enough before. As a child, she couldn't risk an answer that would send her back to a dubious life in an acting troupe. As an adult, she hadn't thought it mattered even though a tiny part of her mind was always devoted to the question.

Today she cared enough to risk it all. Today she brought Lady Rees her hot chocolate and remained in the room to talk.

"Good morning, Mama," she said sweetly.

On the first day that she'd arrived in this house, Lord Rees had insisted that she call him Papa and Lady Rees, Mama. The woman had never disagreed with her husband's pronouncement, had responded when Lilah used the word, but every once in a while—especially when she was young—the lady would pinch her lips together at the word.

She did so now, and Lilah started to duck her head. It was what she always did when she needed to control her emotions. But this morning she was in an unsettled mood. She wanted answers. She needed to know whether the life she lived now was worth preserving.

"You seem displeased this morning," Lilah said as she passed over the chocolate.

Ever perceptive, Lady Rees spoke without even touching her drink. "You have that look on your face. I know we are about to have an unpleasant discussion."

Lilah laughed. "I don't have any look on my face."

The lady arched her brows at her then took hold of her drink. "Did you want to discuss something?"

"Well, yes."

Mama arched her brows, and Lilah had to concede that the woman had a point. Might as well get straight to it.

"Why did you bring me into your home?"

The lady reared back, her brows rising nearly to her hairline. "You want to discuss this now? Today?"

"Yes."

"But I should think the answer obvious."

Lilah's chin rose a smidgeon. "It's not. At least not to me."

"Your father loved you, and I loved him."

"But I'm a bastard."

"You're *his* bastard." When Lilah didn't say anything more, the woman pinched her lips together again then patted the edge of the coverlet. "Sit down. I've been wanting to talk to you about your future for some time, but I kept putting it off."

Lilah did as she was bid. She sat with every measure of composure. She could count on one hand the number of times she'd done this before. Over the years, she'd become the best of friends with her two adopted sisters Diana and Gwen. Her adopted brother Elliott had been away at school most of her childhood, but even they had an ease with one another. It was only Mama who seemed prickly with her, and how could she blame the woman? She'd accepted her husband's bastard into her home.

"I was very young when I met your father," Lady Rees said. "A green girl fresh out of school being courted by an earl. He swept me off my feet."

"You were a beautiful young woman," Lilah said. She'd seen the painting of Lady Rees done as part of her first come out. "I'm sure you enchanted him."

The lady laughed. "My dowry enchanted him, but he was dashing and titled. I thought it was true love. Plus he was a very good lover." She looked back at Lilah and scoffed. "Don't look so shocked. There are worse things than enjoying one's marriage bed...even if it might have been before the vows were spoken."

Now Lilah was truly shocked. She couldn't imagine that Lady Rees had acted so scandalously. The woman had fought daily to instill appropriate behavior in her children. "Act according to your name!" had been her favorite saying. And since Lilah was a bastard, she'd always told her to, "Act *better* than your name."

"Yours was a love match?" Lilah finally managed to ask.

"I was in love, and he treated me well. We had three beautiful children and I..." She shook her head. "I was busy. I was a countess. There were things to do, and the children were growing. He would come to London while I stayed in the country. But I always thought..." She sighed. "When he came home, we always enjoyed ourselves together. I know I should have guessed he had a mistress, but..." She shrugged. "I didn't know. Not until the day he told me about you."

Lilah looked down at her hands and tried not to feel ashamed. She hadn't done anything wrong, and yet it felt like all the blame landed on her shoulders. Until her adoptive mother set her hands atop Lilah's.

"He told me how smart you were and that you had a laugh like Christmas bells. He told me that your mother was dying and that you needed a home. He made you sound like the perfect little child, and then he told me you were of noble birth. From

Scotland."

"My mother was from Scotland," Lilah said.

Lady Rees shrugged. "It wouldn't have mattered if you were from Hades. He loved you, Lilah. And I loved him."

"So you brought me into your home? An acknowledged bastard?"

"Yes."

She made it sound so matter of fact, and Lilah had no reason to doubt it. After all, she'd been well cared for in this home. Her father had certainly adored her, and she'd found her way with her half siblings. But Lady Rees had always been prickly. For all the love Lilah had felt from the others, there was an understandable reserve between her and Lady Rees. One that always left Lilah feeling apologetic for her very existence.

And then her father had died.

Everyone had grieved, but Lilah had an extra worry. Would she be cast out? Not if she was useful. At the young age of twelve, she set herself to become indispensable. She was the youngest, but the most able to handle the servants. She took on every household task she could. She also accepted Diana's anger, Elliott's awkwardness, and Gwen's bookishness, doing her best to ease their way in life. She worked extra hard at being useful because she feared she was one step away from being tossed out if she didn't behave.

"Lilah," Lady Rees said, "we rub along well enough, don't we?"

She nodded. "Yes, of course."

"And now that all the others are married and have homes of their own, there's plenty of money for us to live on." She squeezed Lilah's hand. "Just think of it. We can play with the babies and then send them home. We can host dinners and live a full life, you and me."

What Mama meant was that she would go parties while Lilah stayed at home. That Lady Rees would play with the babies, and then host dinners that Lilah supervised. Lilah would continue managing as an unpaid housekeeper in a home that was warm if not exactly filling. And while Lilah stomach's soured, her adopted mother continued.

"I know you wanted a husband, and I'd hoped you'd take last Season with Gwen's help."

"The *ton* will never accept me," she said.

"I'm afraid not. I've tried, Lilah, every way I could think of. But nothing I did made a difference."

She believed her. Lady Rees had indeed done her best, but even the most skillful society lady couldn't change Lilah's by-blow label. It was time for her to look beyond.

"I thought perhaps I could get a job. Become a housekeeper or companion."

Lady Rees reared back. "Whatever for?" she said looking truly horrified. "You'd work long hours and have no idea what type of company you'd have or even if you'd be safe. Do I need to tell you what happens to such women in so many houses?"

No, she didn't. Daily degradations were commonplace. As were more horrible crimes.

"And for what? Your pin money is as much as they make every year. And now that Gwen has married, I can even increase the amount. Whatever could you find out there, that you don't have here?"

It was a fair question, and one she couldn't answer except that she yearned for a family of her own. She wanted a husband who didn't care who her parents were.

"I need to meet other gentlemen," she said firmly. "Ones outside of the peerage."

Lady Rees set down her chocolate with a click. "Absolutely not. I will not countenance that."

"Whyever not?"

"You are of noble blood—"

"It doesn't matter—"

"It did to your father. He insisted that you be reared according to your station."

"As a bastard?"

"As a lady. And I have. You have the education of a lady, the support of an earl's family. He even set aside a dowry for you."

A small sum that would not keep her housed if she took it to live on.

"I have done everything he asked and more," Lady Rees continued. "Lilah, I have given you love and a home. I cannot understand why you would want to abandon that! And certainly not for a job or a husband who is beneath you."

"You're not making sense," Lilah said, her voice taut.

"And your father would be appalled by the way you're acting. He wanted you to live with us and not go off and marry some… some actor!" She spoke in dramatic accents as was her wont, but Lilah could see that she truly was distressed. What could she say to all this? It wasn't logical, but Lady Rees had taken her in and given her a home. Lilah had food, clothing, and a family who loved her. How ungrateful was she to disdain that? She lived a good life, far better than most.

"I know you're not ungrateful," Lady Rees continued. "I know you understand how you might have grown up if not for us."

"I do," she said. Her mother had died of the pox. Margarite was subject to Jamis' whims. Many women who trod the boards had a very sad, short life. Lilah was much better off here. And yet it wasn't enough.

"I know you love us just as we love you."

"I do," she said as she soothed Lady Rees' hand.

"Good," the lady said as she pulled her hands away to wipe at her tears. "It's settled then. You'll stay here, I'll increase your pin money, and we'll rub along just like two peas in a pod. It will be wonderful."

"Yes, of course." What else could she say?

"Now run along. Have you finished the meals for the week? That fish we had the other day was dreadful. I'm off them for now. Can't even think of having one."

"Yes, I remember. We're going to have some nice mutton."

"What a good idea. And maybe later we can talk about hosting a dinner. I should like to have one toward the end of the Season. Say, twelve guests?"

Lilah sighed. Lady Rees always had an end of the Season dinner with an eclectic group of her intimates. Lilah was always paired with an influential boor. Someone Lady Rees wanted to impress by inviting, but did not want to do the work of conversing with. Lilah was well-skilled at listening politely to whomever was her dinner companion and making sure he, at least, enjoyed the dinner.

She, on the other hand, always went to bed with a headache once the interminable meal was over. "Perhaps this year I could invite my friend, Lady Clara." At least then she would have someone to talk with.

"The odd one? Well, I suppose. But then I'd have to find someone to match her with. A gentleman who isn't very stiff in his notions. Maybe one of Gwen's bookish friends. Would that make you happy?"

It was something, she supposed. But it felt like she was accepting a cup of water when what she wanted was a river. Was she being ungrateful?

"Lilah? Don't you think that's a most generous idea? You can help me choose the man I invite, so long as he is appropriate to the company."

What could she say? "I think that's a wonderful idea. Thank you, Mama."

CHAPTER NINE

AARON'S DAY HAD been absolutely miserable. No one liked drippy, foggy days, but his had come with a full round of chastisement from his party leader over breakfast, bureaucratic delays regarding his successor in the House of Commons throughout the morning, and further fruitless discussions throughout the afternoon. He didn't disagree with his party's general policies, he just preferred a different focus. He saw need everywhere he looked and so many of the country's leaders didn't seem interested in alleviating the suffering. At least not the way he thought they should.

He wasn't surprised when he arrived at his front door to find no butler answering his knock. His staff often disappeared in the evening. He used his key to open his own front door, then stopped on the threshold at the sound of hysterical female laughter. It was so odd that, at first, he didn't even recognize it as laughter. But once he did, he pulled off his hat and climbed the stairs to investigate.

The door was ajar, which was fortunate, because he got a full view of Miss Rees in repose. Her legs were tucked up onto the settee as she leaned sideways against the armrest. Her eyes were bright, and she bit her lower lip in the most adorable way. He had to step closer to see what she was doing. She was spinning an empty wineglass in her hand before she tossed it into the air then caught it again. It was an impressing feat of juggling and his sister clapped her hands in delight.

"That's marvelous!" Clara cried. "Teach me how to do that?" She drained her glass of wine then held it up as if to start spinning it.

"Stop! Stop! You can't start with fine glasses. They'll shatter all over the floor."

Fortunately for his glassware, Clara flopped back into her chair beside the settee. "Oh very well. I'd rather drink more wine anyway."

"Me, too!" agreed Miss Rees. Sadly, Clara had just finished the bottle.

"Bother. We'll have to get another one."

He stepped into the room. "Then you shouldn't have dismissed the staff for the night," he said as he reached for the empty bottle.

"My lord!" cried Miss Rees as she hastily readjusted to a more proper position on the settee. It gave him a glimpse of her delightful ankles, but the end result was less intriguing. He would have to tempt her to relax in his presence.

"Well of course I dismissed the staff," Clara said as she gave him the bottle. "Do you think I want them listening in while Lilah and I talk about bad men?"

His brows rose. "About—"

"We're sharing stories, my lord," Lilah said hastily. "About a drunken footman and—"

"About the barrister who was so drunk he fell asleep in the middle of a trial."

"And a drunken cabbie who forgot he had a fare in his carriage—"

"There seems to be a theme here." Ironic, really, given that both of them were well into their cups.

Miss Rees grinned as she twirled her empty glass. "It seemed like an appropriate topic."

Good lord, but he loved her smile.

"Go get another bottle for us, will you?" his sister begged.

"And guess what!"

He leaned against the side of the door, happy to see his sister in such a state. She normally hid in her books and replied to his inquiries in the shortest of possible conversation. Something—or someone—had brought out the silly in her and he was beyond pleased to see it.

"What should I guess about?" he teased.

"I have engaged a new cook, and she has left an excellent dinner for you below stairs."

His brows rose. He was indeed hungry, but his spirits had been so depressed he hadn't bothered to visit his club. "Has she really?"

Both ladies nodded, and Clara went so far as to tap her stomach.

"It's simple fare, my lord," Miss Rees supplied, "but hearty and well made."

"I don't mind simple. I am pleased that you found someone so quickly."

"It wasn't me," his sister said with a laugh. "Lilah found her."

"I asked our cook if she knew of someone. We were lucky that her niece was available for work immediately."

Aaron frowned. "Her niece? Just how young—"

"Taste the food, my lord," Miss Rees said. "If you like it, then that is a good beginning. She may be a tad young for the usual cook, but she can learn her other tasks quickly. Especially with the right supervision."

The right supervision was the problem. His sister was a disaster with young, inexperienced staff, but Clara interrupted him before he could think of diplomatic way to express his concerns.

"Oh, don't look at me like that!" his sister cried. "It shall work out. Now get us the wine, if you would."

He bowed. "I shall if you will allow me the pleasure of joining you." He planned to make a plate and return to eat it on his lap. It wouldn't be the first time he had made do at his desk. He could do the same here. But Miss Rees was already pushing up to her feet.

"You cannot bring your food up here." She waved at the cluttered room. "Wherever would you sit?"

On the settee right beside her. But he didn't say that aloud.

"Come along, Clara," Miss Rees said as she tugged his sister to her feet. "Let us go watch your brother enjoy his dinner."

"Just like the servants watch me?"

"Exactly like that!" Miss Rees said with a giggle. "Then he will know how uncomfortable it is for you."

"A capital idea!" his sister cried as she gained her feet.

Aaron worried that Clara was too inebriated to stand, but she was steady enough. Then he watched with a growing smile as Miss Rees linked arms with her. He went first, thinking he could catch them if one tumbled down the stairs.

He needn't have worried. The ladies descended carefully and even managed to sing a little ditty as they went. It wasn't until they were on the main floor that he realized what he'd thought of as a childhood song had different words. *Scandalous* words that should not have been in their vocabulary.

And it was really quite funny.

"Miss Rees," he said in mock reproach. "What have you been teaching my sister?"

"Unfair," the lady responded. "I learned that from her."

Really? "Clara?"

His sister grinned. "Do you think my friends at the lending library only talk about books?"

Well, yes, he had thought that. "Just how much wine have you had?" He wasn't angry. In fact, he was pleased because he got to see a side of her he hadn't witnessed in decades. Just when had she stopped being the happy girl of his childhood?

"Oh, don't be like Mother. I have spent most of the year there with her. This is the first full breath I have taken since Papa grew ill." To demonstrate, she leaned back and inhaled a full measure. She might have toppled, but Miss Rees set a bracing hand out just in case.

There was the answer. The minute his sister had grown into a young woman, his mother had begun putting restrictions on her. She constantly picked on Clara's manners, interests, attire. Everything.

"And what else have your lending library friends taught you?" he asked, his brows lifting in interest.

She launched into another ditty that was funnier than it was crude. He laughed along with Miss Rees at that one. He still watched them both as they made their way down the second set of stairs to the kitchen, but now he saw that they weren't exactly inebriated. He'd call it being in jolly good spirits. And so he settled in to enjoy their company.

"I'll get another bottle of wine," he said.

"I'll put together a plate for you," said Miss Rees.

"I'll entertain you with another song," said Clara.

Before long they were all seated around the kitchen table and chatting in the most relaxing way. When asked, he spoke about the day's frustrations and felt the strain melt away from their attention. Clara's day had been filled with the discovery that the registry office she'd been using to hire servants was abominable in its treatment of its clients. They demanded the servant's first month's wages in return for the placement. And that was in addition to the funds they required from the employer.

What he learned about Miss Rees was that she was an excellent conversationalist. She listened closely, was always ready with a witty comment or a sympathetic agreement, and she never, ever spoke about herself. It was frustrating, really, because he wanted to know her better. But when he asked about her day, she deflected it to speak about having a wonderful time with Clara.

He chose instead to watch her body and enjoy her gestures. There was a natural beauty in any person's smile, but he saw sweetness in hers. Her laugh was filled with joy the few times it burst out of her, but she quickly moderated it. And she was prone to ducking her head when mirth overcame her as if she were hiding her happiness. Even her gestures were modest, and he wondered what it would be like to see her fully express herself in body and voice.

She was reserved to a degree that saddened him. Compared to the overly wild gestures of his sister, she appeared to have a cloak of restraint around her that even her jolly good mood could not pierce.

Time ticked away and he found himself more and more fascinated by Miss Rees. By the time the second bottle of wine was finished, Clara declared herself too exhausted to continue. She embraced first him then Miss Rees with a happy exuberance, then wobbled her way to bed. That left him and Miss Rees alone.

"This has been a lovely evening, my lord. I shall—"

"You are not walking alone back to your home," he stated firmly.

She opened her mouth to argue, but one look at his face and she dipped her chin. "Thank you, my lord."

"But first, I should like to hear something about you."

"What?"

"I remember the bold, forthright woman from the masquerade a year ago, the woman who asked me to consider marrying her and I cannot see her in you tonight." He leaned forward. "Who is the true Miss Rees? The shy, self-effacing woman today or the bold one from a year ago?"

Her eyes widened and she opened her mouth as if preparing to speak, but no sound came out. In the end, she pressed her lips together and shrugged. He found that completely dissatisfying.

"Shall I make a guess?" He waited until she nodded then continued. "Something happened today, something to diminish your fire. I should like to find out what that was and beat it into a pulp."

"My lord, I have not laughed so well as I did this evening in a very long time. It was wonderful."

"What happened this day then?"

She bit her lip. "Your sister and I interviewed new cooks. I very much enjoyed helping her find the right one for you." She pointed at his empty plate. "The food was good, wasn't it?"

"Yes, it was, but you cannot distract me. What happened this morning?" And when she did not immediately answer, he covered her hand with his. "You may confide in me. I will not betray you." He had no idea why he was being so bold. If a lady wished to keep her secrets, he had no business pressing her to divulge them. But he wanted to know. He wanted to kill whatever dragon had plagued her.

She blew out a breath and flipped her hand such that they were palm to palm. It was a bold gesture for a woman not attached to him, and he relished the feel of her small hand in his. Her grip was strong though, as she squeezed, and he returned it in full measure—strength for strength—until she took a shuddering breath.

"I realized today that my mother has decided on my future. It is not a bad one, my lord, and she is most generous. But I don't want it, and yet I fear the other options." She released a soft laugh. "So I ran to see your sister today, I took joy in helping her, and then spent the evening laughing about silly things. But tomorrow will come and I will be faced with the same choice as I have been every morning."

"And what is that?"

"Do I do what is familiar or throw it all away on something new?"

His brows rose. "What new thing would you do?"

She laughed. "That is the worst of it. I don't know. I have an idea, but it's just a whisper of a thought. One that your sister gave me."

He had a horrible thought about séances or ghost hunts. His sister had a notorious love of the supernatural, but she also read about practical things. Sometimes. "I am breathless with anticipation."

She chuckled. "She said I had so many good ideas about how to hire a good cook that I ought to open a registry office of my own. One that included teaching women how to pick good servants and that taught servants how to perform excellently at their jobs."

He straightened in surprise. "I suspect you would be excellent at that," he said slowly.

She heard the hesitation in his voice. "But you don't think I can do it."

"Not alone. And not all at once."

She arched a brow, so he eventually conceded the rest.

"And not such that it would earn a great deal of money. Not for a while, at least."

She smiled at him. "At least you have not dismissed the idea."

He took a breath. "I listen to a great many ideas from a great many people. Mostly young men, but the older ones have strokes of genius as well." He shrugged. "The world practically overflows with good ideas."

She arched a brow. "But there is a problem?"

"Money. Time. I believe you would follow through with your ideas. I believe you would be willing to put in the work."

She nodded. "I would."

"But how would you live while you establish yourself? Registries are notorious because they don't make money without bilking their clients. And where would you place your office? People must come and go but a shop is expensive, since you must pay rent for the space. Especially since you would want to be in a respectable neighborhood."

He saw her absorb his words, her teeth pressed into her lower lip. He did not mean to dash her dreams, but he had seen many people lose everything on unmanageable ideas that had not been thought through. And that didn't even begin to address the most serious question.

"Will your family support your ambition?"

She looked into his eyes. "My adoptive mother wants me to stay at home and manage her household." She blew out a breath. "She wants me as an old spinster keeping her company through the rest of her life."

He tilted his head to look her in the eye. "Was that the discussion this morning? Is she the dragon who dimmed your fire?"

"She's not a dragon," Miss Rees hedged. "She cares for me, but she has a vision of my future. Indeed, she's decided what every one of us will do, and she's an expert at managing things to her satisfaction."

"She prevents you from considering gentlemen who might marry you and she—"

"Provides me with enough comfort and pin money to dissuade me from searching for a job." She took a deep breath. "I am not mistreated, my lord."

"But you are not allowed the full choices that you would like."

She laughed, but it was a low, unhappy sound. "No one gets a full array of choices."

"What will you do?"

She shook her head. "I don't know. I have only landed on this idea today."

"Then perhaps you should explore it without spending any money. Think of how you would fashion your registry. Look for a place to have it. Perhaps there are other options of which you are unaware."

"Perhaps I will find that I am not suited to it at all."

"You will never know unless you look."

She smiled at him and this time he saw a full measure of excitement in her eyes. No restraint, no fear. And he felt like the greatest dragon hunter of all since he had been the one to bring her there.

CHAPTER TEN

LILAH'S MIND WAS spinning. She had so many ideas, and none of them would settle. Every idea sparked another and another. She realized very quickly that she would have to get a hold on her runaway thoughts. She itched to start making lists and sort through her options, but she was walking home with Lord Kittrel and as much as she ached to flesh out her plans, she wanted to linger with him more.

"You have given me so much to think about," she said as she spun around on their walk. "I haven't felt this excited since..." She pressed her lips together. She wasn't supposed to talk about her childhood.

"Don't stop now," he said with a grin. "Since when?"

She matched his smile, unable to hold back her thoughts when he looked at her like that. "Since my mother was alive. She was an actress, and I used to sneak down to watch in the evenings."

"You watched her performances?"

"Not exactly. Of course, I saw them, but that part was the same every night. Or mostly the same."

"I don't understand."

"It was everyone else. Actors do such interesting things before they perform. Naturally, everyone cared about what happened on the stage, but I loved the excitement just before the performance. Anything could occur then. The evening was one huge possibility. Afterwards, it was done for good or for ill. But beforehand—"

"You like the anticipation of a thing."

She smiled. "I suppose so. Does that make me odd?"

"That makes you intelligent. I have seen so many young men lost in the constant getting of things. As soon as it is in their hands, they are bored and think of something else to acquire. It is an empty way to live."

How very perceptive of him. "And what of you, my lord? Do you appreciate the waiting or the getting of a thing?"

He flashed her a rueful smile. It made him look boyishly handsome as he spoke. "The getting, of course, but that scarcely matters as I never obtain what I seek. It's incredibly frustrating, I assure you."

"Bah," she said. "You are a handsome earl. You can get whatever you want." Clearly the wine had made her bold. She would never have challenged him otherwise.

"Right now, I want the government to pay better pensions for our veterans."

Oh yes. He was a man who tilted at governmental windmills. "There is no chance for such a thing?"

He shrugged. "I continue to try. I think I shall get money for a new infirmary attached to Royal Hospital. At least those who were wounded can get more care."

"But that is a wonderful thing!" she exclaimed.

"And once I have achieved it, I shall be like all those young men I mentioned. I shall immediately look to the next thing I want."

"I think the getting of a hospital is vastly different than the getting of a new carriage or another horse." *And infinitely more admirable.*

"The process is the same though," he said. "I fear I need to live more like you, enjoying the anticipation more than the getting because my successes are few and far between."

She shook her head as her steps slowed. "Nonsense. I think

you enjoy the work. That is exceedingly rare for a titled gentle-man."

His brows rose. "You think my set is generally lazy?"

And spoiled, sometimes cruel, and often completely useless to the world.

"Don't answer that," he said dryly. "I can see your thoughts on your face."

Then she was definitely inebriated because she was normally much better at hiding her thoughts. "A bastard often sees the worst of mankind. Especially the female ones."

His expression sobered, and he extended his arm to her. She took it with ease, feeling happy with the whole world. Or perhaps it was just the joy of being with her companion.

"May I ask you a personal question?" he asked.

"You may ask me anything you like," she returned, curious at what he might want to know.

"Did your father ever plan for your future?"

"What do you mean?"

"Do you have a dowry?"

"My father used to say that my future was secure. Whatever he meant by that was lost when he died. There is a small dowry that Mama managed, and I've managed to put a little money aside for myself from saving my pin money, but that is not enough to sustain me for long."

He frowned as they walked and even made a disgruntled sound before he spoke. "I should not speak ill of your parents, but I find their choices baffling. You say they care for you, and I believe you."

"Yes, of course they did."

"But your life has been created such that you cannot escape your illegitimacy. It is thrust in your face every day. You train and supervise the servants as a housekeeper, and yet you are family. You are reminded of your lack of status among the peerage, and yet you are forbidden to socialize with the lower orders. No wonder you and my sister get along so well. She cares so little for all of that."

"I enjoy her company more than I can say."

"I should think any time you can laugh among friends would be cherished."

She was startled to realize how clearly he saw her life. Indeed before he had put words to her situation, she had not realized how much her every waking moment was defined by being a bastard. It was a depressing thought.

"My family loves me. I know they do. But I never forgot that I wasn't a full person."

He snorted. "Of course, you're a full person. You think, you breathe." He winked at her. "You enchant."

She grinned at him. He said such things to her that made her warm throughout. Especially when he returned her regard. She should have been more attentive. One should never walk about London without being very aware of who is around you. But he was looking at her so sweetly that she forgot everything but him.

Then she felt him stiffen. She saw his jaw set and he started them walking again at a smart clip. She knew why as soon as she heard the feet behind them.

Robbers!

Lord Kittrel rushed her to a shop doorway and pressed her into the protected place of the door.

"Stay behind me," he whispered, then he spun around to face their attackers.

Three men approached, boxing them all in. They were rough men with a rank smell and bad teeth. Two held knives, the third had fists the size of hams, and all three were grinning.

"Give us yer purse, gov."

Her breath caught, fearing the disaster that would come if he didn't give in. She'd heard tales of men begin gutted for less.

"Very well," Lord Kittrel said as he reached inside his coat. "You may have my purse, just leave us alone."

He tossed his purse into the dirt in front of them. It landed with a heavy clink of coins. Not as much as she would have expected, but the point was made. The brute on the left swooped down and scooped it up.

"Now go," ordered his lordship.

The one who had grabbed it poured the contents into his palm. As she'd guessed, there wasn't a great deal of money in it. A few pounds, nothing more.

"It ain't enough!" the man grumbled. "Ye got more."

"I don't have any more for you. Now leave before this turns dangerous."

For all that Lilah was trembling in fear, Lord Kittrel's voice was laced with authority. He didn't sound remotely frightened. More like a tolerant prince who was growing impatient.

"'E's got a watch. Get 'is watch."

"You will not get my watch," he said, his voice cool. "Go."

As he said the last word, Lord Kittrel twisted his cane. Out whipped a sword which he held up in the dim streetlight. The two men carrying knives seemed taken aback, but the one with the huge fists was not deterred.

"Rush 'im!" he cried, and he shoved his nearest compatriot forward before following on the opposite side. It was a cruel thing to do. The one he pushed forward could have been gutted on Lord Kittrel's sword. But instead of stabbing the man through, his lordship dropped the tip of his blade to the side as he punched the man in the face. That left him vulnerable to the big one, but he turned faster than Lilah thought possible, blocked the attack before following with a fast uppercut.

Lilah wasn't idle. Backed as she was in the doorway, she couldn't help that much. But she gathered some stones from the ground and threw them as best she could at the third attacker. Plus, she screamed with loud purpose calling for the watch.

"Help! Help!"

She needn't have bothered. Lord Kittrel laid out the big one with another fast blow. She saw the man's head snap back before he toppled onto his arse. His head landed on the ground with sickening thud, and everything seemed to stop as all of them stared. Was he dead?

"Take him and go," his lordship ordered as he lifted up his sword. "I've been patient up until now, but my kindness is done." His tone dropped to menacing. "Go."

The other two looked at his sword and then down at their compatriot. By some unspoken signal, they dropped down to grab their large companion beneath the arms and began dragging him away. Lilah remained silent, watching as they disappeared into the shadows.

"Are you all right?" Lord Kittrel asked.

She took a breath, her gaze still scanning the shadows. "I am fine," she murmured in awe. Attacked by three robbers and her only damage was dirt on her hands from the pebbles she'd thrown. "You could have dispatched them immediately," she said. "Your sword could have done quick work—"

"That's a messy business," he said. "And I'll not gut a man if I can avoid it."

She took another breath, using the motion to steady her pounding heart. "You lost your purse."

He shrugged. "A small price to pay for your safety." Then he stepped out of the doorway and squatted down. He was picking up the coins the large brute had apparently dropped. "Besides, that was my spare purse. And they didn't get it anyway."

"Your spare purse?"

"It carries enough money to give to someone who might need it. Or to distract thieves." He shrugged. "The smart ones take what they get and leave." He bent down to retrieve his discarded walking stick, quickly piecing them back together.

"But you didn't have to give them anything. You fought them off so easily."

He looked back at her. "Even stupid thieves can get lucky. A few coins is nothing to me. Your safety, however, is of grave importance." He touched her chin. "Are you sure you're all right?"

"I was behind you the entire time," she said, as he held out his arm to her.

"Let's get away from here. It's clearly not a safe corner of London."

It was with him here, she thought. She stepped closer into his side and he allowed it. She wanted to feel the heat from his body and the strength in his arm. "I am protected by Lord Ares himself."

The gentleman squeezed her arm tight. "I am hardly that, but I am pleased—"

She abruptly pushed up on her toes and pressed her mouth to his. It was an awkward motion, and one that could not have happened if he weren't looking at her. But he was angled in her direction and she needed to press herself against him. To show him her gratitude and to taste, once again, the glory that was Lord Ares.

He caught her about the waist, no doubt to steady her. Her motions were abrupt, but he didn't pull away. Indeed, he let her mouth move against his for as much as three seconds before he pulled her tight against him and took control of the kiss.

His tongue invaded her mouth, his arm supported her entire weight, and it felt as if he touched every inch of her inside and out. It wasn't true, but she reveled in the length of his chest against hers, the balance of their weight on his two very solid legs. What he did with his tongue set her blood on fire.

She wrapped her arms around him, she gripped his coat to pull herself tighter. And when they had to break apart to breathe, she let him kiss across her jaw and to her neck. She even lifted her left knee until it pressed against his thigh as she slid down his body. She went only an inch, but it was enough to burn the feel of his groin.

Her right foot remained on the cobblestones, and she forced herself to hold some of her weight. The rest of her was still wrapped around him. He had found her mouth again and she met him stroke for stroke with her tongue, only to surrender to his thrust.

She wanted this. She wanted him. She had no thought other than that. And if he had the wherewithal to find them a bed, she would have given him everything.

He was the one who stopped. He ripped his mouth from hers and pressed their faces together, temple to temple, cheek to cheek, while his breath came and went in a ragged gasp. Hers did too, but his seemed like a great bellows against her ear.

She wanted to speak. She wanted to apologize or beg or something, but her senses were flooded with the weight of his body against hers, the grip of his arm across her back, and the way her blood rushed and roared through her.

"I'm sorry," he rasped.

She swallowed and tried to force herself to release him. It didn't work. "I kissed you." Now she did tilt her head back so she could look him in the eye. "I want to kiss you more."

He dropped his forehead to hers. "If I were a man to have a mistress, I would move heaven and earth to have you."

She winced. "If I were a woman to be a mistress, I would give myself to you right now."

She felt him shudder at her words. "Do not tempt me."

"It is the honest truth," she said. They had just been attacked. He had saved her with the most casual display of strength. Never in her life had any man done so much for her before. Twice, in fact, because she did not forget the drunkards at Vauxhall who had accosted her. He had saved her then as he saved her now, but he was right. Unless she intended to become his mistress now, she needed to pull away. And yet it was so hard to do.

"I'm shaking," she said more as a statement to herself. She was normally so composed.

"Is that you?" he asked as he eased her back. "I thought it was me."

Was he trembling? The thought pleased her. She liked that he was as affected as she was.

"It's only natural," he said gruffly. "We were attacked and survived. Such a thing stirs the…um…primal needs in a person."

Very logical and scientific. She nodded because she couldn't manage to speak. She felt weak even as her blood still pumped hot and strong in her body. They both took time to awkwardly adjust their clothes, and then he extended his arm to her. Such a gentleman! She touched her fingers to his arm as a lady would, and they resumed their walk back to her home.

But her thoughts would not steady and her blood was still pulsing. She wanted to pretend everything was normal, but it wasn't. She wasn't.

"My lord…" she began.

"Yes?"

"Is…" She swallowed. "Is that an option for me?"

"What?"

"Mistress," she said, her voice soft. And when he didn't respond at first, she spoke more forcefully. "Your mistress."

He still didn't speak. Instead, he pressed his far hand over hers and squeezed her fingers where they were placed on his arm. Finally he spoke, his voice hard. "It is a bad life and the absolute wrong life for you," he said.

"How so?" She knew so little of the life of a demirep. She knew he would house her. He would have her.

"Eventually I will marry," he said softly. "Indeed, the pressure for me to set up my nursery grows every day."

She swallowed. He was an unmarried earl with a significant fortune. That made him the catch of the Season.

"I will not betray my wife with a mistress," he said. "I find the very idea distasteful. When that happens, what would you do for protection?"

She would be a demirep in search of a new sponsor. That was not an enviable position for any woman. "I find your position very honorable," she finally said. "To release a mistress when you marry." So many men would not.

Meanwhile, her body chilled by the second. She was not even acceptable as a mistress.

"Miss Rees," he said.

"Please, call me Lilah. At least while you dash all my hopes."

He turned to her, his expression tight with distress. "You cannot set all your hopes upon me. I have never lied to you, never suggested anything but—"

"I know, I know!" she interrupted. "You will not marry me. I cannot be your mistress—"

"That is not because of any failing in you!" he huffed. Then he touched her face, and she felt her soul still at the exquisite care he took even as he pulled her around to look him in the eye. "You tempt me," he said, his voice low. "But I would betray us both were I to indulge our desires."

She knew it was true. She knew he was being honorable. And yet she couldn't help the wave of frustration that rolled through her. She had never wanted a man more, never felt her heart pound for any man, or her body physically pulled in any man's direction. Just him. And by all accounts he was pulled toward her as well.

Good marriages had been built on much less.

"I would be a good wife to you," she said. "I am a good woman."

"I would never suggest otherwise." He pulled both her hands to his mouth and pressed a kiss onto her knuckles. "But for all that I still desire you, my opinion has not changed."

She frowned. "Opinion? What—"

"I could ignore everything, risk everything if I were in love." He lowered her hands. "But this is lust, Miss Rees, and a surge of feeling after a scary attack. Nothing more."

It felt like a great deal more to her. But obviously not to him.

"Very well, my lord, you have convinced me," she said, her voice excruciatingly dry.

"Of what?"

"I now know that the aristocracy has no good men. I have been accosted by drunkards, dismissed by the educated, and insulted by the cream of the *ton*. But of all of them, I find you to be the absolute worst of the lot."

She felt the shock reverberate through his entire body. He stepped back from her as if he had been struck, and indeed, she had intended such a thing. She had offered herself to him in every way possible, and during all that, he had treated her kindly as if it were the honorable thing to do, when in truth, he could not, would not see beyond the circumstances of her birth.

And that made her furious.

"You have dangled the possibility of love in front of me, you have given me hope, only to dismiss it out of hand when you finally feel something!"

He gaped at her, and then he straightened to his full height. "What I feel, Miss Rees, is simply of the body. It is not love."

"Liar!" she snapped. "You are an honorable man, my lord. The truest I have ever met. You are not ruled by your lusts."

"You are drunk," he said firmly. "That is the only explanation. Damnit, Lilah, you accuse me and compliment me in the same sentence."

Why would he not see reason? "You are not a man to be overcome by passion and yet you have kissed me—"

"You wanted me to!"

"Of course, I do. Because I feel something for you. Because you feel something for me." She might not have a great deal of experience, but she knew it when a man was overcome by lust. And she knew when there was something more in his touch, in the way he looked at her, and in his kiss. What they shared was more than lust.

He clearly did not believe her as he shook his head. "You are an attractive woman."

She snorted. That was how incensed she was. She made the rudest sound she knew. "There are dozens of women more beautiful than me. I will lay odds that you have never touched them as you did me."

"You underestimate your charms."

"You underestimate your feelings."

She stood there then, challenging him in every way she knew

how. She wanted to shake him until he realized that he felt something for her. She knew he did! Just as she was rapidly falling for him. But he stood there like a confused and stupid man, disconnected from his feelings and unable to comprehend the possibility of real feeling between them.

It made her want to scream. Instead, she turned and looked to her house just up the street. She could run there in under a minute. Then bury her face in her coverlet and sob out her frustration.

Before she could take flight, he touched her arm. He held her in place while he struggled for words. "Miss Rees. Lilah. I see you are overwrought."

She arched her brows at him. She was incensed.

"In the morning—when you are calmer—I hope you won't think less of yourself after tonight. Personally, I continue to hold you in the highest esteem."

What was she to say to that? His "highest esteem" was not high enough to consider her a marriage prospect. And it didn't begin to acknowledge the love that was growing between them. Which meant he would never recognize it, never comprehend his own feelings, and never, ever look past the difference in their social status.

"You are an idiot," she said, speaking to herself as much as to him.

Then she curtseyed to him and took her leave. She walked slowly away at first. She wanted to hold onto her dignity. But as soon as she was out of sight, she broke out into a run. And with every step, she vowed to never think of Lord Kittrel again.

How dare she?

Aaron's blood boiled, and yet even furious, he waited until he saw a lit candle in her bedroom. He wanted to see that she returned home safely. *You are the worst of the lot.*

What nonsense. The woman had been overcome after being inebriated. Of course, she spouted all sorts of ridiculousness. He was a man of reason, and that often upset emotional creatures like Lilah.

Aaron ground his teeth at his own lies. Lilah was the least irrational person he'd ever met, and he exposed his own failings when he cast her as such a creature. Was she the one standing in the street staring at a window? Was she the one with a painful cockstand for a woman he'd just labeled overwrought and ridiculous?

You underestimate your feelings.

Hard to underestimate the throbbing in his loins, but that's not what she'd meant.

You are an idiot.

Yes, he was because she was right. He felt more than a physical hunger for her. He had felt protective of her before and after the attack. He felt admiration for her quick wits, not just in conversation but in throwing rocks at their attackers while screaming for the watch. She was not a woman who panicked or became overwrought. He, on the other hand, was a man who controlled his lusts and never trespassed upon a woman's heart. Because a spurned woman could make your life miserable.

Why hadn't he controlled his desire for Miss Rees? Why hadn't he left her alone rather than allow tender feelings to blossom? Feelings that were deceptive. Feelings that promised more than any soul could deliver. Which is why he had lied about them.

His parents had been a love match, and it had destroyed them both. His father—not yet an earl—had fallen in love with a clergyman's daughter. She, in turn, thought him the most refined gentleman to ever come calling. They were "dazzled by love" according to his father. Mother said he'd made her believe in true happiness.

The cost of the mésalliance had not been clear at first, but soon his mother's less refined manners began to embarrass his father. He hid her in the country and blamed her coarse manners every time he was overlooked in his political career. She became shrewish in her demands for London amusements only to find herself associating with milkmaids and clergyman daughters because they were her only company. By the time Clara was five, the two were so steeped in resentment they poisoned the very air.

Aaron had been raised in a household filled with love gone sour. If it were not for the steadying influence of their Nanny, God only knew what kind of man he might have become. Thankfully, he learned the lesson well that love was a trap. Happiness came from a steady temperament that never succumbed to the "dazzle of love."

He'd nearly misstepped with Lilah a year ago. After their kiss at Vauxhall, he'd been so mesmerized he believed he had to marry the woman. A year in the country with his bitter parents had brought clarity back to his emotions.

He felt lust for Miss Rees, nothing more.

You are an idiot.

Guilty. Because only an idiot would fall into the same trap that had destroyed his parents.

Strangely, he was grateful to Miss Rees for bringing his attention to his changing feelings. He was beginning to fall for her. But now that she had declared a disgust of him, he could return to his life and think of her no more.

The first step, of course, was to stop standing like a lovelorn waif in front of her bedroom window. He took a deep breath and forced himself to move. He would go home and think of her no more.

CHAPTER ELEVEN

A WEEK LATER, Lilah accepted the fact that Lord Kittrel would not be banished from her dreams. During the day, however, she had other things to occupy her thoughts. Like Mr. Reuben Bates who was right now taking a turn through her parlor. Never had Lilah met a person with more energy. It should have been exhausting to be in the same room with him, but the constant twinkle in his eye invited her to play even as he talked about outrageous things. They were having tea in her private parlor and though he'd sat down when invited, even drank the tea when offered, he was currently up and pacing about the room.

She found him delightful.

"I don't mind telling you that I've been looking for a solution to the horrendously exploitive registry practice," he said. "People come in from the country or fall on hard times. They think they're getting help when it's just another way to fleece someone already desperate. But now I think you're the one to fix that." He grinned as he dropped back down into his seat. "And I am just the man to help you."

"Mr. Bates, my registry idea is just beginning. I don't even have a location selected—"

He held up his hands. "But that's where I can help. Lucas told me all about your ideas."

Lucas was her brother-in-law. He'd married her half-sister Diana after a courtship fraught with scandal, murder, and love lost. It was a story that still touched Lilah's heart. "I was merely bouncing ideas off Diana when Lucas overheard. I have no set plans. Only possibilities."

"I know," Mr. Bates said as he clapped his hands together. "I have learned a great deal about you in the last couple days, and I believe you are just the woman to run a registry. We need integrity in London, you know. Honest people doing honorable service."

He sounded like he was recruiting her into a nunnery, but that was the opposite of her plans. "I mean it to be a business for profit," she said. "I will have to support myself."

"Yes, yes, of course," he said as he waved his fingers at her. "The thing is, you have an ability with organization, the knowledge to teach your clients how to do their jobs correctly, and…" His eyes seemed to glitter with excitement. "Your family situation sets you in the exact position to place souls in good households for honest labor."

"I am a bastard, Mr. Bates. I don't think that recommends me in any way whatsoever."

"But that's where you're wrong. You've been to several society parties. The *ton* knows you."

"As a *bastard*."

"Exactly!" He pointed straight at her. "They don't want you marrying their sons, but they will take your recommendation on what housekeeper to hire or where to find a good footman. You're above a servant, you see, but below them."

That was something she knew all too well.

"Besides, you will have the backing of your family, yes? Lucas was singing your praises, as did Sayres."

"You've talked with my family?"

He shrugged. "With your brothers-in-law. They have assured me that their wives fully support you."

She nodded. Gwen and Diana were the easy ones to persuade. They were both very independent in their thoughts. It was the rest of her family–her mother and brother—who were more traditional. Fortunately, Elliott wanted her to be happy and he had married an artisan tradeswoman. He might support her. Mama, however, was likely to declare it a calamity of historic proportions. "My mother will not help," she said firmly.

"You will have to persuade her. She has the most reach out of all of you."

Her adoptive mother was indeed the most influential society matron out of all of them. "We are getting ahead of ourselves. There is no business yet to support. I haven't found a location or—"

"But I have! And best of all, it's already established by a drunken sot who has somehow managed to survive these last years." He grinned as he sat back down. "Your dowry is enough to buy him out. Then you can take over his business, train his clients so they are good at their jobs, and voila! You have a thriving career and a happy life."

"My dowry!" she gasped. "But that is all the money I have!"

He leaned forward. "One must spend money to make money. Surely you know that."

She knew nothing of the sort. What she did know was that no one did something for free. "What is your part in all this, Mr. Bates?"

"Mine?" he grinned. "I'm doing my friend Lucas a favor."

"That cannot be all."

She expected his expression to dim, but strangely, he brightened even further almost as if he were cheering her on. "I shall give it to you straight. I want the drunken sot gone. He is a blight on my neighborhood."

He paused then, and she arched a brow. Did he really think she would accept that as his sole purpose? She did not.

"Ah, you're a canny one," he said with a sexy drawl.

"And you sound more and more like a swindler. I cannot believe you and Lucas are friends."

He touched his hand to his heart in horror. "You wound me, Miss Rees." When she did not change from her severe expression, he winked at her. "But I do have another purpose beyond being a help to yourself and Lucas."

He took a deep breath as he dropped his elbows forward onto his knees. "I should like to be an investor in your business."

Her eyes widened in surprise. "An investor? How?"

"Alas, I cannot offer you money. That you will have to find on your own, but I can offer you protection. The neighborhood is not the best for a gently-reared lady. I have a vast network of friends throughout London. We shall keep watch over you, to the best of our ability, and in return, I should like you to help my friends and family in obtaining positions." He grinned. "I should require you to teach my friends their skills for free. That is fair recompense for your protection. And naturally—because of our great friendship—they will get preferential treatment for any jobs."

Truly this was a man who could charm a bird from the trees. The way he said things made his words sound as if they were eminently reasonable and he the most beneficent of souls. She did believe him when he said he was a friend of Lucas's. Diana had even mentioned him a few times, though this was the first time she'd met the man face to face. But she did not believe that he was acting out of the goodness of his heart. This was clearly a business transaction for him and one she would do well to investigate.

"Let us take this one step at a time," she finally said. "Where is this registry that you think I can buy? What makes you think the…the drunkard you speak of will sell to me?"

"Oh well," he said as he held up his hands. "As to that, I can negotiate on your behalf—"

"For a small fee, no doubt."

"The smallest, I assure you."

She snorted. "The smallest amount is free."

"Ah well," he demurred, "my time is valuable, you know. I am only here—"

"Out of your great friendship with my brother-in-law."

"And a civic duty to oust that sot from blighting my favorite London street."

She shook her head. "I will negotiate myself."

He arched his brows in a doubtful expression. "You know what permits are required to run a registry? You know all the things that a man or woman must do to establish a London business? What taxes are to be paid and to whom?" He leaned back in his chair. "Miss Rees, the requirements are daunting, and I am here to assist you with all of it."

Of course, he was, but thanks to her discussion with Lord Kittrel a week ago, she'd already researched a great deal of what was required.

"Actually, Mr. Bates, I do know what is required, and I will manage it myself." She folded her arms across her chest. "Do women always fall for your charm?"

"Indeed they do."

"Not me."

"Lucas said you were smart." He pushed up from his seat. Then after a quick turn about the room, he came to a stop across from her. "I shall do you a favor, Miss Rees. A free favor from a man who hopes that one day you will have cause to return it."

She waited, wary but still curious. "I am listening."

"I shall tell you the best way to negotiate with Mr. Palmer. He's a veteran gambler. Can't resist a challenge no matter how stupid, which means he's got notes throughout London. The right contest will have you buying his business for much less than it is worth."

"Why should I buy his business? You said it is a stain upon your neighborhood."

"*Mr. Palmer* is a stain upon my neighborhood, but he has put advertisements for his services all over England. Nearly every new resident of London has heard of Mr. Palmer's Path to Prosperity. They flock to his registry with nary a soul to send them elsewhere." He snorted. "It's the one thing the man did right. His registry—if it were run correctly—would be an asset to my neighborhood."

She agreed with him. She'd already discovered that Mr. Palmer's registry was the most well-known and in the best location, but it hadn't occurred to her until now that she might win his business in a wager. "It cannot be that easy," she said.

He chuckled. "It won't be easy, but if you can win the business from Mr. Palmer, I will support you with my protection."

"But I don't gamble—"

He laughed as he leaped to his feet. "Everyone gambles in some way. You more so than most, I think, else how would you have landed here?"

Lilah winced at his perception. She had indeed gambled when she'd pressed her father to bring her home with him when she was nine. She'd gambled again when she'd pressed Lord Ares to marry her, but she'd lost that bet.

"Find a way to win against Mr. Palmer," he pressed. "Otherwise, I shall have to employ more drastic measures to oust the blighter, and that is not something I want to do." On that enigmatic statement, he pulled an address from his pocket and passed it to her. "That's where you'll find Mr. Palmer most nights, but mind you don't go alone. I'd bring a large, brute of a man with you. Mr. Palmer negotiates with his fists first."

She looked at the address and frowned. She'd heard of the Lyon's Den gaming hell from someone, but she didn't recall the exact details.

"And don't bring Lucas," he said grimly. "They've got a past and Palmer would likely cut off his own nose rather than help anyone associated with your brother-in-law. Which means, I wouldn't let him know who you are."

"Then how am I to negotiate with him? I'm related to Lucas!"

Mr. Bates bowed to her as if he hadn't heard her question. Then he left, moving down the stairs with surprising speed. He had gathered his hat from their butler and was out the door before she could decide if she were insulted or amused. A little of both, she supposed.

Either way, her next steps were clear. After a little more research and a discussion with her brother regarding her dowry, she needed to find a large, powerful man to accompany her into the Lyon's Den. Someone who wouldn't be appalled at the idea of her going into a notorious gambling den.

Her brothers wouldn't do it, that was for certain, even if Mr. Bates hadn't explicitly warned her against using them. Her servants weren't large enough to be intimidating. She needed someone she trusted, someone who would see it as a lark, perhaps, and would still provide some measure of protection.

In short, she needed a lord who laughed when most of his compatriots would scowl. She needed Lord Loughton.

CHAPTER TWELVE

"**A**BSOLUTELY NOT! I won't do it."

Aaron frowned as he heard his sister's voice through the door of her parlor. He was coming home after another long day's work. He had no wish to step into an argument with his sister. At least he didn't until he heard the voice of the other half of the argument.

"I could think of no one else. You needn't join us. In fact, I much prefer you didn't. You have a reputation worth saving."

Miss Rees. He had not spoken with her in the eight days since their last kiss, though he had done that and much more with her in his dreams. She had been to the house. That much was certain from his daily conversations with his sister, but he had not crossed paths with her. Indeed, he had worked to avoid her. Unless he could find a way to marry her—and he had thought often on the possibility—it did neither of them any good to stay in each other's company. But his efforts had failed tonight. She was here, and he wanted to see her.

Without thinking too hard about it, he knocked once on his sister's parlor door and entered. His sister was standing in the center of the room. Her face was flushed, and her hands fisted as she spun around to glare at him. Miss Rees was sitting in the far corner and she looked chagrined. Also, she looked adorable as she bit her lower lip while her chin sat firmly in the palm of her hand. She straightened upon his entrance, but that didn't stop him from mentally recording her expression such that he could recall it whenever he wished.

"Aaron! Why are you here?" his sister gasped.

"Because I live here?" he returned.

"But you're never home before…" Her gaze turned to the clock. "Oh. My. It is late."

Meanwhile, Miss Rees stood up. "I need to be going. Good evening—"

"I'm coming with you!" Clara cried. "You cannot go there alone."

"I will have to learn how to do many new things alone," Miss Rees said gently. "I shall be perfectly safe."

Clara dropped her hands on her hips. "Aaron, there is food downstairs waiting for you. Now if you excuse me, I shall be accompanying Miss Rees to a fleecing."

"Don't be so dramatic," Miss Rees said. "You have gone alone to all sorts of strange places. I am merely emulating your bravery."

"My séances are perfectly safe!"

He held up his hand. "Perhaps one of you should tell me what's going on."

Miss Rees shook her head. "It is nothing of import. I merely asked your sister to contact Lord Loughton on my behalf. She has refused, and I am—"

"Lilah is going to a gambling den to out-swindle a swindler. She's going to lose all her money and maybe die."

The silence in the room after that pronouncement seemed to echo in his head. Contrary to his sister's mode of argument, Miss Rees did not try to out-yell or out-dramatize Clara. She smiled warmly as she collected her things and made as if to leave. Naturally, he couldn't allow that, but he did appreciate that she wasn't trying to create a Cheltenham tragedy out of her plans.

"You know I must have the truth now," he said. "Clara will never give me any peace if I allow things to stand."

Miss Rees paused and blew out a slow breath. "I have done as you asked, my lord. In the last eight days I have visited all the registries in London pretending to be a client. I have looked into the way they do business, figured the prices and expenses, and even taken steps to claim my dowry. And now, thanks to a suggestion from Mr. Ruben Bates, I have learned—"

"Bates! Wherever did you meet him?"

Miss Rees tilted her head. "Do you know him? He visited me last week on the pretext of offering his help. I gather he learned of my plans from Lucas, my brother-in-law."

"Yes," Aaron grumbled. "He and Lucas are fast friends, though I cannot understand what he was thinking to introduce the two of you."

Clara frowned. "Is he a blackguard then?"

"No, no," Aaron rushed to say. "I believe his heart is in the right place. Generally."

Miss Rees smiled. "But he is an interesting person. Seems to straddle the line, I think, between self-interest and general good."

He did not like the way she smiled when she spoke of him. Unfortunately, he could not disagree with her statement. Reuben Bates had made a business out of being aware of everyone else's business. He was related to half of London and was friendly with the other half, including the *ton*, though he couldn't imagine many would admit to the association. "He is not respectable, Miss Rees, and I cannot understand what Lucas is about to allow you the association."

"Lucas has no authority to allow or disallow my companions," she countered firmly. "The question is, do you think Mr. Bates is reliable?"

He would rather chew glass than answer that, but he could see she would not be deterred. "He will honor his word."

"Excellent—"

"But did he give it?" Aaron pressed. "Did he say you would be safe at this gambling den? Will his men protect you?"

"No!" Clara huffed. "That's the problem. He has tossed her to the lion's den and waits to see if she gets eaten."

Aaron folded his arms. "I believe I need details. What lion? What den?"

Miss Rees laughed. "Oh, sorry. She means that literally. I am to find my quarry most nights in the Lyon's Den. It's a gaming hell that—"

"I know it," Aaron interrupted. Every young man of means knew of the Lyon's Den. It was where the unwary went to enjoy gambling on unusual things. The usual as well, but the place was notorious for unusual games.

"Mr. Parker is there most nights," Miss Rees continued.

Clara folded her arms. "Tell him what you intend to do."

Miss Rees shrugged. "I intend to gamble with him. I have pin money, and he has debts." She grinned. "I intend to win ownership of his registry."

He gaped at her. "You cannot be serious."

"I have limited options."

"You told me you were going to explore the feasibility of—"

"And I have. His place has the best location and the worst management." She lifted her chin. "I think I can do it."

"Why not get a job there?"

"And work for the reprobate?"

No, of course not. That would be dangerous. "Why not go to the second-best place and make improvements? Why not—"

"Because they aren't hiring." She held up her hand. "I have considered every possibility. Indeed, I have thought of nothing else for these last eight days." She took a step forward. "You gave me excellent advice, my lord, but given my situation..." She shrugged. "I have opted to try the big risk that is available to me rather than wait for another opportunity to arise."

"And if you lose all your money?"

She shrugged. "Then I shall remain with my adoptive mother and try to save up again."

He stared at her. He held her gaze and he waited. She looked like she meant it, as if it were the easiest thing in the world to lose money she had scrupulously hoarded for years. Eventually, her gaze wavered, and she sighed.

"Men win and lose fortunes all the time with nary a thought."

"You are not them." He touched her arm. "I think this is very foolish."

"Nevertheless, I am determined."

He could see that. "Why don't you try to purchase the registry from him?"

"I haven't enough money."

"How much do you need?" The words were out before he could think them through. The earldom was well heeled, but he'd sunk a great deal into improvements. He did not have a lot of ready cash. Nevertheless, he would find a way to help her. She did not need to take insane risks at a notorious gaming hell.

Miss Rees waved his offer aside. "Mr. Palmer won't sell. I already tried. But Mr. Bates said he would gamble it away if I was clever."

Mr. Bates excelled at finding clever ways to trick people. That didn't mean Miss Rees could do it too. "Gambling is not so easy. You cannot be sure to win. Indeed, the odds of success are very small."

Miss Rees leveled him with a hard stare. "I know that. I have decided to take the risk anyway."

He could see that she was intent on going no matter what he said or did. Damnation, she was going to lose every penny she owned, but he was not her nanny. He couldn't stop her. What he could do was make sure that she lost only her money and not a thing more.

"When do you mean to go?"

Clara huffed out a breath. "Tonight!"

He'd guessed as much. "Very well. I will accompany you."

Her eyes widened. "You'll stand with me in a gambling hell?"

"I won't let you go alone."

"You're not going to try to stop me?"

He shook his head. "I'd like to discuss it with you more on the way there."

"I would like that."

"But I am not your parent and you are of age. I cannot stop you."

Her smile was slow in coming, but dazzling when it finally appeared. "You are a rare breed, my lord."

He frowned. "I beg your pardon?"

"A man who does not insist upon his way. One who respects my choices. It gives me hope for the human race."

He snorted. "I don't think the race is in any danger, but I accept your compliment. Though I find your choice baffling and incredibly unwise."

She laughed. "You have the entire drive to convince me of your thoughts."

He nodded. That was exactly his plan. Then he held open the door to her. She passed by him close enough that he could feel the heat of her body as she brushed past. What he wouldn't give to have her in his bed for one night.

He pushed aside those thoughts as he stepped to follow her, neatly cutting off his sister. "Not you, I'm afraid."

"What?" Clara gasped. "Aaron, you just said you would respect her choice."

"I did. I also agree with her statement."

She lifted her chin. "Which was what?"

He winced in advance. She was not going to appreciate this. "You have a reputation to lose. You cannot be seen in a gambling hell, Clara."

"Don't be ridiculous—"

"Plus, I have the carriage. You have no means to get there."

She sniffed. "If you think your carriage is my only means of transport, then you are sadly mistaken."

It was true. She had money for a hackney if she could find one at this hour. She also had friends who would likely offer to take her wherever she wished. "You will be of no help there," he said gently. "A gaming hell is a man's domain, and you have no experience in it."

"I should like to learn!"

That wasn't in the least bit true. She had no interest in gambling. Never had. Never would. "I can protect Miss Rees better if I am not watching to see that you are safe. As my sister, you are my first obligation. If she gets in trouble, my priority would be to make sure you are safe first. That would leave Miss Rees unprotected."

It was a lie. He would see them both safe, but it would be much easier if he watched only one woman, not two. Fortunately, he knew that Clara respected logic. She was temperamental, not unreasonable.

"You will not abandon her?" Clara stressed.

"I swear it." Then because he felt bad about leaving her behind, he pulled her into a quick, brotherly hug and whispered into her ear. "Allow me to be human, Clara. I cannot protect two women at once."

"I understand," she said as he drew back. Then her gaze went to Miss Rees. "Pray do not do anything stupid. Do not spend a penny of your dowry. Just your pin money."

"I shall be very practical," Miss Rees returned.

"If that were true," he muttered, "then we wouldn't be doing this at all."

She chuckled as they left Clara's parlor. He called for his carriage and she served him his dinner in the kitchen while they waited for it to be brought around. Between bites of the still-warm meat pie, he asked her about the details of her plan to run a registry office. She answered easily enough, and he could find no fault in her conclusions. This mad gamble might indeed be her best choice.

He worried, of course, what his sister was doing. It wasn't like Clara to remain in her room while they were still here. But he was more interested in Miss Rees, and so he let himself forget his sister and focus instead on what Miss Rees was saying.

"I know it sounds ungrateful," she said. "But I cannot accept the life my adoptive mother has declared for me. I don't want to be her companion for the rest of my life."

"But are you sure you want to run a registry? You haven't been working on this idea for very long. Perhaps a new idea, a better idea will strike—"

"I cannot spend my life waiting for inspiration. This is what I've decided upon, and I will never forgive myself if I don't try."

He admired that determination. So many risked foolishly while the others never took a chance at all. He hoped she was that rare creature who straddled the middle line. "Tell me about your calculations."

She did. She walked him through all her thoughts during the rest of the drive to the Lyon's Den. She'd certainly been thorough. She'd been very analytical, and he was impressed by her methodical approach. It was too bad, really, that her dreams would never be realized.

No man, even a drunk, would gamble away his business when it was his only means of income. By all accounts Mr. Palmer was a veteran in the hells. Aaron knew many such men who had markers all over town yet managed to survive through fair means and foul. Such a man did not lose to a woman, even one as enticing as Miss Rees. Especially her.

It would be a painful lesson for the lady, but one that might not cost her everything. He vowed to find a way to give her back whatever money she lost this night. It wouldn't gain her the registry, but it would minimize the damage. It also meant that Aaron would have to stand stoically by her side while her dream was destroyed.

It was going to be the hardest thing he'd ever done.

CHAPTER THIRTEEN

LORD KITTREL UTTERLY disagreed with her plans. That much was clear. But he didn't stop her. He allowed her to express her opinion, and—this was the best part—he vowed to stand with her despite his utter disagreement.

This was a man she could trust. She entered the Lyon's Den gaming hell with a buoyancy to her step. She was taking a chance on her future, and that felt exciting in a way nothing else had for a very long time. She wondered briefly if this was how her mother had felt before every performance. Had her belly tightened with excitement while her heart pounded in her throat? Lilah's cheeks flushed, and her hands pressed against her stomach, but she walked with firm purpose up the steps of the den.

They were stopped at the door by a large man with a scar running through his right cheek, and that gave him the look of an angry dog. But his tone was bored when he spoke to them.

"Women's door be around the corner," he said as he pointed.

She smiled. "Yes, but I'm looking for a man. Mr. Dalbert Palmer. I'm told he's here most nights."

The man didn't even blink. In fact, his gaze lifted over hers to Lord Kittrel. "Women's door around the corner."

He was dismissing her, but she refused to budge. "And will I be able to find Mr. Dalbert Palmer in the women's area?"

"No."

"Then why would I go there?"

His gaze returned to her. "Because yer a woman, and we don't like any fracas here. Find him somewhere else."

"I don't intend to make a fracas." She reached into her purse. "Perhaps I could convince you—"

"I don't take bribes either. Mrs. Dove-Lyon would toss me out for it, and I like it here."

Well, hell. She could admire the man's ethics, but that wasn't going to help her get inside. Then Lord Kittrel stepped forward.

"Mrs. Dove-Lyon does enjoy a certain kind of sport, and we are here to provide it. If you let us through."

The man's gaze sharpened. "You're here to see the mistress? Have you an appointment?"

"Yes—" Lilah lied.

"No. But we offer something worth her while." Then he passed over his card.

Lilah flushed and mentally chastised herself for trying to lie. She'd been thinking only of getting through this one barricade, but even if it worked, it would damage her five minutes from now when someone discovered the truth. Meanwhile, the door guard looked them both over and nodded.

He passed the card to another large gentlemen behind him and said, "Philostrate will take you to her." Then he looked at Lilah and the side of his mouth curled up. "There's lots that the missus can do to help, if'n you don't lie to her."

Lilah nodded and felt her cheeks flush hot as her confidence slipped. This was a new world for her, and things were already not working out as she'd planned. She resolved to be even more careful as they walked in Philostrate's wake. She also glanced at Lord Kittrel for reassurance. He returned her look with slightly raised brows as if to say, *Are you sure about this?*

Of course, she wasn't sure, but she was determined. She lifted her chin and walked with more purpose in her step. He matched her pace with a set expression, and—she now noticed—his gaze was never still. They were walking around the main gaming floor while cigar smoke thickened the air. Fortunately, this made some sense to her as she had seen the card room at many balls. This place was no different, just larger. She noted men playing, very handsome men dealing, and coins or markers always changing hands. If she recognized any of the men here, it was in a distant sort of way. Lord Kittrel, on the other hand, seemed to recognize several of the players and that made his jaw tighten and his hands twitch. He also moved closer to her as if protecting her, and she welcomed his nearness and his large size.

"Stay close to me," he murmured barely loud enough for her to hear.

He needn't have said anything. She had no intention of leaving his side.

In time, they made it to a parlor on an upper floor. Philostrate gestured for them to remain where they were—outside the open door—as he went in and passed Aaron's card to a lady dressed all in black where she sat at the back of the parlor drinking tea.

"That's Mrs. Dove-Lyon, the owner of the Lyon's Den," Aaron whispered to her. "She is known to be a champion of women."

There was no time for him to say more as the widow gestured them forward. They entered and Philostrate left, closing the door behind him. They were not bid to sit down. Indeed, they stood there like poor parishioners before a priest. It was a lowering experience for her, but it had to be a fully insulting one for Lord Kittrel. And yet he stood by her side as her support without any appearance of anger.

Yet.

"Good evening, Mrs. Dove-Lyon," she said. "I appreciate your seeing me."

"You have a need?" the lady said. Her face was obscured by the dark lace of her veil, but her words came out clear enough.

"I wish to see Mr. Dalbert Palmer."

"Why?"

"I want to buy his registry office. It is run terribly. He abuses his single employee, he takes advantage of his clients, and he never trains them in their intended careers. It's criminal." In her time between Mr. Bates' visit and tonight, she'd visited the office under the guise of looking for work. What she'd found there had set her teeth on edge.

Apparently, it didn't bother Mrs. Dove-Lyon.

"It's not criminal. It's completely legal, though I agree his actions are deplorable. Either way, a purchase offer should be extended during the day at his place of business."

Lilah took a deep breath. "I intend to gamble him for it."

The lady was silent for a long moment. Then she set her teacup back in its saucer before turning to his lordship.

"Lord Kittrel, it is lovely to see you again. I cannot remember the last time you came to my humble establishment." She extended to her hand to him.

As was proper, Aaron stepped forward and bowed over her hand. There wasn't anything intimate about his actions, and yet Lilah found herself annoyed by the interaction even as he spoke in neutral tones with the lady. "I'm afraid the work of the country takes up all my time. Personal amusements are rare for me."

"And yet you come here with a lady who means to challenge one of my most loyal customers."

"I do." He turned to Lilah. "Miss Rees is true to her word, and her money is good."

"You endorse her?"

"Yes."

Absurd to feel warmed by his statement, but she did. And it was far easier to focus on her gratitude toward Lord Kittrel than the anxiety that churned in her gut. What was she thinking to try such a crazy thing? She wasn't a gambler. She knew how to dust a room and plan meals. And yet, she would never be more than a bastard housekeeper if she didn't take this risk. And though Aaron was against this, he was here endorsing her. She had to take comfort in that as she waited for Mrs. Dove-Lyon's approval.

It took a long time.

"How do you gamble, Miss Rees? Cards? Dice?"

"Mathematics."

She saw Aaron's eyes widen in surprise. She hadn't told him of this part of her plan, but clearly Mrs. Dove-Lyon was intrigued. She sat forward in her seat.

"Mr. Palmer is well known for his ability to figure in his head. Indeed, he has often challenged the Abacas Lady to a mathematical duel."

Even Lilah had heard of the Abacas Lady. She was the mystery woman behind the cage door who kept track of all the den's money. The click-clack of her abacas was a constant here.

"And the lady has refused, much to the disappointment of your clientele," Lilah said.

"So you wish to duel him. In mathematics?"

"Yes."

"What will you put up in return?"

"Five hundred pounds. In cash."

The woman was silent for a moment, then she set down her teacup. "You have it on you?"

"I do."

"Then I will allow it—"

Lilah blew out a breath of relief.

"—But there is a price."

Naturally. "Yes?"

"I know who you are, Miss Lilah Rees. Indeed, Mr. Bates appraised me of your intention several days ago."

Really? He'd only had the discussion with her yesterday. "How interesting."

Mrs. Dove-Lyon didn't appear to think it interesting at all. "I require you to teach several of my employees the details of household management."

Lilah jolted. "What?"

"I wish you to teach the maids how to dust, the footmen how to serve, and all of them how to keep accounts."

"What?"

Mrs. Dove-Lyon gestured to the floor below them. "There is

space below the den for such classes. I have cleared a space for you there. At present, I have seven students in mind beginning next week. You may consider them your first clients whether or not you succeed in winning Mr. Palmer's registry."

Lilah frowned. "But if I win, I must spend all my time setting things right there. I did not intend to start classes this early. I won't have the time."

Mrs. Dove-Lyon was not swayed. "That is my price."

What choice did she have? It was the only path to Mr. Palmer. "Agreed," she finally said. "For seven students, one class." She lifted her chin. "Any more will require payment."

"One class lasting a full day. We shall discuss the details of your instruction beforehand."

Lilah winced, but could find no reason to disagree. "Done."

"Excellent." The woman pushed up to her feet and walked regally toward the door. "Follow me."

Things proceeded quickly after that. The lady paused at the door to her parlor to whisper to one of the large men stationed there. He nodded smartly then ran off, presumably to do her bidding. A minute later, the orchestra stopped what they were playing before abruptly sounding a fanfare. Then, still poised at the door to her parlor, Mrs. Dove-Lyon spoke to the entire gallery below.

"Mr. Dalbert Palmer, I have a challenge for you. Do you accept?"

If the gallery had gone quiet before, it was now absolutely silent. Plenty of time for a corpulent man at a whist table to lean back in his chair. His gaze ticked to where the Abacas Woman sat in her cage.

"Does the lady of mystery accept my challenge?"

"No," Mrs. Dove-Lyon said as she took a step toward the stairs. "She stands as judge."

"Then who challenges me?" demanded Mr. Palmer.

Damnation, this was a great deal more attention than she expected. Lilah was used to slinking about the background, not stepping forward into the center of attention like this. Every part of her body urged her to run and hide. Fortunately, Lord Kittrel was there bracing her with more than his body.

"Make it entertaining for the crowd, and Mrs. Dove-Lyon will help you," he whispered. "Make it dramatic," he said. Then he pushed her out the door such that she stood at the top of the gallery next to the woman.

Good God, standing there with a hundred eyes on her was horrid. At that moment, she knew she had not a drop of her mother's acting talents because she was nearly frozen with terror. And yet what choice did she have? She'd embarked on this path against all advice. And so here she was, just now realizing how much more would be required of her than simple mathematical figuring. And that, she knew, would be hard enough.

"Say it!" Mrs. Dove-Lyon hissed under her breath.

"What?"

"Idiot," she said, in a kind of curse. "Say your challenge."

Oh. "Um…I do," she said.

"Dramatically!" whispered Aaron from behind her.

Right. Of course. Damnation, why couldn't she think?

She raised her voice. "I do!" she said loudly.

The chuckles began slowly, but they quickly gained speed. All around the gallery, the gamblers were laughing at her. They knew nothing of her abilities, but already they dismissed her. Damnation, she might be a bastard, but she wasn't a fool. For all they knew, she could be a genius at figuring. In fact, she was damned good at it!

Strangely enough, Mr. Palmer didn't laugh. Instead, his gaze seemed to rove over her. "I like the stakes," he said.

It took her a moment to realize that he thought she was offering herself as forfeit and she stiffened at the insult. She watched in horror as the rest of the gallery looked over her figure as well, adding their own ribald comments.

Only one man didn't laugh. Lord Kittrel. Up until now, he had stood behind her, likely hidden by the shadows. But as the jeering got louder, he set his hand to the small of her back. He didn't push, but the warmth of his palm steadied her. Then he spoke in a low tone straight to her.

"Give me the word, Lilah, and I will step in. I can get you away now, and you will lose nothing."

Nothing but her chance at a future. Nothing but her own self-respect. Far from giving her an out, Lord Kittrel was giving her the strength to forge ahead. Taking a deep breath, she pitched her voice until it filled the gallery. Her first words shook a bit, but they steadied soon enough. And before long, she was giving everyone the kind of show her mother had done so effortlessly. And what a surprise to find that she was capable of such a thing.

"Mr. Palmer," she began. "I submit that you are a terrible owner of a disastrous registry office. You have abused your one employee, your files are a mess, and you fleece your customers every possible moment."

It was a dangerous statement, mostly because it was guaranteed to raise Mr. Palmer's ire. She knew from her discussion with his one employee that many of the gentlemen here in the den got their servants through Mr. Palmer's business. They did not take kindly to the suggestion that they had been fleeced. And from the man's hurried denial, he knew she was striking at the core of his business.

"The devil I do!" he cried. "I'm as honest as—"

"A wolf in sheep's clothing," she said, though she had no idea if she was heard over him.

"—My sainted grandmother!"

She couldn't afford to keep him scoffing at her. She needed him to agree to the challenge, so she pressed forward, first to the railing at the edge of the platform, then following Mrs. Dove-Lyon as they both descended the stairway to the gallery.

"I would run your business better," she said. "I would ensure that your people are trained before they are sent into service. That none were thieves. And that every lord or lady could be assured of proper respect when they hired from me." She glanced about the room. "How many of you have received a rotten worker from this man?"

Every man here had likely griped about his servants. It was what aristocrats did. They complained about the staff. It felt good to turn that ire against a man who deserved it for putting out untrained people.

"I will own your business, Mr. Palmer. And I will match mathematical wits with you to get it."

Far from being enticed, the man rolled his eyes at her. "You aren't worth it."

No, from his perspective, she probably wasn't. She drew out her purse and fanned the pound notes. "Five hundred pounds, Mr. Palmer. Is that worth it to you?"

If there was one thing the gallery respected, it was money. The greed was palpable as she waved the notes in the air.

"Goodness, Mr. Palmer," said Mrs. Dove-Lyon. "With that kind of blunt, you could pay of your gambling debts. Maybe even have something left over for later."

"My debts aren't that large," he said, but the desperation in his eyes belied the statement.

"Then do you accept her challenge?" Mrs. Dove-Lyon pressed.

Lilah smiled. "Or do you fear being bested by an ignorant woman?"

"Pshaw," he blustered. "You're hardly worth the effort."

She didn't say anything. She simply fanned out her money again. That was more than Mr. Palmer could resist.

"Accepted," he said as he reached for the money.

"Accepted!" Mrs. Dove-Lyon cried as she grabbed the money. Then she waved the others at Mr. Palmer's table aside, pulled out a chair for Lilah, and gestured her to sit. "And now," she declared in dramatic accents. "Let the game begin."

Chapter Fourteen

Aaron couldn't keep track of all the threats at once. Bloody hell, whatever had possessed the woman to bring 500 pounds here? Even if she won, they'd probably be attacked, robbed, and beaten to a pulp before they made it out the front door. But there was no help for it now. The stage was set and all he could do was stand behind her and try to block every attack.

All while praying she somehow managed to win.

The rules to the challenge were simple. The surrounding crowd threw out mathematical questions while Miss Rees and Mr. Palmer wrote down their answers on small chalkboards. The Abacas Woman was the judge as she figured the correct answer. First wrong answer lost everything.

It began simple.

"Five times thirty-seven."

Neither competitor could make notes. They had to figure in their heads. Which meant Aaron would have lost immediately. Fortunately, Miss Rees was smarter than he. At least in this area.

"185," she said as she revealed her chalkboard.

"Child's play," Mr. Palmer said as he turned his board around showing the same number.

From the upper deck where the Abacas Woman click-clacked away came the shout from one of the dealers. "The correct answer is 185!" The Abacas Woman never spoke above a whisper, so she needed a dealer to bellow her judgement.

The crowd erupted in cheers, but they were just getting started. There were so many suggested computations, that Mrs. Dove-Lyon had to pick one and repeat it.

"Add 372, 193, and 8,221."

"And five pence!" laughed someone.

"And five pence," she dutifully repeated.

With so much chaos in the room, Aaron wondered how Miss Rees managed to compute these things in her head. He was impressed when she wrote down *8791*, then rapidly corrected it to *8786.05 lbs.* He was also nervous. No one had claimed the full numbers were pounds, but there wasn't time to ask as Mrs. Dove-Lyon called for answers.

"What say you Mr. Palmer?"

He turned his chalkboard around. It read, *8791.*

"Miss Rees?"

Lilah turned hers around. Damnation, it was already over, but Aaron wasn't sure who had won. They all looked to the Abacas Woman who passed her answer—also on a chalkboard—to the dealer.

"The correct answer is 8786 pounds, 5 pence!"

The outcry of displeasure was nearly deafening. No one wanted it to be over so fast, and certainly with a woman as winner. But no one was louder than Mr. Palmer himself who scribbled a quick P after his number to indicate pence, and then he bellowed, "You said pence! No one said pounds. Only pence!"

"That's right!" bellowed someone. "Palmer only has pence, these days!"

There was a great deal of laughter throughout the room at that, which only made Mr. Palmer's face redder. He loudly denounced the entire game and bellowed how he refused to be cheated. Truthfully, the noise was louder than a heated argument in Parliament, and Aaron feared for Lilah's hearing. Fortunately, Mrs. Dove-Lyon was well used to such commotion.

She raised her hand and waited for the laughter to die down.

"Mr. Palmer has a point. We did not specify pounds or pence, and so this round will be forgiven him…" She paused for dramatic effect. "Provided he buy a round of drinks for all." She arched a brow at the man and though he clearly didn't like it, he nodded his agreement.

"A pint of ale for all who will have it," he grumbled. Naturally, he selected the cheapest drink available.

Quick as a wink, she pulled several chips from in front of him. Apparently, he had been winning at whist, but now his pile was severely diminished. The crowd was very pleased as waiters quickly served one and all. A pint was set at Lilah's elbow. She clearly didn't realize she was expected to drink it because she smiled her thanks, but didn't touch the glass.

"Drink! Drink! Drink!"

On cue, Mr. Palmer lifted his glass and drained it. Then he banged his glass on the table and glared at Miss Rees.

"Bottom's up, chippy," he growled.

Her eyes widened as she turned to the ale. She was not a woman known to drink, and Aaron knew she'd already had wine earlier. Given her small stature, she'd be bleary-eyed within minutes. But she had little choice given the mood of the crowd. With a worried frown, she reached for the glass, but Aaron stopped her.

"This is not a drink for a lady," he chided loudly. Then he lifted the ale in his own fist and drank it, clapping the tankard down on the table with as much noise as Mr. Palmer had made.

The crowd loved it.

"Next test?" Miss Rees asked when the noise died down. "And be specific, if you please."

"A monkey divided among all of us!"

"And five p!"

Mrs. Dove-Lyon looked to the front door. "How many souls in here tonight, Lysander?"

"132 ma'am."

"Very well," she said, lifting up Miss Rees' bag of pound notes, often called a monkey. "500 pounds and 5 pence, divided by 132."

Lilah frowned, especially as Mr. Palmer began scribbling immediately. But then she scrawled. *3.78 to all with 1.04 remaining for Mrs. DL*

Smart. And far more than he could do off the top of his head. Unfortunately, Mr. Palmer was equally smart. Both had the same answer except that Mr. Palmer claimed the leftover for himself. And indeed, the Abacas Woman had the same result.

"Another round!" called a loud gentleman, and Aaron did a double take. Was that Reuben Bates? What was he doing here?

"This time the lady drinks," growled Mr. Palmer.

Reuben Bates stepped into the light. "Wine, Mrs. Dove-Lyon, on me." He held up a small purse and tossed it to her.

She caught it easily and immediately, wine was served all around, including a large glass to Miss Rees.

"Perhaps some bread as well?" Aaron ventured. It might soak up some of the alcohol, but his suggestion was loudly hooted down.

"Fear not," Lilah said as she lifted her glass. "I am not so poor a specimen that I cannot drink wine." So saying she drained her glass, much to the enjoyment of the audience. When she was done, she set it aside and pitched her voice to the crowd. "Perhaps we should finish with the simple questions, eh? How about some algebra or geometry?"

Aaron looked down at her flushed face. "You know algebra and geometry?"

"Lady Gwen and I passed many afternoons making a game of such things."

Truly? Impressive. And a smart suggestion, given that he very much doubted Mr. Palmer had any understanding of advanced mathematics. Unfortunately, the crowd had very little under-standing of it as well. It was no fun for them if they couldn't at least guess the answer. And since the crowd created the prob-lems, Lilah was left to battle it out in arithmetic.

"How much fer a night upstairs fer each o' us?"

"Wot's a year's pay fer a coachman who don't know nothing 'bout horses?"

"What's the pot if seven of us here pay in a quid and one of us falls out each round?"

"What's the pay out on red seven if I drop a quid?"

Questions flew fast now with Mrs. Dove-Lyon picking the ones she liked. Lilah answered the mathematical ones with relative ease, but the gambling questions were a struggle, much to the delight of the audience. She was hesitant, and she looked to Aaron in panic. Worse, each round was celebrated with wine or ale. He drank what he could for her, but she had to imbibe the wine. And given that he was already feeling unmoored, she had to be thoroughly foxed.

And yet she persevered. Bloody brilliant of her. Then came the dice question.

"What's the odds of nicking in the first Hazard throw?"

"That's not mathematics," she protested, and he winced at the way she slurred her words. "Give me something to add or subtract."

The crowd roared its disgust. This was a gambling lot and odds-making was their lifeblood. Fortunately, Mrs. Dove-Lyon decided to rule in her favor. "We gave Mr. Palmer his pounds to pence argument. I shall give to Miss Rees this one. And this next question shall be mine." She grinned as she pointed at one of the nearest gentlemen. "Mr. Wicker, how much money did you win last week?"

"Ten quid, Mrs. Dove-Lyon. At faro."

"Well done, Mr. Wicker. And what of you, Mr. Lidst?"

"Twelve quid, 17 pence."

She continued to ask gentlemen one after the other how much they'd won last week. The numbers got larger and larger, with derisive laughter following each outrageous amount. Figures flew fast around the room with people arguing what exactly someone had won and who owed someone else something. It was dizzying, and he rapidly lost track of it all. Even if he'd had pen and paper, he couldn't have kept track. Certainly not with his head swimming in ale.

Then Mrs. Dove-Lyon judged it finished. "Very well, Mr. Palmer, Miss Rees, how much did my customers win last week?"

That was not a mathematical problem. It was a memory problem, and he could already see the panic on Lilah's face. Fortunately, Mr. Palmer was also sweating, his brows drawn into a fierce scowl.

"I don't know, I don't know," Lilah whispered. He could see her hand shaking where she pressed the chalk to the board.

"Guess," he whispered back, though he doubted she heard him. She was already writing down a number. Mr. Palmer, too.

After a dramatic pause, Mrs. Dove-Lyon turned to the Abacas Woman. "How much did they win?" she cried.

The click-clack of the abacas stopped, and everyone leaned in to hear the whispered answer. A moment later, the dealer turned to the gallery and bellowed.

"239 pounds 87 pence."

"Oh no," Lilah moaned. She'd written down 209 pounds, 85 pence.

"Mr. Palmer?"

Mr. Palmer wiped his brow and seemed unable to turn his chalkboard around. Fortunately, there were many hands forcing him, and eventually everyone saw what he'd written.

"256 pounds, 3 pence is incorrect!" Mrs. Dove-Lyon cried. "What do you have Miss Rees?"

Lilah's hands shook as she turned around her chalkboard. "It appears we both got it wrong," she said, relief in her voice.

"That's true," agreed Mrs. Dove-Lyon. "But it appears you got it *more wrong* than Mr. Palmer. That is most unfortunate for you, Miss Rees. Most unfortunate, indeed."

"What?" she cried. "There aren't degrees of wrong."

"She's right," Aaron tried. "Wrong is wrong. Give them another problem."

Their objections fell on deaf ears. Mr. Palmer was already

celebrating, Mrs. Dove-Lyon was giving Lilah a sympathetic look, and everyone was cheering that the challenge was done. After all, it had taken up too much time. They wanted to get back to their own gambling.

"But that's not fair," Lilah pressed. "Wrong is wrong."

"*Wrong* is something only nobs think," Mrs. Dove-Lyon said. "We know there's degrees of everything." She patted Lilah's cheek. "And *fair* is a word used by children."

"No," Lilah said, shaking her head. Tears were running down her cheeks, and there was nothing that Aaron could do to help. Nothing but squeeze her shoulder and wish that it were different. But he'd known this would happen from the beginning.

"It was a good plan," he offered. "Mr. Palmer doesn't know anything about geometry or algebra. If they'd asked those questions..." His voice trailed away. This wasn't helping her at all. Her shoulders were shaking as she tried to suppress her sobs. And her gaze was on Mrs. Dove-Lyon as she bounced Lilah's purse of pound notes in her hand.

"Five hundred pounds, Mr. Palmer."

He reached up eagerly to grab it, but she held it away from him. "But first, I think I'll take what is owed me for your drinks and food." She pulled out a few notes and pocketed them quickly. "And—"

"He owed me forty quid," came a voice from the side.

"I spotted him twenty-two quid."

"'E owes me thirty quid for..."

On and on it went as creditors lined up. And while Mr. Palmer watched with an increasingly sick look on his face, Mrs. Dove-Lyon peeled off pound notes like she was handing out candy.

"I've just paid off all his debts," Lilah said. "It took me years to save up that much."

Aaron cursed under his breath. He had to get her out of here. She didn't need to see this disaster unfold before her. He pulled Lilah to her feet, but the floor was crowded with everyone grabbing for a piece of Mr. Palmer's windfall. There was no easy way out of the den, and he was now drunk enough to be unsteady on his feet. Especially as she was too distraught to stand easily.

"This way, gov," said a low voice.

He looked to see one of the bouncers holding his arm and gesturing toward the stairs.

"We need to get out of here," he rasped.

Then he noticed one of the dealers sliding up on Lilah's other side. The man cupped her elbow and steered her in the same direction.

He dug in his heels. "That's not outside," he pressed. "That's upstairs."

"Yes," agreed the bouncer. "You're in no condition to manage outside. She had 500 quid. Someone is going to try to rob her."

Lilah shook her head. "I don't have it any more."

"They'll think you do. Or they'll want yer lordship's coin and watch." The man jerked his head at the group of men trying to grab at whatever remained of Lilah's purse. If it weren't for the three large bouncers surrounding Mrs. Dove-Lyon, the woman would be in serious danger. "Safest place is upstairs until tomorrow."

"Tomorrow!" Aaron said, shocked. Miss Rees could not be out until tomorrow. It would destroy her reputation. But then he looked down at her. Her skin was ashen, her eyes wide, and … bloody hell. She was going to be sick.

Fortunately, the staff at the den were well used to that as well. A bucket appeared just as Miss Rees lost control of herself. And when she finally emptied her stomach, Aaron understood the truth. She was in no condition to go home. At least they could have some privacy upstairs in which to recover.

He pressed a coin into the bouncer's hand. "The best room you have for the night."

CHAPTER FIFTEEN

F IVE HUNDRED POUNDS. Her entire savings.

Gone.

Five hundred pounds.

Gone.

Lilah's thoughts kept revolving around those words. Over and over. And when she pushed those thoughts aside, she returned to the last question. The numbers people had shouted, the words Mrs. Dove-Lyon had repeated, and she re-calculated them in her mind. Over and over, never coming up with the same answer.

Where had she missed? How had she gone wrong? Why hadn't she been more forceful to have them ask geometry or algebra questions? She should have insisted. She should have asked for more clarity on the rules.

Five hundred pounds. Her entire savings.

Gone.

Her chest was tight, her legs wobbly. She had awareness of where she was going – up the stairs, into a room with a bed – but she relinquished all control of her body to Lord Kittrel's guidance. He would see her safe. He was even now tucking her close such that she could clutch onto his waistcoat.

Her breath was heaving. Or maybe that was her stomach. It didn't matter. She'd made her big gamble and lost.

Five hundred pounds. Gone.

It wasn't so bad. She still had a life with her adoptive mother. She had food and clothing. Ridiculous of her to think she'd been destroyed simply because her big gamble had failed. And yet, the ache of that loss overwhelmed her.

"Can you get us some food?" Aaron was saying to someone. "Anything to settle her stomach?"

She had a tonic at home that she used to give to Gwen when her stomach was upset, but obviously, it wasn't here. She looked around. Where was she? This room was bare except for a large bed and a small bedside table.

"Right away, my lord."

"Thank you." Lord Kittrel guided her to set on the edge of the bed. Then he squatted down before her, his gaze troubled. "Miss Rees...Lilah. Please say something."

What could she say? She'd just gambled everything she had and lost. It had been a stupid, stupid risk, and she was a fool for having done it.

"It was a good try," he said gently. "If I'd had the chance, I would have bet on you."

"You would have lost," she said, her voice broken.

He touched her cheek, stroking away the tears she hadn't even realized were falling. "So many people are afraid to risk. You made a bold move. You believed in yourself and made the leap. I find that inspiring."

"I *lost*."

"I know."

"I lost *everything*."

He didn't argue with her. He didn't tell her that she still had her health, her home. She still had friends and family who loved her. She had so much, and yet all she could think was that she had nothing left.

"I have five hundred pounds," he said to her. "I will give it to you."

Nice of him, but not the point. She was trying to win the registry office. Another five hundred pounds meant nothing if she couldn't use it to gamble against Mr. Palmer. "I made this choice," she said to herself. "I knew this could happen." But she hadn't really thought it would. She had a better memory than even her bluestocking sister Gwen. She could do calculations in her head. And she had a good understanding of the higher levels of mathematics. She could certainly hold her own against a drunkard like Mr. Palmer.

Such had been her thinking, but obviously, the man held his liquor well. Plus he had a good memory and a savant's ability with calculation. And she...she had made a mistake. She had thought wrong was wrong. She had thought so many stupid, ridiculous things.

"Stop it." Aaron's hard voice brought her out of her own thoughts.

"What?"

"You're blaming yourself. You're going over it all again in your head."

Her chin lifted as her gaze met his. "Yes."

"Stop it."

"But—"

"You can't change it. You miscalculated. You lost."

She winced and when she would have looked away, he touched her chin and held her gaze with his own.

"It does no good to chastise yourself now."

"If not now, then when?"

He shrugged, his mouth curving into a sloppy smile. "I have no idea. Except that you can't be angry at yourself for doing something I admire. It makes things clash in my head."

She felt herself echo his smile. Then she pressed her hand to his cheek. "My head is swimming."

"Mine, too." Then he frowned. "Food is coming."

"May I lie down until it gets here?"

"May I lie with you?" he asked. "There's only the one bed."

She nodded, and he placed his hand on the edge of the bed as he shoved himself upright. He wavered there slightly, and she frowned. "How much ale did you drink?"

"Too much." He dropped down on the mattress, adjusted his large body until his head on was on the pillow, then stretched out his arms to her. "Come here. We'll rest together."

An excellent idea. After all, she'd spent a year wondering what it would feel like to rest in his arms. She crawled carefully up the mattress and settled against him. He was large, he was warm, and he cradled her like she was the most precious thing in the world.

She'd lost everything.

Grief hit her broadside, burying her beneath a tide of regret and shame. What had she been thinking?

"It's all right," he whispered against her forehead. "We'll figure out something new for you."

"Without money? Without resources?"

"I will give you—"

"No!" She had made her choice to gamble. She would accept the results of her mistake. "I will live with Lady Byrn until I am shriveled and gray."

He chuckled against her temple. "I think you will be very attractive shriveled and gray. I think you will still be full of life then and even if you are not married, you will be managing those around you such that everything moves smoothly and is allowed to grow to absolute perfection."

She snorted. "You have a romantic mindset."

"You have a practical mindset." He tucked her closer against him. "I posit that we fit together very well."

There was no doubt about that. Their legs were intertwined, their hips and sides were pressed tight. If she tilted her head a few degrees, she could press her lips against his chin. And if he tipped his head down, they would be kissing.

"A practical person would not have risked everything on tonight's gamble," she said.

"That's what made it so brave."

"I lost," she said again. And the two words felt like they imprinted themselves ever deeper in her soul every time she thought it, and every time she said the words aloud.

"Take it from someone who is perpetually tilting at windmills. Yes, you lost, but the effort was worthwhile nonetheless."

She thought about that. She tried to take his words and make them her own. She tried to feel like she'd done something more than throw everything away.

She couldn't do it. "I shall never, ever do something so foolish again."

"Hmmmm. I think you will," he said gravely. "It may take you some time, but you will take another leap."

"Never," she vowed. And she meant it. She couldn't withstand this kind of failure again. Her heart wouldn't take it.

"Aren't you the woman who boldly asked me to marry her during a masquerade party?"

She snorted. "You refused."

"I'm here, aren't I? You caught my attention, and that is something that is very hard to do."

She lifted up onto her elbow to look him in the eye. Her vision swam and her head felt heavy, but she waited it out until she could see the way he looked at her. "I wanted…I *want* a husband."

His free hand stroked her arm, the caress seemed casual, but she felt it all through her body. "You want stability. A home, a family, and the respect that comes from having an aristocratic husband."

She couldn't deny it. "But you want love."

He winced. "I do not. I'm simply aware that sometimes it happens."

She searched his face, wondering how he could still seem so handsome to her. She saw strength in his face, kindness in his eyes, and a sexy tease with his mouth. "Could you not find a way to love me?" she whispered. "I could love you."

The wine had loosened her tongue. Indeed, the whole evening had turned her upside down and inside out. But she still had the wherewithal to temper her words. She couldn't say that she loved him. Only that she might. She couldn't declare her feelings, only that she wanted to. When inside, she knew with startling clarity that she had long since fallen in love with him. He was everything that was noble in a man, and if he would only soften the tiniest bit, she would be his faithful wife until the day she died.

"The day after our kiss at the masquerade," he said softly, "I went to see Sayres. I told him that I had ruined you and was forced to marry you."

She blinked. "What?"

He nodded, his expression wistful. "That was how deeply you impressed yourself upon me. One kiss, and I was prepared to throw everything away for you."

She straightened off him. "What?"

He nodded, his expression wistful. *Wistful!* When he was talking about handing her everything she had ever wanted. "But I had to go to my father's bedside. I left the very day, so I asked Sayres to keep you safe, to watch over you until I could come back and claim you."

Now she was sitting fully upright, and she pressed a hand to her temple. She couldn't believe this was real. The man she'd dreamed about had wanted her! "Sayres did everything he could to introduce me to eligible bachelors," she rasped.

"I know." His hand dropped down to the coverlet. "He lied to me, but he was right to do it."

"Right?" she gasped. "You were ready to marry me!"

He nodded. "I thought I was. You were clearheaded and bold. Capable and…" He released a soft sigh. "So beautiful. I believed I could love you."

She could tell by his tone that his feelings had passed. "What happened?" she asked.

He looked up at the ceiling. "I remembered that love is not enough."

She swallowed, her entire body going cold, especially when

his gaze returned to her and he repeated those words.

"Love is not enough."

"Enough for what?" she pressed. "Happiness?"

He frowned, then elbowed his way into a sitting position leaning back against the wall. His body looked large against the wall, but also defeated as his shoulders slumped and his expression grew sad. "My parents loved each other. Theirs was a love match, and I wanted that for myself. But once I got home, I remembered all the things I'd forgotten since moving to London."

She winced. She'd heard plenty of tales from Clara about their parents' rocky marriage. Lilah guessed it was the main reason that Clara refused to entertain the idea of a husband for herself. Apparently, both siblings felt the same.

"You are not doomed to repeat your parents' problems."

He looked at her. "Their marriage was a mésalliance. My mother was a clergyman's daughter. Perfectly respectable, you see, but hopelessly countrified. My father loved her, and so he married her."

"Exactly as it ought to be," she said.

He shook his head. "Politics was his real love. He should never have married at all or married a woman who knew how to support his ambitions. She crippled him politically, and he resented her for it." He blew out a breath. "Until the day he died, he blamed her even though he loved her."

What was she to say to that? That his father's love was weak? That blaming another for his own failure was wrong. But she knew that wasn't true. She more than anyone knew that society threw up walls that no one could break. "So he was unhappy?"

Aaron lifted a hand in a gesture of futility. "He felt a failure."

"He raised two children, cared for his lands, fought for what he felt was right."

"He felt like he failed." His gaze turned piercing. "Just as you feel like you failed tonight."

"I did fail!"

"And yet you are loved by your family, you will manage Lady Byrn's household, you will live a full life."

She swallowed, seeing his point, but she didn't want to acknowledge it. She didn't want to feel like she'd nearly attained something wonderful—marriage to him—only to have circumstances rip it away. Just like tonight when she'd almost won her registry office. And while she was still rejecting every one of the feelings churning inside her, he showed her that he felt the failure just as keenly.

"I've thought about marrying you, Lilah. Ever since I got back to London, I've thought about the possibility, and so I tried to learn what the women do." He looked at her. "Do you know these women?" He rattled off several names. "Do you have a friendship with them?"

Friendship? One had spit in her tea. Literally. The others had never deigned to look at her, much less claim an acquaintance. "No. They won't... They don't..." She didn't have the words to express how very solid the societal wall was against her. Those women would not accept her into their ranks. Ever.

"They are the political women, Lilah. The ones behind the scenes who will marshal their husbands for or against my work."

She snorted. "You give them too much credit. Surely the men have minds of their own. Surely you can convince them on the merits of your arguments. It has nothing to do with their wives."

He shook his head. "You know that's not true. You know the women have extraordinary influence. Only a fool would deny it."

And he was no fool. Thankfully, a knock at the door spared her from giving an answer. She rolled off the bed, though she was still unsteady. Opening it allowed a servant to bring in a tray with cheeses and bread. Another followed behind him with a bottle of wine and two glasses. The wine was set on the table. The tray was plopped on the bed. She watched as Aaron slipped them each a coin, and then both bowed themselves out.

"Come eat something," he urged as he waved her back to bed. And when she shook her head, he shifted to sit completely upright. "Do you think I want to break your heart?" he asked. Then he looked at her. "Do you think I want to break mine?"

"Do you love me?" she asked. The words slipped out.

He shook his head. "Not yet."

She turned away.

"But I think of you all the time. Tonight, you amazed me."

Her eyes suddenly filled with tears. It was all too much. Fifteen minutes ago, she'd thought she'd lost everything when her 500 pounds went to Mr. Palmer. How much deeper the pain now that she lost Lord Kittrel, too. He'd been willing to marry her, but now couldn't see a way. Not at the cost of his political ambitions.

Her knees went out from beneath her as a sob tore through her throat. He leaped off the bed. He was too slow to catch her, but he found a way to wrap his arms around her while she sobbed on the floor. She didn't want to turn to him in her pain, but how could she refuse his strong arms? And when he pressed kisses into her hair and against her forehead, she cried even harder.

"I love you," she whispered, and the pain of that admission shredded what little composure she had.

Chapter Sixteen

WHAT THE HELL was wrong with him? Aaron held Lilah as gut-wrenching sobs tore through her. Her every shudder condemned him. Every tear burned him.

Why the hell had he told her that? Why had he confessed that he could love her? Drunkenness was no excuse. And he was definitely inebriated. He'd come up here to make her feel better. He'd wanted to show her how much he admired her. And somehow that had led to his admission. And somehow that had led to her devastation.

The process wasn't entirely clear to him. Certainly not to his befuddled mind. All he knew was that he'd hurt her, and he couldn't forgive himself for that.

He lifted her up and carried her to the bed. He set her down on the mattress and she curled into herself, wrapping her arms around her belly as she sobbed. He had to move the food tray, but once he'd set it aside, there was nothing to do but hold her.

Her body was rigid as she gripped herself. Didn't matter. He wrapped himself around her and held her. He said things to her. No idea what. Anything that came to mind as he tried to ease her pain. And while he murmured to her, his mind finally let him face the words she'd said as she'd collapsed.

I love you.

She loved him, and he felt guilty for feeling such happiness from those words. She was such an impressive woman that the idea of her love buoyed him even as it seemed to devastate her. Which tore at him. Which destroyed his ability to think of anything but making it better for her.

He wanted to fully surround her, but his size was such that he didn't want to crush her. So he lay his head down on the pillow behind her and pressed kisses into the back of her neck. He pulled her close and tried to get her to turn toward him.

"Lilah, please," he said for the thousandth time. "Please let me help you."

He didn't know what that meant. How was he supposed to help? He wanted to give her the money to buy the registry office, but she was right. Mr. Palmer would not sell his only livelihood now, especially since she'd just paid off a stack of his debts. And he wasn't sure she'd take money from him anyway. It would declare to the world a very different relationship between them.

He thought about marrying her. Of course, he thought about it! Who wouldn't want the love of a good woman for the rest of his life? But in his mind, that was choosing his own selfish needs over the good of the veterans, the poor, and the people of England he'd sworn to aid. He had a very clear agenda for his life's work. He believed it was his God-given purpose. How could he damage that in favor of the very selfish desire to have Lilah in his life? He'd seen the resentment that built in his parents' marriage because his father had chosen love over his goals. He didn't want that for Lilah or himself.

What was left? Nothing but holding her. Nothing but whispering to her that it would be all right. That he was here. That he…

He didn't say that he loved her. That would be too cruel since he couldn't marry her. He said instead that he wanted to help. How could he help?

Eventually she quieted. A body could only withstand so much grief before it fell into exhaustion. Her breath evened out, her body unclenched, and her weight sank back against him. His words stopped. He didn't want to disturb her if she slept, but in this she surprised him. She spoke to the wall, but her words were clear enough.

"And now I have done the one thing I swore never to do."

"What is that?"

"I have turned my life into a Cheltenham tragedy." She took a shuddering breath. "If I were watching this from the audience, I would tell the heroine that she is a fool."

"Never that."

"Oh yes," she said. "The hero doesn't love you. So what? Unrequited love is the most common of emotions. Incredibly boring."

He swallowed. "I am not bored."

"I am," she said. She slowly stretched out her body. The motions were halting, and her breath continued to hitch, but she spoke in bracing tones as if she were trying to discipline herself. "I have lost all my money," she said. "I willingly gambled it away. How many times have I shook my head at such a tale? Never gamble with something you cannot lose."

"Everyone thinks they will win."

"Oh, I am fortune's fool," she quoted, her voice mocking herself. It was from *Romeo and Juliet*, and she clearly hated the way that cast her. She wiped her eyes and squared her shoulders for all that she was still lying down. "I will not become this wretched thing," she said as she pushed herself upright. "I will not pine away for lack of a man." She didn't look at him, and he didn't force her. Instead, he moved away from her, feeling the chill in the air as they separated.

She peered at the tray of food. Her hands were unsteady, but she was able to bring the tray back onto the bed between them. She tore off a hunk of bread and ate it with a sliver of cheese. He took his cue from her. He lifted the wine bottle and poured them both full measures.

"I don't know if I should," she said.

"Neither do I," he admitted. "But if ever I felt the need to get completely foxed—"

"It is tonight." Her lips twisted into a wry smile. "I think I already am."

"If so, then you are remarkably composed."

She had been looking at the food in her hand, but at his words, she finally looked straight at him. Her eyes were red and still sheened with tears. Her shoulders were slumped in defeat, and yet she resolutely chewed and swallowed her food as if it held the answer to all her problems.

"Shall I call for water?" he asked.

She shook her head and took the glass of wine. "I don't want anyone else to see me like this." Then she smiled. "I don't want *you* to see me like this."

"You've never looked more beautiful." He meant it. She looked resilient, and that was powerful indeed.

"Then I have looked woefully bedraggled whenever we met before."

He smiled. "You know that's not true."

She didn't answer except to take another delicate bite of cheese. He ate as well. He'd drunk a great deal of ale on her behalf. He needed something else in his stomach. But as he chewed, he couldn't help but imagine what it would be like to eat with her every night. Her hair was a tangled mess, her cheeks were ruddy from her tears, and yet he was seeing how the candlelight made her skin glow gold. He saw the curve of her neck, the length of her spine, and the sweet movement of her mouth.

So beautiful.

"Why are you looking at me like that?" she asked.

"What?"

"You look like…You look…" Her words failed her.

"I am thinking that you are beautiful. That I want to make love to you." Honest words loosened by wine. Or maybe spoken aloud because he wanted her to know.

She frowned. "You want me as your mistress?"

He laughed. "I want you every way I can have you, Lilah."

Damnation, his clothing was already uncomfortably tight, but he didn't move from his place on the opposite side of the bed even as his fantasies made him ever more uncomfortable.

He watched as her nostrils flared and her cheeks darkened with heat. The way she looked at him made his blood pulse.

"I am not a man to be ruled by my lusts," he said gently, though desire pounded in his veins. "I will not dishonor you that way."

She pulled another morsel of bread from the roll, but she didn't eat it. Instead, she just looked at it. "And what if I wanted you to?"

Lord, how she tempted him.

"My reputation is already gone," she said. "I was a bastard before. Now I am a bastard who gambled and lost a monkey, then spent the night in a brothel."

He acknowledged the truth with a shrug. Though the Lyon's Den was not known as a brothel, there were rooms above the main den for that purpose. And even if they left right now— which they couldn't—Lilah had already spent enough time here to destroy her respectability.

"Shouldn't I do the crime," she asked, "if I am already damned by it?"

"If you think lovemaking is a crime, then you are sorely misinformed."

She arched a brow at him. And wasn't that the most devilishly sexy sight? "Perhaps I need someone to enlighten me."

And perhaps he wanted to do exactly that with a pounding drive, but he still didn't move. "Lilah," he said, startled by how husky the word sounded. "Tonight is not the night to make such decisions."

She laughed and threw up her hands. "Then tell me, my lord, exactly when I should make such a choice? Back when I am at home, an unpaid housekeeper whose days are filled with Lady Byrn's needs, and whose nights are empty and dull? Or perhaps you mean when I begin a fruitless search for a husband among the less-than-elite? Do you think a barrister will have me now? I tell you, even the lowest fishmonger will reject me now."

"You underestimate—"

"Don't say it!" she interrupted. "Don't lie there in your shirt sleeves not an hour since you rejected me and say that I have some mysterious appeal! I do not! I have not! I am—"

He exploded across the bed, upsetting what was left of the cheese. He was on all fours and an inch from her face. "You are!" he all but roared. He could not bear to hear her discount herself. Torturing himself, he flowed the very edges of his lips against hers. "You are," he swore.

"What?" she whispered back. "What am I but a failure in all my hopes and schemes?"

She was herself, and that was more than enough for him. He meant to say more. He meant to convince her of her worth. But the moment they were lip to lip, his words evaporated. Whatever his noble intensions were, they disappeared beneath the heat of her breath, the caress of her lips, and the gentle stroke of her hand across his jaw.

"May I not have this one night?" she whispered. "I know what tomorrow brings for me. I know what the rest of my life will be. Will you deny me this one thing that I want? One night for the rest of my life? Especially since everyone will assume we have done it."

Such logic when his body was on fire. Such need to please her flooded his thoughts. "You will regret this tomorrow," he said. It was his last grasp at rationality before desire completely overran him.

"Such arrogance," she said as her hand cupped his face. "To think that you know what I will think on the morrow."

He pulled back enough to see the honesty in her eyes. "You have me there," he admitted. Here and everywhere. "But I will not take your virginity. Leave me with some small measure of honor."

She smiled, her expression softening such that he saw her

strength and pain mixed with relief and joy. It was the measure of joy that convinced him. Especially as he intended to make it blossom until she felt nothing but ecstasy.

"I have seen your honor, my lord. But now, please, cast it aside." She touched his mouth. "For tonight, at least."

He smiled. "For you."

CHAPTER SEVENTEEN

LILAH FELT HIS lips on hers, his body as he surrounded her, and his need in the frenzied domination of her mouth. She'd known he was holding back. She'd seen him reach for her a dozen times only to stop while his gaze roved over her body with obvious hunger. It fired her blood to see him want her. And when he finally cast aside his restraint, she waited for his frenzied possession. She *wanted* his possession.

He did not disappoint.

He held her head, he thrust inside her mouth, and while they dueled tongue to tongue, his free hand curled over her breast. His fingers shaped her flesh, rolled her nipple, and squeezed just enough to make sensation burst through her breast, straight to her womb. She gasped against his lips. Such feeling! And he used that moment of startled amazement to push her back against the mattress.

She went willingly. She did everything he wanted eagerly. When he pulled at the buttons of her gown, she helped him strip it away. She tugged at the ties of her stays, frustrated when the bindings knotted. He soothed his hands over hers and did what she could not. And then they both cast them aside. She'd long since removed her shoes, but now he stroked her stockings and rubbed his hand up the inside of her thighs as he claimed her mouth again.

Such heat she felt, such wetness as he pressed her down. Her shift still covered her. He untied her stockings but did not wrest them down. Instead he kissed her longer, deeper, while she surrendered her body to whatever he chose. And when he broke the kiss to scrape his teeth along her jaw, she arched her back and whispered, "I don't know what to do."

"I do," he said as his hands rolled over her hips. He was pulling her shift over her head, his hands spanning her belly, her ribs, and up to her breasts. "Tell me if anything upsets you." He paused, his hands large as he spanned her ribs. He looked into her eyes and spoke clearly. "Tell me if it hurts."

"Your clothing," she said. "It rubs me raw."

It was a lie. His shirtsleeves were the finest linen and a sensuous caress beneath her shift. And yet it was also true because she wanted his skin against hers. She wanted him to feel as exposed as she did.

He nodded then pulled himself back. He withdrew his hands slowly, letting her feel his touch across her vulnerable belly. Her muscles rippled in reaction, sending sensation to her womb.

"Don't stop," she whispered.

He grinned. "I'm not."

She watched as he removed his waistcoat and shirt. He was above her on the bed, his broad shoulders and trim waist now revealed to her. She drank in the sight and marveled at the muscles that defined his body.

"There is no fat on you," she murmured as she stroked her hand across his torso.

"You know how abysmal our cooks have been. I have had no temptation to overeat."

She chuckled as continued to touch him. What heaven to feel a man's body in its prime. "It's more than that," she mused as she pushed up on her elbow to get closer. "Your muscles are..." Words failed her. They were big and thick, like a laborer's, and yet more fluid as he moved.

"I did plenty of work this past year. My father was too frail and much had been neglected."

He let her touch him, let her press kisses to his chest and roll her hands across his ribs. She touched the flat disks of his nipples and teased them with her nails. As his breath caught, she grew bolder. She kissed them next and teased them with her tongue while his hands tightened on her shoulders.

Before long, he tightened his grip and set her away from him. "My turn," he said with a grin. Then he pulled her shift off and she sat naked before him except for her stockings. His gaze grew hot, and he looked at her with such intensity. Not moving. Not even breathing. Just staring.

"My lord?"

"Aaron," he rasped. "Use my name."

She smiled. "Aaron, then." She tilted her head. "Is something wrong?" It was a coy statement. She could tell that nothing was wrong by the way his nostrils flared and his expression was near awe, but she had to say something to break the tension. Never before had anyone looked at her like that and it thrilled her as much as it made her shift uneasily on the bed.

"Now that we are here," he said softly as he extended his hand. "I want to remember everything."

He touched her left breast, his caress mesmerizingly slow. He outlined the shape of her, lifting her breast in the palm of her hand while he stroked left and right across her nipple. She tingled where he caressed her, her flesh burned where he held her, and the brush against her nipple felt like the strike of flint. Each spark built upon the other until her chest was on fire.

And then he put his mouth to her body.

She braced herself on her hands, arching her back as he kissed her throat, her collarbone, and then down to her breasts. He sucked her left nipple into his mouth, then alternately pulled and nipped at the pebble.

Her breath shortened, her body trembled, and she wanted more, more, more of whatever he wanted to do.

She set her hand to the back of his head. She felt him wrap his arms around her back as he eased her down. He did such things to her breast and then he did the same to the other one. And while she gasped at that, she felt the heat of his skin against hers. She gripped the bulge of his biceps, and she pulled herself up against him however she could.

Sensation flowed, one experience building to the next as he touched her all over. Breasts, ribs, stomach, and then at the juncture of her thighs.

First it was his whole hand over the base of her, then his fingers slipped between the folds. Such long, thick fingers explored her. They spread her open, they coiled against the nub at the tip, and they pushed inside her.

Her legs widened and her stockings slipped lower. He continued to suck on her breasts, but her attention—even fractured as it was—centered on where his fingers stroked, pushed, and entered.

He lifted off her breast, watching her face as he rolled across her nub. She cried out as he did that, unable to form a true word. And just like before, the sensations built until she was writhing beneath his hand, but his weight held her down. The palm of his hand kept her pelvis from accidentally bucking him off. His chest against hers kept her from twisting away when she wanted to be closer.

And his fingers kept moving, kept touching, kept building the tension inside her.

She clutched him then. Not his body, but lower down his back until she gripped the fabric of his falls. "Off," she said. "Take them off."

She wanted to feel him. She wanted him as open as she was. She wanted him.

"Not for your first time," he said. "Not yet."

She had no idea what he meant. And soon, she had no ability to do anything but feel. His fingers moved in a steady rhythm now. Inside and out. Inside and out. She understood what he mimicked. She knew the mechanics of this, but never had she thought it so all consuming.

He rolled his thumb against her nub. His thick, powerful thumb. Up and over, back down. Up and over, back down. Faster and harder while her legs spread and her back thrust upward. Her breath caught, her eyes shuttered closed.

Her belly rippled.

And then he abruptly squeezed her nipple.

Light shot through her entire body. A flashflood of sensation, an explosion of something, a taking and giving of... of...

Everything. And nothing.

He was not inside her. He was merely watching. His hands were not still, his gaze was fixed upon her, and though he was right there, she felt as if she had missed something important.

She felt exquisite. She was soaked in pleasure. And yet, she was alone in her bliss even as he lay pressed against her.

She breathed in the sensations. She shivered in continued ecstasy. And when the floating was done, she rolled her head to him.

"That was wonderful," she whispered. "But it was not what you promised."

He frowned. "What?"

She touched his face, felt the scrape of his beard against her palm, and the tension in his jaw. "Can I not be a whole woman? Just this once?"

He pressed a kiss to her palm. "You are a whole woman. You are more woman than anyone I have ever known."

She shook her head. "Not in this. Not yet."

He held her gaze and his expression turned tortured. "Do you know how much I want to?" he rasped. "Do you know how hard it is to deny you? Deny myself?"

She shook her head. "Explain it to me."

He straightened off the bed then. He stood up before her and slowly, deliberately, unbuttoned his falls. His cock popped free, large and thick. It bobbed before her. She saw the ruddy color and the cross of veins along the stalk. A drop of moisture coated the slit, so close she could taste it if she chose. But then he moved away.

He stripped himself of his clothing until he stood nude before her. Bare and with so much power in his naked form. She saw thick ropes of muscles in his thighs. His legs spread and his feet gripped the rug, giving him a broad base. And when she finally lifted her gaze up past his organ and sculpted chest, she looked into his eyes which seemed to burn with intensity.

"Touch me and I will explode like a boy in his first heat."

She reached out to do just that, but he gripped her wrist and held her back.

"Aaron—"

"A man does not take when he knows it's wrong. A man thinks about tomorrow."

"But—"

"A man does not dishonor that which he most prizes." He dropped down below the bed such that they were eye to eye. "You are precious to me, Lilah. How can I—" He strangled his words, and his expression turned anguished. "I am giving you what you want, Lilah—"

"Not everything."

He took her mouth then. He possessed it and plundered it like a ruthless pirate. And she gave him it all because she wanted it. She wanted him.

But then he drew back.

"I—" Again the word was tortured. She saw the need in his eyes, the tightness in his body, and the way he kept himself back. She knew that he wanted her, but that everything he valued in himself as a man would prevent him from taking what she freely offered.

It made her want him even more. And perversely it made her furious that he would reject the one thing she had of value that she wanted to give to him. Just to him. The one man who valued her.

But just as he would not dishonor her, she could not break what made him so wonderful. She would not take his honor. So she pulled herself up onto her knees and faced him squarely.

"Teach me."

"What?"

"Teach me how to pleasure you. What do I do to give you… to…" Words failed her, but he understood. He took a step forward and caressed her face.

"Would you touch me?" he asked. Then he held out his handkerchief. "I'll tell you when to back away."

She took the fabric from his hands. She was not ignorant. And though she had never done it, this was something she understood. She dropped the handkerchief and set her attention on him.

She touched him first. Light strokes to outline the scope of him. Long strokes to measure the length of him. Deep strokes to explore the sac beneath just as he had held her breast and played along its contours.

Then she gripped him. She hadn't expected his gasp, but she enjoyed the sound of it. She'd meant to hold it steady for the next part, but in this she learned what he liked, especially as his hands went one to the wall, the next to her shoulder to steady himself.

"Lilah," he rasped.

She flashed him a grin, then she leaned forward and tasted him. She licked the tip and noted the salty taste. She rolled her tongue along the edge to feel the dimensions of him. Then she sucked him in because that was what she'd been told men liked.

He did.

She heard his tortured groan. She felt his buttocks tighten as he thrust against her. And then she held herself steady as he quickly built tempo in her mouth. There wasn't time for more though she reveled in the strength of his thrusts. She gripped his organ with one hand and the thick contours of his thigh with the other.

Faster, harder, he was close now. She knew it.

She had brought him to this. She had done—

Suddenly he broke away. He ripped backward so fast, surely

she hurt him as he tore from her grasp. But he didn't seem to notice. Instead, he grabbed her by the thighs and pulled her to the edge of the bed.

Yes!

She was open for him and so wet and empty. She gripped his shoulders and tried to pull herself up on his body.

He held her back. He gripped her ribs and pushed her down into the mattress. Then he squeezed her breasts and she arched into his need. Sensation shot through her as he pinched her nipples. And then—*yes*—he pressed his organ against her lower flesh.

He rolled his cock up her wet folds, slipping between them, and rolling against her most sensitive spot. She spread herself as wide as she could, trying to manipulate him inside, but he wouldn't do it. And while his hands played with her breasts, he thrust against her. His shaft rolled up between her folds, but not inside.

She wrapped her legs around his buttocks. She drew herself hard and tight against him.

And he thrust.

His hands dropped to the mattress. His face was tight, his jaw hard, and his eyes bore into her.

He thrust.

Sensation burst from him to her. Or so it felt. Over and over, he slammed himself against her, but never inside.

She lost the ability to fight him. He was too strong. He was too determined. And so she opened herself up to whatever he wanted.

He stroked himself against her folds.

He thrust against her nub.

And she burst into light.

This time, he joined her. His body shuddered against her and with a guttural cry, he let go. His seed spilled on her belly.

And while she floated, he shuddered, then slowly dropped his forehead to hers.

She kissed him, and he returned it in full measure.

Then he kissed her cheeks, her nose, and her brow.

Ever the gentleman, he cleaned her up, and then he lay beside her. He tucked her close, and covered them both with the blanket.

It wasn't the fullness that she'd wanted. He wasn't her husband and there was no possibility of children.

But it was enough.

He was enough.

CHAPTER EIGHTEEN

ARON WAS AN early riser by nature, but the sun was streaming in through the dirty window by the time he opened his eyes. He felt remarkably relaxed and languidly appreciated the body curled against him.

Lilah.

He revisited anew her remarkable performance yesterday during the bet, and then let his mind relive the wondrous moments in this bed. He shifted and realized she still had her stockings on, and that made him grin from ear to ear.

She stirred against him as well, her eyes opening as she tilted up to face him. He watched as awareness dawned, and then she appeared to fall into the same memories he had. Her eyes softened, her body flexed against him, and the temptation of her lips drew him.

Bang bang!

A fist pounded twice on the door, jolting them both apart.

"Up ye get," came a rough voice. "Ye got a visitor in the mistress's parlor."

"What? Who?" Aaron asked, his voice thick.

He waited for an answer. They both did, but none came. In the end, they both leaped out of bed, performed their ablutions behind a screen, and dressed as quickly as they could. That did not prevent Aaron from watching her with hunger as she moved. Neither did it stop her from looking back. Her gaze dropped to that large and very inconvenient part of him thrusting forward as he tried to button his falls. And his lingered on the curve of her bosom and the length of her leg as she retied her stockings.

"Do you regret last night?" he asked.

She looked up, her expression fierce. "Not for a second."

"Thank God," he breathed.

"Do you?"

"Not unless you do."

She smiled. "Then we are agreed."

"Yes."

He held out his arm to her, and she took it. She stepped right up to his side and smiled. He felt his loins surge as she stepped close. The scent of her returned his mind to the night before, and he paused before opening the door.

"One kiss," he whispered. "One last…"

She stretched up her face to his and he set his mouth upon hers. He moved slowly, trying to savor the moment, but he couldn't stop himself from wrapping an arm around her back as he thrust inside her mouth. Damnation, he wanted to take her straight back to bed. His blood surged, he pressed her against the wall, and if he'd had the right, he'd have lifted her skirts as he… As they…

He didn't have the right. He forced himself back as he smoothed his hand down her flushed cheek.

"Are you sure, Aaron?" she whispered.

"What?"

"Are you sure that love is not enough?"

He swallowed, his gaze canting away. "This is not love, Lilah. This is desire and by God, it is the most potent feeling I have ever experienced."

Her expression darkened into sadness. "You still have no understanding of your own feelings."

He winced. He did not want to be his father. He would not lose everything for love, and then endure decades of pain in his own home. And yet, he feared it was already too late. His heart might already be engaged, and she was perceptive enough to know it.

She sighed when he didn't speak, then pushed him even harder. "What if it is love for me? What if I love you?"

She could not have cut him more deeply if she'd sliced him open with a knife. The last thing he wanted to do was hurt her. He should have refused her last night. An honorable man would have, but he'd been foxed, and she was so beautiful.

"You cannot love me," he said firmly. "You don't know me well enough."

She arched her brows above eyes that seemed to mock him. "So last night was not, um, getting to know one another?"

He owed her the truth, such as he understood it. "Last night was pleasure." How small a word for what he experienced! "The most exquisite of my life."

"But it was not love," she finished for him. There was definite mockery in her voice.

"It cannot be," he said gently. "Because if it is, then we are both doomed to unhappiness. And I would never do such a thing to you."

The humor that sparkled in her eyes cooled until her entire expression closed down. That cut him yet again.

"Lilah," he whispered.

"Still an idiot," she muttered as she pulled open the door. "But this time, I cannot blame you."

When had he let down his arm? When had she stepped free of him? He didn't remember, but now there was no remedy. She was already out in the hall, quickly walking past rooms where other voices stirred. Most were women's voices, but a few had men's. One door in particular opened as Lilah passed it. A gentleman stepped out, his hat pulled low over his eyes and his shirt points stretched high. He saw Lilah's back, then turned and gave Aaron a jaunty grin. Aaron didn't return it.

It sickened him to think that he had put Lilah in this position. She was walking the halls alongside these women as if she belonged here. She did not. And yet now, thanks to his inability to protect her, she would be damned as one of them.

He rushed ahead, thinking to wrap her in his coat or give her his hat. Anything to hide her identity. Fortunately, he didn't need to. They'd come to Mrs. Dove-Lyon's parlor and were bid to enter.

They entered together because he'd caught up to her. And they both stopped short when they saw that Mrs. Dove-Lyon was not alone.

"Reuben!" Aaron said in surprise. "Whatever are you doing here?"

"Been here all night. It's one of my favorite places in London," he said with a wink to Mrs. Dove-Lyon.

As she was wearing her typical widow's weeds, Aaron couldn't see if the mischievous expression pleased her or not. But he did see her gesture to the chairs set in a circle for their use. Aaron was quick to hold Lilah's seat for her as she settled. Then he found his own and gratefully accepted a cup of tea. Given that Reuben was here, he gathered he was going to need his wits about him.

"How are you feeling this morning?" Mrs. Dove-Lyon asked once they were all settled and drinking their tea.

He knew the question was directed at Lilah, so he remained silent.

"I am well," Lilah responded. "Chastened, but not harmed. And newly committed to never gambling again."

"Yes," responded Reuben dryly. "If people failed so spectacularly on their first foray into a den, many estates would be the better for it."

She nodded but didn't respond, so it was left to Aaron to try to move things along. "I should like to get Miss Rees home immediately. It does no good to keep her here while the rest of the world wakes."

"On the contrary," Mrs. Dove-Lyon said sternly. "I should like her to remain here for the day at least."

"Unacceptable!" Aaron said as he set down his tea. He would not allow her reputation—whatever was left of it—to be further damaged. But before he could say more, Lilah set aside her own tea and folded her hands in her lap.

"What do you want?" she said.

"We want to employ you," said Reuben, his tone jovial. "And not at all in the fun way."

Mrs. Dove-Lyon waved a dismissive hand at her companion. "You left last night before the rest of the show," she said gently. "So you are unaware that all of Mr. Palmer's debts were called in."

"I saw that," Aaron said. "Her money went to pay them off before the man could even touch the purse."

"Yes," Mrs. Dove-Lyon said. And this time he could see her grin.

"But there were more, weren't there?" Aaron asked, his mind already working out the financials. He looked at Reuben. "You bought up the rest of his debts, didn't you? I wondered why you were there."

Reuben grinned at him. "You've always been clever. Deadly dull, but exceptionally clever."

Given what Reuben liked for entertainment, Aaron took that as a compliment.

Meanwhile, Lilah looked back at him, clearly confused. "I don't understand," she said.

"Reuben did what you couldn't. He bought Mr. Palmer's business."

"More accurately," Reuben said, "I bought off his debts while you set the public display to make him pay. When he couldn't, I took the forfeit you had already forced on him."

"His registry business," Mrs. Dove-Lyon said. "My part was to enforce it. So an hour past midnight, Mr. Reuben Bates became the new owner of London's most used registry office." She leaned forward. "I own a small part as well," she confided. "Especially as I am giving you a room on the main floor of this building to teach employment classes."

"What employment classes?" Aaron pressed.

Mrs. Dove-Lyon turned to him. "Well, she already agreed to that yesterday. She's to teach my ladies how to become proper housekeepers—"

"Maids and footmen," Lilah corrected.

"Or better," Mrs. Dove-Lyon said. "Depending upon their abilities."

"Depending," Lilah echoed. Then she twisted in her seat, adjusting herself so she faced Reuben directly. "Why would you do this?"

"Do you think you're the only one who can see a good opportunity? Miss Rees, I know you wanted to keep all the profits for yourself, but you have no experience in running a business. Mrs. Dove-Lyon and I do. This way, you can do what you do best—teach servants how to do their jobs well. And we can—"

"Take all the profits," Aaron said.

Reuben looked back at him. "She will be well-compensated for her work. It's a fair offer, given how unproven she is."

Of course, it was. Downright generous, truth be told. But Aaron wasn't willing to give ground so easily. "It's a fair offer if she's paid what she's worth." He leaned back. "What are your terms?"

It was presumptuous of him to negotiate on her behalf like this. She hadn't asked him to, but he'd be damned if he let her come out of this with a pittance. She could stop him whenever she wanted. Fortunately, she remained silent as she listened to him dicker with Reuben.

They haggled like fishmongers.

He kept an eye on her expression, watching to see when her eyes widened in surprise or narrowed in disagreement. She gave a slight nod when she approved, or so he assumed, and her fingers tightened on her teacup when she rejected an idea. He wouldn't have known these small gestures a month ago, but he had made a study of her in the last weeks. He recognized her feelings in these small ways, and he prayed he guessed correctly.

"Are we in agreement?" Reuben finally asked after the details were hammered out.

Aaron turned to Lilah. She was the one who had to agree. Everyone waited on her, and he was struck anew at her regal demeanor. She was quiet, composed, and in the end, she had one question.

"When would I begin?"

"Today," said Reuben.

"Immediately," said Mrs. Dove-Lyon.

She shook her head. "Tomorrow. I must set my affairs in order at home first. This is a change, and I require a day to make the adjustment."

It was more than a simple change. She was about to embark on an entirely different life, and she spoke as if she were swapping horses at an inn. He had to give her credit for nerve. So did the others as they exchanged a glance and nodded.

"You continue to impress, Miss Rees," said Mrs. Dove-Lyon.

And even Reuben gave her a nod of approval. "Good show, Miss Rees." Then he leaped up from his seat. "Well, I need to be off. There are more dragons about, more damsels in distress."

"And are you helping the dragons or the maidens?" Aaron asked.

Reuben gave him a wink. "Depends on who has more gold."

That was likely the dragons. But before he damned Reuben too much, Aaron had to admit that the man had come through for Lilah today. And he'd been a significant help to Diana and Lucas two years ago. That counted for something. So he stood up from his chair and shook Reuben's outstretched hand.

"It's never dull when you're involved," Aaron said with good humor. "I thank you for your efforts."

"I expect to be richly rewarded for my work this night." He bowed over Lilah's hand. "Don't forget that, Miss Rees."

"I won't, Mr. Bates."

Then he turned to Mrs. Dove-Lyon, whispering something

into her ear that made the woman giggle. And with a last bright smile, he headed for the door only to pause as he looked at Aaron. "You really are trying to help the veterans, aren't you?"

Aaron nodded. "More than just them. But at the moment, they're the highest priority."

"Hmmm. Perhaps we should talk about that."

"About what?" Aaron asked.

"Your priorities. I have some suggestions."

Of course, he did. But Reuben also had a unique perspective on the people of London. One that was not ruled by the peerage or the royals. That was valuable to Aaron. "I should enjoy that immensely," he said.

"I'll be in touch," he said. Then he winked one last time at the ladies and left.

Which left him and Lilah to make their excuses as well. He pushed to his feet, but she remained seated, her gaze on Mrs. Dove-Lyon. "You engineered this," she said. "Why?"

"Goodness, no. I simply listened to smart people like yourself and Mr. Bates. I recognized an opportunity, and I enjoy doing favors for people in power." She tilted her head toward Aaron.

"A favor?" he returned coldly. "You made sure she lost her bet against Mr. Palmer."

"On the contrary. I made sure she could make that bet safely. As did you. And she now has the running of the business she wanted with the security of a salary while she finds her feet."

He couldn't disagree, but Lilah did. Or rather, she could question it.

"And what do you get out of it? Besides what I am sure is a very tiny bit of profit. Mr. Bates does not seem like one who would have given up much to you."

Mrs. Dove-Lyon sniffed. "My arrangement with Mr. Bates is my own. What I get, Miss Rees, is access to a Member of Parliament who had never before stepped inside my doors." She looked at Aaron. "Just like Mr. Bates, I should like to call upon you, my lord. We share a reforming spirit, and I have ideas regarding the treatment of women."

Ideas? Everyone had ideas! But like Reuben, she had a singular view on society. One that he would be foolish to discount if only as a source of information.

"You will find that I cannot be bought, and I do not take kindly to threats," he said.

She laughed. "I never thought anything different."

"Then I should be happy to discuss your ideas. Once. If they are interesting, I will be open to discussing them in more detail."

"Excellent," she said with a smile. Then she looked at her watch. "I'm afraid you should be going now. All of London shall be about soon and you should be at home when that happens."

Yes, they should. He held out his hand to Lilah, and she took it with a worried kind of smile. They departed quickly, down a back stairway and out to a quiet side alley. A carriage was waiting there for them as a final gift from Mrs. Dove-Lyon. They quickly climbed in. Once Aaron had given directions to Lilah's home, they settled down in silence. So much had happened, it was a struggle to wrap his mind around it. Harder, it appeared, for Lilah because she was twisting her fingers in and around the fabric of her skirt.

He touched her hands, soothing him as best he could. "You needn't do this—"

"I want to."

He nodded. "If it doesn't work for you. If you hate it or you feel in danger—"

"I will tell you. I promise."

"Good."

She looked up at him. "I don't like you beholden to them on my account."

"What?"

"To Mr. Bates or Mrs. Dove-Lyon. You promised them—"

"A meeting, nothing more. I assure you, this is how I spend most of my days."

"But—"

"Don't worry. This is my stock and trade."

She nodded and appeared to be reassured. They travelled that way in silence for a bit with his hand wrapped around her two. In time, she flipped her hand over and they were palm to palm, their bodies pressed together against the squabs.

"I don't regret last night," she abruptly said. "Not one moment of it."

"Not one moment?" he asked. He could think of several moments—before they were together—that could have gone much better.

"It all led to my time with you," she said. She twisted so she looked him in the eye. "And I wouldn't change that for the world."

He saw the honestly in her expression and felt his heart twist. How brave she was to embark on a new life so easily. How beautiful she was to face her uncertain future with excitement instead of dread. And how much he wanted to keep her in his life.

"May I call on you?" he asked.

"When?"

It was a good question. She was going to be working night and day to set things to right at her new registry office. And he had a great deal of work to do as he set up in the House of Lords. "Whenever you want. Whenever you are free."

"Why?"

Damnation, he should have known she would ask that question. "Because I want to see you, of course." And because he wanted so much more.

"But you don't love me. You said as much. I have a respectable job now. I will not be your mistress."

"I wasn't offering you carte blanche! I wouldn't insult you like that."

She nodded as if she understood. "Then why?" She touched his face and it felt like the ring of a bell. His entire body reacted to her single caress. "Why would a new earl call upon a shopkeeper?"

Because he liked how he felt when he was with her. Because he wanted to see what extraordinary things she would do to make the registry office her own. Because he wanted to hear her voice and listen to her laugh. And he also intended to find a way to replace the five hundred pounds she had lost.

But he couldn't say those things. They were inappropriate from a single man to an unattached female whom he did not intend to marry. So he swallowed them down. But that left him mute in the face of her question. Why did he want to see her?

"I think," she finally said, "that it would be best if I concentrated on my new responsibilities."

If she had cut him open before, now she pulled out his heart. By his own words, he did not love her and would not marry her. Therefore, he had no right to keep her from whatever future she chose to pursue. And yet he wanted to. How desperately he craved it.

The carriage pulled to a stop. He glanced outside and saw that they had come to her home. She needed to get inside soon, but he didn't want to release her. She didn't give him a choice. When he didn't move, she opened the carriage door on her own.

"Say you will visit Clara. She would be devastated to lose your friendship."

"As would I," Lilah said.

That was it. There seemed to be no more words between them. She stepped down and turned to shut the door. He was pushing forward so he could follow her and wasn't that insane? He couldn't be seen with her at this time of day.

She waited while he held her gaze. If only the situation were different. If only he could believe that they wouldn't eventually make each other miserable. If only the political world could allow him to be an effective Member of Parliament while married to the woman of his choice.

His career or his heart?

His life purpose or a woman? A beautiful, brilliant, capable woman.

If only he could believe they wouldn't end up miserable, despising each other for things they couldn't change.

With a sigh he looked away. Duty, responsibility, and purpose outweighed his personal concerns. That was the life of an earl.

"Goodbye," she said, and the word broke his heart.

"Let me know if you need..." His voice trailed away. She'd already shut the carriage door.

CHAPTER NINETEEN

LILAH HAD A great deal to do, but first she wanted a few moments to herself. Something extraordinary had happened with Aaron last night and she wanted to savor it. She wanted to steep herself in the memories because they were delicious, exquisite, and now over.

She'd confessed her love, and he'd refused her. There was only so long she could carry a torch for a man without becoming ridiculous. It was time to move on. Today marked the fresh start she'd been praying for. She just hadn't expected it to be punctuated by her first glorious sexual experience.

Which was now over.

She called for a bath. It was a luxury, but one she needed. Not all the scents from yesterday had been pleasant. Cigar smoke clung to her hair overpowering the more delicious scent of Aaron on her skin. Unfortunately, she wasn't able to keep one and wash out the other. And since he was no longer part of her life, she would clean it all off.

Which is exactly what she did, though she lingered over a small bruise and a few new aches. But in the end, she rose from her bath and dried herself before the fire. She needed to focus on new tasks, first and foremost of which was telling her adoptive mother about her changed future.

So it was that she supplanted the maid and brought the Dowager Countess Byrn her morning chocolate.

"Good morning, Mama," she said as she set down the tray. Strangely, the lady was already awake, and her expression was not in the least bit welcoming. Lilah saw the reason why a moment later when the countess' dresser, Carter, stepped out from behind the changing screen carrying a pile of linens. The woman shot Lilah an arch look, then made her way past and out the door. A moment later, Lilah heard the heavy thud as the door was pulled shut.

Lilah sighed. She and Carter had never gotten along, but they hadn't actually been enemies. At least Lilah hadn't thought so, until now, when her adoptive mother gestured her forward with the chocolate.

"Carter has been giving me news."

Of course, she had.

"She says you made a spectacle of yourself at a gaming hell with Lord Kittrel." The lady sat up straight, poured herself her own chocolate, then pinned Lilah with a heavy gaze. "Very well. Tell me everything."

Lilah folded her hands across her stomach. "Carter is correct."

Lady Byrn narrowed her eyes. "I didn't doubt it. The servants know everything."

It was true, especially since Lady Byrn often rewarded Carter for sharing good gossip.

"Well? Come on, don't be coy. Tell me it all." She leaned forward eagerly. "Is Lord Kittrell going to marry you?"

Lilah was startled by the pain of that question. It cut sharp enough that her throat closed down, and she could only shake her head by way of an answer.

Lady Byrn pursed her lips. "He's an honorable man, and he's ruined you. I think we can find a way to force him."

"What?"

"Don't be so naïve. If any other man had seduced you, you'd be out of luck. But Lord Kittrel? Carter claims he carries a purse specifically to give to thieves when he's attacked. Can you imagine? But he's got a level head, no vices beyond his strange sister, and best of all, he's an earl."

She didn't need anyone to sing the man's praises to her. "Lord Kittrel won't offer for me," she said firmly. "And in case you're wondering, he did not… we did not…" She struggled to find a way to explain exactly what had happened, but apparently Lady Byrn didn't care.

"I'm sure you didn't. He's not one to debauch anyone."

"Then—"

"But your reputation is still ruined."

Lilah shrugged. "I didn't have much of one anyway."

At that, her adoptive mother dropped her cup down on the saucer with an angry click. "Good God, Lilah, I cannot understand why you continue to fight me on this. Day in and day out, I hear you say, 'They won't accept me. I'm a bastard. They won't invite me.'" Lady Byrn huffed out a breath. "I have worked tirelessly to show you as more than *just a bastard*. I've told you of your Scottish nobility, and your father's ancestry is above reproach. You've grown into a capable woman, and I won't hear another word about you not having a good reputation before last night. I worked too hard to ensure it!"

It was true, and Lilah acknowledged that with a quiet apology. "I have not thanked you enough for that. You brought me in when you didn't need to. I would have an entirely different life—a much poorer one—without you."

"That's right."

Lilah stepped forward and pressed a kiss to the lady's cheek. Their relationship had never been easy, but there was affection on both sides. "I am sorry I have disappointed you."

"You haven't disappointed me yet!" the lady cried as she encouraged Lilah to sit down on the edge of the bed. "But we must execute our campaign precisely. It is no small thing to capture an earl, Lilah, but somehow you have done it. And now we must force him to come up to scratch. It's the honorable thing to do."

"Forcing a man to marry me is not honorable."

"Pish-posh. I'm talking about his honor." She adjusted her position on the bed such that she no longer lounged but sat forward with clear determination. "Now tell me everything. Don't leave any detail out. I want to know why you went to that gaming hell and what exactly Lord Kittrel's part was. There will be something there to trip him up." She grinned. "I had a note from his sister, you know. Last evening. She said you would be spending the night with her. Very smart of him to cover your tracks like that. Nevertheless, if Carter found out that you were at the Lyon's Den, then everyone else will know, too. We haven't a moment to waste."

Lilah looked at her adoptive mother. The woman was focused and happy. She was planning a social campaign, and she was thrilled that Lilah might force an earl to the alter. What a coup that would be to get a bastard wed to an earl.

"I thought you wanted me to live with you for the rest of my life. I would manage the house. We would bounce the grandchildren on our knees."

Lady Byrn tilted her head in confusion. "Well naturally that's what I thought. I'd done everything to make you take, but it didn't work. Even Sayres couldn't force it, and I know he worked very hard at that."

"You and he together waged an aggressive campaign."

"Well, it worked for Gwen," the lady said with a wave of her wrist. "That was one worry off my mind, I can tell you." She clapped her hands in delight. "I never imagined you would get an earl as well. We shall make the rounds this afternoon. We must tell everyone that he took you to that place, and in your innocence, you agreed."

"No, Mother," she said. "I forced him to take me."

"That doesn't matter. He's a man, and it was his responsibility to stop you. That's what we'll say—"

"No."

"Don't be difficult. We'll start with Lady Jersey. She loves it when the gossip comes to her first. We'll show up early to Lady

Castlereagh's musicale tonight and tomorrow I'll get you into the Willrich ball somehow—"

"No! Stop!" Lilah held up her hands. "Lord Kittrel is not responsible for my choices."

"Very egalitarian of you, but that's not how society works. I thought you understood that. Now—"

"He will not marry me!"

Lady Byrn grinned. "That's where you're wrong, Lilah. We can make everyone believe—"

"I've taken a position at a registry office. Starting tomorrow, I'll run the place. You needn't worry about this house. I'll make sure that everything is in order for you here." She squared her shoulders as she continued. "I won't be calling on anyone, and I won't go to any balls. I'll be a working woman from now on."

Her adoptive mother's eyes widened in shock. Her mouth even hung open for a few very long moments. Then she snapped out a very firm response. "Absolutely not! If you're working, you'll never marry the earl."

"He's not going to marry me in any event. He said so quite specifically." And several times, no less.

"What do men know about these things? I can count on one hand the marriages that were the man's idea first. It's always arranged beforehand by the women." She leaned forward. "It's fortunate that Kittrel's mother isn't in London. She would be the difficult one to persuade."

Lilah leaped off the mattress. "Stop it!" she cried, startling herself at the violence in those two words. It took her a few deep breaths, but she managed to moderate her tone. "He has said no."

"But—"

"I say no."

"Now you're being difficult!"

"I'm going to work in the morning. I am going to run a registry office. It's a respectable position that I'm proud of." She swallowed. "And maybe I'll meet a respectable man with a position of his own. We'll marry, have children, and be happy."

"Now you listen here," Lady Byrn said as she pushed herself out of bed. With every word, she advanced on Lilah. "I didn't bring you into my home, raise you as my own, just to have you throw it all away. So stubborn!" Her hands clenched into fists as she banged them down through the air. "You, of all of my children, have been the most biddable, and yet here you are, being stubborn. I cannot understand it!"

Neither could Lilah. That was the first time that Lady Byrn had named her one of her children. Never had Lilah been lumped together with her half-siblings as if she were one and the same with them. It stole her breath enough that she barely processed the lady's next words.

"You are of noble birth, and you will not shame me by acting beneath your station!"

"I'm illegitimate."

"I know it! And yet, if you would but listen to me, I can get you a good match. An earl!"

Lilah shook her head. "But you can't. He won't marry me."

"Have a little faith in me. Haven't I proven myself? Diana and Gwen married spectacularly. I can do the same with you." She squared her shoulders in much the same way Lilah had. "Indeed I promised your father that very thing. He loved you. He wanted the best for you, and I will provide it. But you must do exactly as I say."

The lady was so fierce in her determination, so absolutely confident of her abilities, that Lilah believed her words. The woman could find a way to force Aaron to the altar. She could manipulate the *ton* such that he would have no choice.

Part of her wanted that. To marry Aaron would be the fulfillment of so many dreams. But to force him into that would poison the very marriage she wanted.

"I won't do it," she said. "I won't force him."

"Don't think of it like that. Think of it as the proper remedy after he ruined you."

"He didn't!" Lilah swallowed her protests. Facts made no

difference here, only appearance and the pressure of public opinion. Lady Byrn was a master manipulator when it came to that.

"I can make it work for you," the lady said. "Now that you have baited the hook, I can see him reeled in."

And that was the end for Lilah. Whatever temptation she'd felt disappeared at the image of Aaron hooked like a fish. Whatever guilt she felt at denying her adoptive mother faded to nothing at the image of Aaron hung on a line and dropped into a church.

"I won't do it," Lilah said. Then she invested strength in her words. "I know you don't understand it, but my future isn't with the peerage. I'm going to run a registry office and be happy there."

"No, you won't," her mother declared. "You've been raised with much finer things. Do you know how they treat those women? Do you know what happens to women who work?"

"I do," she said firmly. "Better than you do."

"Then why?" the words were screeched at her. "Whyever would you want that?"

"Because you were wrong!" she cried. She'd never spoken these words out loud. She'd never dared allowed herself to utter her darkest secret. But suddenly, when offered the one thing she truly wanted, the ugly truth spilled out. "You were wrong to bring me into your home. You were wrong to lift me above my station."

"Don't be ridiculous. We love you. We gave you a home."

"You did, but it was a cheat. You pulled me into a world that won't accept me. And the only way I can marry is if you cheat Lord Kittrel as well." She shook her head. "I'm the illegitimate daughter of an actress. And by taking me away from that—by lifting me above it—you've made it so I can't find happiness here without cheating someone else."

"You'd rather we left you in the acting troupe? You'd be dead in the gutter by now!"

Maybe. Maybe not. After all, Margarite wasn't dead. As far as Lilah could tell, her childhood friend was happy in her hard life. She certainly wasn't tricking any man to the altar.

Lilah pleaded with her mother to understand. "I know you meant well. I know you love me." At least she knew that now. "But it's too hard," she confessed. "Living like I have been, existing on the edge of things. I see what Diana's found, and Gwen and Elliot." All of her half siblings were blissfully in love. "You and father were the same. You loved each other."

"But there is affection between you and Lord Kittrel. There must be or how would you have gotten him to that gaming hell in the first place?" The lady dropped her hands on her hips. "There are many pathways to a happy marriage."

Lilah shook her head. "Maybe so, but I will not do this to him." She lifted her chin. "I start work tomorrow."

"You'll humiliate me. Everyone will know. Everything I've done for you will be for nothing!" Lady Byrn's voice rose with every sentence.

Lilah knew it was true—at least from Lady Byrn's perspective—but there was nothing she could do about it. "I'm sorry," she said. Then she turned toward the door.

"If you do this, you won't be welcome back in this house. I'll bar the door to you."

Lilah jolted. "You'd do that to me? The child you claim to love?"

Mama nodded her head, tears flowing down her cheeks. "You're forcing me into it. I can't let you do this. I can't let you throw away everything I've done for you."

"I'll live with Elliott or Diana." She would have said Gwen, except she and Sayres were right then in Lincolnshire.

"You'd embarrass them then just like you would me. They'd be harboring a tradeswoman, and it will bring down their status." Lady Byrn scrambled out of bed. "Damnation, why can't you listen? I can get you an earl!"

They were going in circles. As much as she loved her adoptive mother, Lilah now saw how limited the woman was. She was fierce in her own right, determined to manipulate everyone she loved into the world she knew. The idea of going outside of the tiny circle of the peerage meant diminishment, and she would do everything in her power to keep Lilah in that suffocating circle. Even if it meant trapping Aaron into a marriage. Especially if it meant that!

"You're right," Lilah finally said. "My working will always have a negative effect on your status."

"Exactly!"

"Best to distance ourselves from one another immediately."

"What?"

"I'll pack a bag." She had no idea where she was going to live, but she'd think of something. "Thank you, Mother, for everything you've done for me."

"This isn't what I want!" the lady bellowed. She even stomped her foot as emphasis.

It wasn't what Lilah wanted either, but it was the only solution she could stomach. "I won't hurt your status, and I won't keep begging to be let inside your level."

"But—"

"And I won't trap any man into marriage."

She sobbed as she packed her bag, but she didn't linger. It would be too painful. If she still had her purse, she would go to an inn or a rooming house. But she'd lost all her money last night. Which meant there was only one place left to go. One friend who wouldn't lose status by "harboring a tradeswoman." After all, Clara was already known to harbor all sorts of odd ideas and friends.

Chapter Twenty

ARON WAS NOT an emotional man. And yet as the carriage took him on to his home, he felt as if he were being battered by a dozen different emotions, all of them intense, and all contradictory. The bliss of the night before was tinged with guilt and lust. He knew both pride that he hadn't thoroughly debauched Lilah as he'd wanted to, and worry that it didn't matter. After all, they'd spent the night together in a gambling den. Someone probably noticed and would talk. The unknown man who had seen them in the hallway this morning, perhaps. He also felt enormous relief that Lilah had a future now, though naturally he was concerned that she was not in control of her fate. Reuben was, and that was always a worry.

And over it all was a maddening pall of depression from the way they'd separated. Goodbyes spoken as if he would never see her again. He knew it was for the best. And yet the ache he felt at never laughing with her again, never sharing tales of their day over evening meal, and never kissing her again, made him want to dash his brains against the carriage wall.

That was the most ridiculous thing of all. He was an earl and a respected Member of Parliament. Whatever was he doing feeling like he wanted to dash his brains against anything?

Thankfully, he arrived at his home and was able to bury such concerns under action. Or so he thought. He intended to spend his day working on estate matters received yesterday from his steward, but the moment he entered his home, he realized nothing was as he expected.

Lord Loughton was snoring in his front parlor.

He looked at his butler in confusion, but Binner merely shrugged. "I believe Lady Clara left him there last night."

The irregularity of that statement momentarily rendered him speechless. Eventually, he recovered enough to look up the stairs. "Where is my sister now?"

"In her bedroom, presumably asleep."

"And where were you, Binner, that you don't know these things?" he asked. "You're the butler of the house. You should know all the comings and goings. When did Lord Loughton arrive? When did Lady Clara go to bed? Why did Lord Loughton choose to sleep in my parlor?"

Binner flushed dark red, and his eyes narrowed in hostility. "I cannot say what your sister chooses to do or with whom. It is not my place."

"Wrong. A butler knows what happens in the house. Unfortunately, you probably choose to spend your evenings in the pub, returning here barely before morning. I daresay you learned of Lord Loughton's presence the same way I just did."

"The devil you say!" the man blustered. "I have toiled for you, my lord. Sweated and worked my fingers to the bone on your behalf, and this is the thanks I get?"

"You get no thanks for a job badly done."

Aaron was a patient man, one who had promised the management of his servants to his sister. It was a task she took great pride in and so because of his love for her, he would usually stop here. He would discuss Binner's bad performance with his sister and firmly suggest the man should be turned out. Then he would leave it in her hands because that's what he'd promised.

But he was done with that. If he was an earl, then by God, he would be served like an earl. If he had to give up the woman he wanted because of his status, then he would be treated as a man with status. Especially in his own home! And if his sister—

beloved, scatterbrained, lost Clara—could not perform her duties accordingly, then she would lose those responsibilities until such time as she proved she could do them.

"Binner."

The man had been walking away in a huff, but he stopped to turn back with an obsequious gesture. One that might have been sarcastic. "My lord?"

"You're sacked. Pack your things immediately and go."

Far from being shocked, the man drew himself up to his full height. "I don't believe that's wise, my lord."

"I beg your pardon?"

"I know things. I know what your sister does in this house and outside it. It would be unfortunate indeed if such things got out." He gave an oily smile. "Think how that would affect her marriage prospects. And your political—"

He didn't get another word out. Aaron punched him hard enough to slam him into the wall. He didn't check the impulse as usual. Didn't even bother thinking about it before he chose to act. He simply punched the man straight in the face. And if the bastard stood up, he'd get punched again.

"Is that how you managed to keep your job this long?" Aaron sneered. "By threatening my sister?"

"I'll tell 'em! I'll tell everyone!" Binner gibbered as he used the wall to straighten up. "Orgies and knife throwers! Rituals to the devil—"

Another blow straight to the bastard's face. And while the idiot was down, Aaron stripped him of his keys. Then he tried to yank the man's livery off his body. He'd be damned if the man wore the Kittrel colors ever again. But in this, the blowhard had too much bulk to effectively strip his clothes. So Aaron satisfied himself with shredding the fabric with his bare hands.

Then he hauled the man up by what was left of his collar. "One word," he growled. "One word against my sister or myself, and I will have you gutted."

Far from being cowed, Binner shouted obscenities. He cursed

everything and everyone while Aaron shoved him against the wall. And then he drew him close enough to whisper into his ear.

"I'm good friends with Reuben Bates. I will pay him to have you silenced."

Binner choked on his inhale as he seemingly tried to pull back his curses. Aaron held him one moment longer to show that he was in deadly earnest, and then he used one hand to open the door and the other to toss the man onto the street. Binner tumbled arse over teakettle onto the walk. And Aaron took great pleasure in slamming the door shut.

Then he turned around to confront a handful of people gaping at him from the front hallway. Most of them were staff—two footmen and one maid—and they scrambled away at his dark look. Another was Lord Loughton who leaned negligently on the doorframe to the parlor. He was silently clapping his hands. But Aaron's attention went to his sister who stood with her mouth hanging open at the top of the stairs.

"Clara!" Aaron cried. "Why didn't you tell me he was threatening you?"

His sister blinked then pulled herself together enough to descend the stairs. "He wasn't threatening me," she said. "He said he'd destroy your work in Parliament." She glanced worriedly out the door. "Do you think—"

"He can't," Aaron huffed. "Do you think no one knows me in Parliament? Damnation, Clara, they make jokes about how boringly upright I am. No one's going to believe anything he says." He blew out a breath and turned to the other man in the room. "And why are you sleeping here? Don't you have a home?"

Lord Loughton straightened up, but it was Clara who answered for him.

"I asked him to stay. I was worried when you didn't come home last night."

The gentleman spoke up. "I told her you likely couldn't—"

"Is Lilah all right?" Clara interrupted. "We saw her lose all her money. Five hundred pounds! It's all she has. Can you help her,

Aaron? Can you—"

He held up his hand to silence her as he thought through her words. Damnation, she'd gone to the hell last night. She'd risked her reputation and her safety, and he wasn't sure if he was grateful or furious that she'd had the wherewithal to bring an escort.

"Clara, you try my patience," he growled.

"Me!" she exclaimed. "When you—"

"Best to let the man have his say," interrupted Lord Loughton, his words obviously meant for Clara.

Aaron shot the Scot a dark look simply because he could, then crossed down the hall enough to open the door that led down to the kitchen. "Could someone bring me some tea?" he bellowed.

"Right away, my lord!" responded the cook.

"Thank you."

Then he shut the door and turned back to the main hallway. Lord Loughton was in his shirtsleeves and stocking feet as he crossed to Clara. Even Aaron had to admit that the morning light made his rumpled hair and devilish grin handsome. Clara, on the other hand, wasn't paying the least bit of attention. She was wrapping her arms around herself as she kept looking out the front door.

"It's all gone wrong," she murmured. "Binner deserved it, of course, but I didn't know how to stop him. And Lilah—"

"There, there," Loughton murmured, the two words taking on a slightly musical tone when touched by his Scottish brogue. "I'll make sure that bastard won't say a word against you."

Clara shook her head. "You can't stop him."

"I can, an' I will." He looked over to Aaron. "I'll help however you need."

"I don't need help," Aaron growled. "I need an explanation as to why you are here." Then before the man could answer, he pointed into the parlor. "In there. Both of you."

All three of them tromped into the parlor. The cushions were rumpled since it had been his lordship's bed, but there was a wingback chair next to the fire. Aaron claimed that, which left his sister and Lord Loughton to cozy up to one another on the couch. And they did. Cozy up, that is. They sat near enough to touch, and it was clear that Lord Loughton would have welcomed the woman into his arms if Clara had wanted it. She didn't. Or at least she wasn't willing to in front of her brother. She sat straight as an arrow beside his lordship at the polite distance of a scant few inches.

It was unsettling. He was used to Clara pressing herself forcefully to the farthest end of any couch such that she wouldn't be near any male. Obviously, she'd had a turn of heart regarding His Lordship.

"Out with it," he said grumpily. "What has happened such that my sister doesn't hate you?"

Lord Loughton turned to Clara, clearly waiting for her to explain. When she remained resolutely silent, the Scotsman spoke up. "She sent me a letter last evening asking me to help her get to the Lyon's Den."

Yes, so Aaron had gathered. "I asked you to trust me to handle it," he said to Clara.

Her chin lifted, and she spoke in haughty accents. "I wanted to help, and you wouldn't take me."

Aaron glared at Lord Loughton. "And you thought that was an appropriate place to take my sister?"

The man arched a brow. "She was going whether I took her or not. I kept her safe from discovery." Then the bastard had to point out that he'd made the exact same choice when it came to Lilah. "I'd wager you faced a similar problem with Miss Rees."

"No one knew I was there," Clara said. "Everyone was watching Lilah and you. Is she really all right?"

"Better than all right. She starts work tomorrow running the registry office she wanted."

Both people on the couch straightened up in surprise. "What?"

"But she lost—"

He held up his hand for silence as a footman brought in the tea tray. He was more appropriately called a footboy given his youth—barely into his teens—but he was strong enough for the work even when his gaze seemed to hop all over the room in his nervousness.

"Who are you?" Aaron demanded.

"Don't be mean," Clara snapped. "This is Rogers. He's new. Lilah recommended him and he's—"

Young.

"—Learning his duties very well."

The boy straightened up and then flushed bright red to the tips of his ears. "I'm here to serve, my lord."

He sounded like he was reporting to the military, but Aaron had the grace to realize his surliness should not be poured over this young man. "Very well, Rogers," he said with as much warmth as he could muster. "There's going to be extra work until I can find a suitable butler—"

"I'll do that!" Clara exclaimed.

Aaron ignored her. "I'll be watching to see if you know your responsibilities."

"Yes, my lord," Rogers snapped. And again, it felt like he was responding to a commanding officer. *Good enough*, Aaron thought as he waved the man away.

Meanwhile, Clara started to pour tea, but her expression was mulish. "That is my job, Aaron. I'll not have you doing it."

"Well, I'm changing your job," he said. "I'm an earl now, and I can't have a butler threatening me and a boy serving tea." He matched her stubborn expression, glare for glare. "It's time for us both to step into our proper status."

"What does that mean?" she cried.

"It means that I'll oversee the getting of a proper housekeeper and butler. It means that you won't go writing midnight letters to gentlemen so you can visit a gaming hell. And it means said gentleman won't be sleeping in our front parlor!"

"I was frightened for you!" Clara cried. "I got an escort and arrived disguised. You, on the other hand, let them banty Lilah's name about while she lost all her money!" She leaned forward. "I'd wager you're the one who acted badly, not me."

She had a point, not that he was going to listen to it. "I'm a man and an earl. I'm allowed to be an idiot. You're an unmarried lady in want of a husband."

"I am not!"

"You are." His voice was hard. "I've let you run wild here, hoping you would settle down. And what do I find? A gentleman sleeping in my parlor!"

He wasn't even looking at Lord Loughton. His glower was completely reserved for his sister, but at that last statement, Loughton exhaled in a loud, long breath. Almost like a bull preparing to charge. "I'm getting a wee bit tired of being the villain in all this."

"It might surprise you to know that I don't care. It's not proper for a man to sleep—"

"She asked me to! She was frightened for Miss Rees," Loughton interrupted. "And worried about you, though I cannot understand why. You seem churlish enough to do well in that crowd."

His gaze narrowed on the Scotsman. "Have a care, sir. You have to go through me to get her." It was a threat, spoken low and angry, but the bastard met his growl with a firm jaw and a challenge of his own.

"Do I? Are you sure?"

"Oh my God!" his sister declared, suddenly dropping her teacup onto her saucer. Her tones were dramatic and horrified.

Aaron blew out a breath. Now what?

"Clara?" Lord Loughton prompted.

"This is a hangover, isn't it? That's why he's acting like this, right?"

"What?" Aaron snapped. "Don't be ridiculous." He certainly did have a sore head, but that wasn't affecting him in the least.

"But you're never like this. Punching servants and ordering me to become proper. That's what Mother used to do, and you swore you'd never treat me like that."

Aaron pinned his sister with a hard stare. "Perhaps Mother was right. You're twenty-three now, Clara. Long since time to grow up."

She shook her head. "Do you have a fever? Does your tummy feel bad?"

"Damnation, Clara!"

"And you're cursing!"

Lord Loughton leaned forward. "He doesn't curse?"

"He curses all the time," she returned, "but not at me." Then she turned to him, her expression softening.

"Tell me what happened with Lilah."

He exhaled a breath. "Mr. Reuben Bates ended up buying the registry office and has hired Miss Rees to run it."

Lord Loughton pursed his lips. "A difficult boss there. I've heard tales about Mr. Bates."

So had everyone. "His reputation is darker than the man."

Loughton took that with a nod, but his sister was the one who leaned back in her seat and regarded him with vague eyes. "Lilah has chosen to step down from the peerage and make a life for herself?"

"Yes," Aaron said, his throat unexpectedly tight.

"Good for her. Finally, she can find a social circle that will accept her."

"She's still…still…"

"Illegitimate?" Clara said. "You'd be surprised how very unimportant that is outside of the peerage."

"Which is why," Aaron said, his voice heavy, "she can be known in a gaming hell, and you can't." He looked down at his hands knowing how his next words would be received. "I would never stop you from any of your friends, Clara, but it's high time we both began acting according to our status. You are a lady, a member of the aristocracy, with a name and a status to uphold."

His gaze rose to meet his sister's. "It's high time we both accepted that."

To his surprise, his sister didn't leap to her feet and scream at him. She didn't protest that he didn't understand her or run crying to her bedroom. He had witnessed all of these things whenever their mother had tried to impose proper behavior upon her. Instead, Clara held his gaze and slowly shook her head, no.

"Clara, please try to understand I'm saying this for your own good. For both of us."

"Do you know," she said softly, "that whenever I visit a psychic or consult a tarot reading, I ask about you as often as I ask about me."

He frowned. Honestly, he hadn't thought about it at all. He'd merely hoped she'd lose her interest in the occult over time.

"It's one of the ways that I tell if the reading is legitimate," she continued.

"I don't understand," he said.

"If I'm told you're going to have a brilliant career, climb to the heights of respect and power and on and on." She waved her hand in dismissal. "I know they're lying to me and there is no true sight there."

He didn't know how to respond to that. She obviously thought he'd be a failure at his career.

Lord Loughton was equally surprised. He twisted to regard her directly. "What would be a true reading for your brother, then?"

"He has a choice. They've described it different ways, but it's always a fork in the path." She looked at Aaron. "One is the wild path, one is the path of bricks and hard stone. One is lush with wild creatures and beautiful forest, the other is proper with coal-dirtied air and the bang of a gavel."

"Well, I can certainly see which one you'd pick," Aaron said. As much as she loved London, his sister had always craved unusual things. "You want wild things that completely overflow their boundaries."

"And you try to tame the wildness."

"Not true," he said. "I have allowed you to explore according to your heart's desire. There is a time and place for untamed forest."

"For breaking boundaries," she pressed.

And here they disagreed. "Boundaries allow the wild ones to grow as they will and the ones who prefer structure to thrive." He finished his tea then set it aside. "If people are given support, they will grow as they were meant to grow, but one cannot interfere with another. That's what boundaries are for." And that is what he fought for daily in Parliament: to give those who need it adequate support and boundaries against those who would take advantage.

It was his guiding principle. How shocking that she would have discovered that through her unorthodox spiritual explorations.

"And now you've chosen," she said softly, "the brick path where the gavel of judgment constantly bangs down."

"You are simplifying matters to a ridiculous degree."

Lord Loughton frowned. "And what of you, Clara? Do you pick the wild path always?"

She smiled at him. "We are talking about my brother's life, not mine."

"Really?" he returned. "I'm not so sure." But rather than press the issue, he pushed to his feet. "Either way, I should return home now that your brother and Miss Rees are safe."

"I didn't need your help," Aaron grumbled.

"I wasn't trying to help you," Lord Loughton said, his gaze firmly fixed on Clara's. "And I shall return at four for my reward."

Clara winced. "Very well. I'll promenade with you at the fashionable hour. Provided you agree to the rest of the evening's entertainment."

"I wouldn't miss it for the world."

Aaron leaned forward, abruptly feeling alarmed. "What rest of the evening? What's the entertainment?"

"Perfectly safe," Clara said.

"Perfectly fair," Lord Loughton said at the same time. Then at Aaron's scowl, he continued. "We are sharing interests, my lord. She will walk with me if I will accompany her to a true séance." He winked at Clara. "She assures me no one will throw knives at me."

"Unless you're wretched to the spirits."

"Unless I'm mean to the spirits," he echoed as he bowed over her hand. And Clara, to Aaron's shock, giggled like a schoolgirl when he pressed his lips to her hand.

Was it possible? Was the Scotsman finally making headway with Clara? Obviously yes, and Aaron was remarkably unsettled by that. He'd been for the union from the beginning, and yet finally seeing it play out before him left him irrationally grumpy. Just what kind of man was he turning into? Why would he be irritated by the idea of his sister finding happiness with an eligible suitor?

He had no answer as Lord Loughton took his leave. And none either when his sister turned her now cool gaze to him.

"You're going all wrong, Aaron, and you're trying to take me with you. But I won't do it. I won't let you turn me into something I hate."

"Everyone hates growing up," he snapped. "It's hard. You have to be responsible. You have to make good decisions because the consequences hurt."

"Who has been hurt? You want me to change because everyone else thinks I should. You want me to marry because everyone says I must. That's not being an adult. That's letting everyone else decide your life for you."

He slowly pushed to his feet, his gut churning with acid. "Do you think I like coming home to this disaster of a house? That I like listening to the sneers about my unmanageable, unstable sister?"

"That's a hurt to your pride, and that doesn't bother me."

"Well, it should," he said firmly. "As I am the one who pays the bills. I feed and clothe you. I allow you to run to séances without a proper chaperone." He rubbed a hand over his face. "Good God, what was I thinking?"

"That you love your unorthodox sister. That you were proud that I cared for more than just throwing parties and marrying a title."

Why wouldn't she understand? "I care about parties! Because parties allow discussions which lead to the policies and laws that change the world. And I can't host any while my home is in disarray."

She nodded slowly while tears seeped from her eyes. Normally he would think she was forcing the show of emotion, but in this he knew she was genuinely distressed. "I thought you valued me over your politics. I can see now that you have turned away from love."

"How can you say you love me if your actions are destroying my life's work?"

"You're turning into father. You see that, don't you?"

"What are you talking about?"

"He's the one who talked about his life's work and how Mama ruined it. And now you're doing it to me."

"I'm doing nothing of the sort. You've been allowed to run wild and—"

"It was awful, wasn't it? The way they yelled at each other. One minute arguing, near to killing each other, and then the next—"

"I know what they did," he interrupted. His parents were passionate in all things. Eventually the bitterness overwhelmed any tender feelings, but for much of his childhood, their arguments ended in passion that sounded as violent as an attack. "I am nothing like father. I keep my temper restrained."

"Which means you've locked down your heart as well. It's become as hard as stone."

"You're being ridiculous," he snapped. "I am the reasonable one here."

"So reasonable you're going to make yourself and everyone else miserable. Just like father."

He stared at her. Not an hour ago, he'd felt like Lilah had cut out his heart. Now he knew that she'd left a small piece behind for Clara to pulverize. He could not possibly be like his father. Indeed, from his earliest years, he'd resolved to keep his temper in check and to never spread misery like a bad smell to everyone he touched.

Meanwhile, Clara gathered her wrap and turned from him. As she passed through the doorway, she intoned her final pronouncement. "I will get you a butler and housekeeper to give you the home you want. Then I shall remove myself to better accommodations."

"On what money?" he asked.

She didn't answer. He wasn't even sure she heard, but it didn't matter. They both knew he would not allow her to be destitute, but what kind of disaster would her home become? Would he find her frozen to death some winter because her servants forgot to buy more coal and she had no idea how to light a fire? He didn't want to think so. Clara was an intelligent, capable woman, but sometimes he wondered.

And with that horrible fear heavy on his mind, he headed for the library and the papers from his steward. He would need to find a way to maximize the income of the earldom. And he remained there for the rest of the day becoming more frustrated by the second.

He nearly leaped from his chair when heard the knocker sound and Lilah's voice in the hallway. What was she doing here? Of course, she came to visit Clara. Hadn't she told him as much? He could not, would not poison his tenuous relationship with Lilah by speaking to her when he was so ill tempered. That was his plan at least. Until he several hours later when Clara entered his library without knocking and spoke in hard angry words. "Lilah will be staying with me for the next few weeks. I think it best for everyone that you reside at your club until she and I have found alternate lodging."

"What the devil—" he began, but he cut off his words the moment he saw Clara's face. She had on her brave face. The one she wore after every explosive argument between their parents. She even hunched her shoulders the way she did after their angry words spilled onto the servants, the tenants, and Aaron and Clara. It was the expression he'd sworn to eradicate the minute he established himself in London and brought her to live with him. He'd thought it was gone forever, but now he saw its return here as she faced him. In it, he saw bravado as she covered the pain he had caused. He didn't even fully understand what he'd done, but the expression was unmistakable.

At that moment, he knew he'd become his father.

"I'll leave immediately."

CHAPTER TWENTY-ONE

WHAT A RELIEF!

That's the phrase that Lilah repeated to herself as she set Clara's spare bedroom to rights.

Finally, the worst thing in the world had happened to her, and it wasn't nearly as bad as she'd feared as a child. It was a relief. That's what she felt. Total relief.

After all, she'd spent much of her life believing she was one disobedient outburst away from the street. Even when her father had been alive and she'd known he loved her, she'd still walked eggshells around Lady Byrn. The woman cared for her, even showed true affection for her, but Lilah was convinced that was because she'd never truly challenged the woman's dictates. She left that for Gwen who had constantly been at odds with her mother. Lilah was the peacemaker, the housekeeper, and the one who faded into the background so that no one had cause to quarrel with her.

But now she'd quarreled with her adoptive mother. She'd forged a path for her life that was opposed to Lady Byrn's ideas, and she'd been expelled.

It was a relief, she reminded herself. After spending most of her life in terror of such an event, it had finally occurred. And the reality was so much better than she'd feared. She had a job starting on the morrow and a place to live until she could find something of her own. Clara had even suggested that they combine their resources to find a home together. When Lilah had raised her brows in question, Clara had clammed up. It didn't matter. She knew she'd get the story eventually. And in the meantime, they'd cleaned the books out of this spare room and aired the linens.

In short, the axe had fallen, and she was still alive.

Relief.

And yet despite all the times she said the word to herself, the reality felt very different. When all the cleaning and airing was done, when Clara left her to rest after her full day, Lilah sat down on her bed and cried. She tried to fight the tears, but they came anyway. Pretty soon, she was heaving sobs into her pillow.

She didn't feel relief at all. She felt utter devastation.

It took a long while for the sobs to end. Time when she gasped for breath, when her knees came up to her chest, and when the world felt it consisted of nothing but pain and loss. But eventually the turmoil ended. Soon, her breath eased, and her body stopped shaking.

It was only then that she realized a hand was resting on her shoulder. It was large and steady, with a warmth that seeped into her body. It could belong to only one man.

Aaron.

She hastily wiped her eyes and turned to look at him. He was seated on a chair pulled up next to the bed, and he was leaning over as he touched her. Now that she moved, he straightened up a little, but not enough to separate them. And for that she was grateful. So grateful, in fact, that she put her hand over his.

"My lord?"

He winced. "You called me Aaron this morning."

"Aaron," she whispered. God, how sweet his name was on her lips. More, how she longed to throw herself into his arms and sob out the rest of her pain. But he had chosen to sit in a chair beside the bed then to lie beside her. That alone set a barrier between them.

"Lilah, I came up here to pack a bag, then I heard… I saw…"

He squeezed her shoulder. "How can I help?"

She smiled, though the muscles felt weak. And she turned on the bed such that she faced him completely, though it crushed her dress and likely worsened the mess of her hair. Then she entwined her fingers in his.

"You are doing everything for me, Aaron. I have a place to live now thanks to you."

"That was Clara. She didn't even tell me until an hour ago."

Lilah lifted her head. "Oh no—"

"I want you to stay. And I'll stay at my club so you need not fear for your reputation."

She didn't fear for it anyway, but she knew Aaron did. Meanwhile, he pressed on, his expression tight as he spoke.

"I don't understand what happened. Why would your mother throw you out for getting a job? Where did she think you would go?"

"She probably thought I would go to Diana who would convince me to change my mind."

He grimaced. "She doesn't know you very well, does she?"

On the contrary, Lady Byrn knew the former her very well. The old Lilah had been happy to do the household work while living on the fringe, neither in the working class nor in the aristocracy. "She doesn't understand how I don't want the life she offers." Lilah looked up at the ceiling. "I'm not sure I understand it either."

"Because you want something of your own, that's why. It's very admirable given how much you've had to fight for it."

She nodded. It was also fairly stupid given what she'd done before coming here. "I went to the registry office this morning. I wanted to see what was involved in the work." She blew out a breath. "It was overwhelming."

"Worthwhile endeavors usually are."

She shuddered, too tired to do anything more than lay there and speak with him. "Have I been a fool? I could have lived a very good life with Lady Byrn."

He touched her cheek with his thumb, wiping away some of the wetness that lingered. "It's the easiest thing in the world to do what you've always done. But that doesn't make it the right choice."

"I didn't think she'd throw me out." Her voice broke on the last word. Eventually her throat eased enough for her to continue. "She has always fought for her children, stopping at nothing to see that they succeed."

"Whose idea of success?" he asked.

Trust him to see the truth. "Hers, of course, and she does not allow any disobedience."

He drew his knuckles down her jaw, spreading a tingling heat across her skin. "I'm so sorry, Lilah."

She closed her eyes to better feel his touch. "I will look for a place to live—"

"I won't hear of it. You will stay here. Get the registry office working as it ought. Then we will discuss things further."

She opened her eyes, startled to see how vehement his expression was. "I will not oust you from your home," she said.

"I was going anyway," he said glumly. "I believe Clara needs some distance from me."

"Why?"

He ignored her question. "Did you want any dinner? There is plenty to eat. You'll need something to sustain you tomorrow."

She swallowed. She didn't want to eat. She wanted him to kiss her until she forgot all of her pain. She wanted to be his mistress if it meant she would never be tossed aside ever again. Especially if it meant he would grace her bed and teach her such things as they had done last night. But that was the future for a mistress. What she wanted was to become a wife, and that was not something he offered.

She pushed up until she could face him upright. She brushed the hair out of her eyes and tried to smooth the creases out of her gown. She wasn't very hungry, but he was right. She needed something in her stomach before tomorrow. And she would very much like to spend what time she could with him.

"I should love to join you at table."

He smiled as he offered her his arm. She took it as if she were the queen accepting the escort of her favorite knight in shining armor. Of all the people in her life, he was the one who had helped her with her tasks, who had fought beside her and protected her from harm. If she couldn't be his wife, then she would be thankful for his friendship and try so very hard to not wish for more.

They ate together in the kitchen. With Clara gone to her séance, it was just the two of them and both had worked long past the usual hour for dining. With no butler to maintain order, the staff had disappeared to their own pursuits, leaving Lilah to serve them both in the most casual of manners.

"I need to put my house in order," Aaron grumbled over his tureen of cold soup. He looked up with a desperate hope in his eyes. "Please say you will help me with that. I will happily pay whatever your registry wants to get a good butler in place."

"I have already promised Clara I'd help." She tilted her head. "Do you truly mean to force her to wed?"

"Of course not." He gave a helpless gesture. "I simply want her to act with more maturity. I cannot live like this any longer. Servants gone, meals taken in the kitchen, my butler threatening me in my own hallway!" He dropped his fist onto the table. It didn't bang down, but the thud reverberated with frustration. "It's long past time for me to host dinner parties, evening drinks with my compatriots, private discussions at home. It's the way the business of the nation gets discussed and prioritized."

"And you have not been able to do that," she said, seeing the depth of his frustration.

"Would you bring Lord Castlereagh into this house? What would he think of the dents in my table, the dust on the mantle, and the unlaid fire in the library?"

She swallowed her cold soup out of reflex while her mind processed the depth of his problem. Certainly, he could have dealt with this before. He could have wrested the control of his household out of his sister's domain from the very beginning. But that would have hurt his sister and left Clara with even more time on her hands to wander into trouble. Right now Clara and Lord Loughton were at a séance with only her maid as chaperone. Lilah trusted Lord Loughton to keep Clara safe, but that wouldn't stop any gossip from shredding her reputation. And though Clara didn't seem to care about that now, Lilah knew that someday she might have cause to need a good name. If only because it made the way easier for Aaron.

"I'm sorry," Lilah said. "You're in a difficult position. As long as I'm here, I will pay my way by setting your house to rights. I promise."

"You don't need to repay me—" he began, but she cut him off.

"I want to. It won't change things between you and Clara, but if I can find you a good butler and housekeeper, then they can do the work for her."

Relief and gratitude washed through his expression. "I will take any help I can get." His expression turned pensive. "And if you are amenable, I know of several veterans who could use some training and help in finding a position."

She nodded. She had already thought of such a thing. "Of course…" Her voice trailed away when she saw a pile of pound notes on the table. "Aaron?"

"I would like to pay you for the classes. For the veterans. I understand that you aren't quite ready to do it, but this is for when you do."

She didn't have to count the pile to know that five hundred pounds sat on the table before her. He was making up for the money she lost. "I cannot take—"

"Money for classes?" he interrupted. "Of course, you can. Indeed, that is exactly the business you are in." He leaned back in his chair. "I insist. And don't share that with Bates. I'm hiring you, not his registry office. You're not employed there until tomorrow, so this is between you and me."

She smiled and wondered how such a good man had come to be. Aaron had the money and status to force people to do his bidding, and yet he spent his political time fighting for the poor and his evenings burying his needs as a way to show love to his sister. She'd never met a man so generous with his heart, and yet so closed to his own personal needs.

"Thank you," she said as she gratefully accepted his money. Now that she was on her own, she needed the funds. "I will do everything I can to help you and your veterans," she vowed. Someone needed to. Someone needed to give to him as thoroughly as he was giving himself to others.

They spent the rest of the evening discussing their jobs. She wanted to know why it was so hard to get government monies for the hospitals, and he wanted to know how she planned to run the registry office. They spoke over their meal and while cleaning their dishes afterwards. The task was beneath an earl, but he didn't even blink as he picked up a towel to dry off the wet china. And when the task was done, he offered her his arm and escorted her to his library. There he laid the fire while she poured his brandy. And they sat together for hours still talking.

Until he caught her stifling a yawn.

"I'm a beast," he said as he set down his glass. "You've had a full and difficult day."

"I don't mind—" she began, but he cut her off.

"We both have early days." He extended his arm again, and she set her hand upon it. She had had her share of wine this night and swayed unpredictably for a moment. He held her secure, and in that moment, they were face to face. Nearly lip to lip.

Her heart stuttered and her breath caught. Would he kiss her again? Would he touch her as he had last night? Please, please, *please*!

His nostrils flared and his body tightened against hers. She wanted to lean into him. She wanted to drape herself across him as she had last night. And oh, what pleasure they had shared. Could they do it again? Just one more night.

"Lilah," he whispered, and her name came with a strangled kind of groan.

"Aaron," she echoed, her lips curving as she teased him.

"This is madness. We have already decided."

She nodded. She agreed. He needed an aristocratic wife. It was the only way to further his political passions. And she wanted respectability and the family that came from a marriage. She had to remain a virgin for that. She could not be what he needed, and he could not give her what she wanted.

"What if I chose differently?" she asked. "What if I want to be your mistress?"

"You would give up everything you want for me?"

Would she? Did she love him that much? "Maybe," she whispered. She had lived all her life as illegitimate. How hard would it be to become a courtesan? If she were his mistress, it would not be so bad.

Until he found a wife. Then it would be unbearable.

She needed to back away. She could not do this. And yet, she found herself staring into his eyes with longing. What cost for one more night?

"I want you more than I have ever wanted anyone," he said, "but I will not dishonor you." He cleared his throat as if his words pained him. "I. Will. Not."

She was startled by the force of his words. Surprised more by the way he stepped back from her. His arm was still extended, but now at the maximum distance. And when she touched her fingers to his forearm, he walked her out of the room and up to her bedroom. The moment they arrived at her door, he bowed to her and stepped away.

When she looked at him, she felt all her clashing emotions inside her. Confusion, desire, resolve, and love. None of them would settle, and she couldn't find the words to sort through them.

"You deserve everything, Lilah," he rasped. "Everything."

Then he walked away. Ten minutes later she heard him leave the house for his club.

CHAPTER TWENTY-TWO

HOW ODD THAT with time and repetition, even the most overwhelming emotions become the mundane fabric of life. Such was Lilah's thoughts two weeks later. That first day in Aaron's home, Lilah had experienced such violent shifts of emotions from grief to gratitude to lust. Those same feelings had continued the next morning when he had arrived with his carriage to drive her to the registry office. He had stayed with her that day, along with Mr. Reuben Bates, as they had cleaned and sorted the place into a healthy if not quite orderly office.

The two men had then departed together as they discussed London's lack of urban planning while Lilah got to the business of organizing the classes she would teach to people who looked for work. Fortunately, word of the office's new ownership had already spread, and possible employers arrived hourly if only to get a look at her.

Naturally, she took advantage of that, placing as many servants as she could after they proved to her that they could perform the job. It was time-consuming but rewarding work. Good people needed good jobs throughout London, and she was doing her part to see that it happened.

Every evening, Aaron arrived with his carriage and waited while she closed up the office. They spoke about their days in the companionship of the carriage. They came home at the same time to an excellently prepared meal and a brand-new butler who was proving his worth every day. He'd been refused a post time and time again because he'd lost his arm at Waterloo. No one would hire a one-armed butler, but neither Aaron nor Clara had cared. And better yet, the man's wife had leaped at the position of housekeeper. Soon Aaron's home was running with an efficiency that made everyone happy.

Clara rarely joined them in the evenings as she was off on her own amusements. That clearly worried her brother, but he took no steps to limit her beyond making sure she had adequate escort wherever she went. With Reuben's help, Lilah suggested he employ a burly new footman—also a veteran—to accompany her wherever she chose to go. It wasn't exactly proper, but it kept his sister safe and so Aaron relaxed. That allowed Lilah and Aaron to have an amiable evening together before their inevitable before-bed routine.

Every night they hovered on the edge of kissing. Every night the longing felt like it would bury her. And every night he looked at her as if she were the answer to all his prayers.

Until the moment he escorted her to her bedroom and backed away. She was beginning to despise the words, "Sleep well, Lilah" because she never did. After he left for his club, she spent the night tortured by dreams of his hands on her body, his organ filling her belly with children, and of the bliss they could have in each other's arms.

And so it went for two weeks until the night that Clara informed her that she was having a few respectable gentlemen for dinner in two nights' time. "My first true dinner party," she said with pride. "Will you be able to attend?"

Lilah frowned. It wasn't exactly a true dinner party since—as far as she was aware—there had been no formal invitations, no discussion of the meal in question, and no adjustments to the staff to accommodate the extra work. Worse, the new staff livery had yet to be delivered and the current uniforms were sadly outdated. Clara didn't seem to care as she waved at her brother. "You won't approve of anyone I've invited, Aaron, so you should probably remain at your club."

Aaron shook his head sadly. "This is not the way things are done, Clara. I'm sure you know this."

"It's the way I want to do things," she said firmly. "I have chosen the wilder path, and we don't go for all that folderol. There's food enough for those who want to join. And those who don't, needn't come." She pointed a finger at him. "That means you."

Lilah winced. She had heard all about the wild path versus the organized one, and personally she preferred the organized one but understood her friend's need to do things her own way. "You can't bar him from his own home, Clara," she chided.

"It's my home, too, and he's made his opinion of my friends abundantly clear."

"I like Lilah," Aaron said, his tone heavy. "She's your friend."

"Yes, she is," Clara said with a grin. "And this night is for her." She turned toward Lilah. "Ask me who's coming."

Lilah smiled. It was hard not to in the face of Clara's obvious excitement. "Very well. Who will be in attendance?"

"Gentlemen!" Clara said with a cat-in-the-cream grin. "Eligible ones. Smart ones. Funny ones." She clapped her hands. "I've a few lady friends who will round out the evening, of course. They want to talk about a fascinating novel we've all just read." She waved at her brother. "You'd hate it."

"I'm sure I would," he said without heat. "Clara, have you discussed the meal with—"

"I have it all in hand," she said as she looked at Lilah. "Say you'll come. I've done it all for you."

"Of course, I will."

And so, she did. She adjusted her work such that she could be home in time. She checked on the staff and discovered that they had indeed risen to the occasion. And the new livery arrived in time, which was a delight to see. She dressed in her best gown, laughed as Clara fixed her hideous attempt at cosmetics, and then hurried downstairs in time for their first guest.

He was a barrister with a booming voice and a delightful laugh. She found him interesting but a little too fond of his own voice.

The next two guests arrived together. A shy man who manufactured carriages with his father and a boisterous young artist who sang as he painted portraits. They were surprisingly clever about all things mechanical and were both very excited about a new type of mechanical gear.

Two ladies in the company of a solicitor knocked a few moments later. All three laughed easily and talked constantly about a milliner they knew who was detained because of a minor accident while adjusting a bleaching formula.

Clara came down then, late to greet her guests, but was warmly welcomed by all. Then more arrivals, more drink, and more laughter. And everyone seemed genuinely curious about Lilah. Several had heard about her from Clara, but there was no animosity toward her. No subtle jabs about her parentage, and not a harsh word directed toward herself, their butler, or even the fact that their dinner was plain by the standards of the elite and the decorations non-existent. Lilah had been to enough balls to know that each hostess tried to out-do the next. In truth, she had worried that Clara hadn't thought to pick up flowers for their table or even beeswax candles that reduced the smoke. For Clara and the others, the evening was about companionship and not the extras.

And about her. They asked about her childhood in the troupe and the transition to Lady Byrn's household. They quizzed her about her new job and begged her to give gossip about her adoptive family. They wanted details and stories—fodder for the gossip that they freely exchanged about each other—and though they accepted her, she was still left feeling at odds.

They talked about each other and the stories of their lives. She didn't understand the details of bleaching fabric which was discussed after the milliner arrived. And when she asked, one began to answer for half a breath and then another would pick up the tale, only to have a third interrupt with a statement that began, "Remember when…" And off it went.

These people were all good friends, and she was the one left with no understanding of their shared laughter. She ended up resorting to her old tactics of playing hostess without intruding. Smiling without joining. And though she felt no animosity from them, she also was soon forgotten amid their animated conversation.

How lowering to realize that the circumstances of her birth were not the reason she so often fell into the background. These people cared not a whit about her parentage and yet here she was again existing on the fringes of a party. One that Clara had, in fact, created to help her find a husband.

Obviously, the fault lay within her, if only she could understand what it was.

And then, while she was still in the midst of that horrible realization, everything changed. His lordship came home. And not just him. He arrived with Lord Loughton, both of them talking with animation as they stepped into the front hallway. They cheerfully greeted the butler, disposed of their outerwear, and then entered the parlor with every sign of good cheer.

Lilah tensed, wondering if the tension between the siblings would translate to Clara's friends, but if anyone appeared awkward it was Clara herself who jumped to her feet and then stood there in confusion. Lilah stepped into the breach, of course, introducing everyone who then made the two newcomers welcome. And though Lilah caught several arch looks coming from Lord Loughton toward Clara, he eased into the conversation as if he were thrilled to be among them. Because, apparently, he was.

Aaron too settled in once he'd poured himself a brandy. He asked about the carriage business and the milliner's chemical experiments. He turned his agile mind to discussions of science as easily as he pondered the difficulties of advertising. And all the while, Lilah wondered what was wrong with her. Why did everyone else appear to be having the most marvelous time while she stood on the edge and provided a listening ear to the self-important barrister? Once again, she was left to entertain the boor while everyone else made merry.

Was she cursed?

Of course not. That was a fanciful idea borne of Clara's current discussion of ancient pagan religious practices. No, the fault lay entirely within herself.

Her thought trailed off. It didn't matter that she'd been chewing on the idea for more than an hour. Suddenly it faded away beneath Aaron's steady regard from across the room. He appeared to be listening to his sister's commentary of paganism, but his gaze was on her as was hers upon him.

In that moment, she felt seen.

Her body relaxed, her breath eased, and she smiled with true feeling.

The barrister caught his attention then, and they began a discussion about an important legal case. There had been broadsides about it, but Lilah had been too busy in the registry office to pay attention to it. Not so for Aaron who apparently had a clear opinion that differed from the barrister's. But far from being put out by the disagreement, he asked about the legality of something or other. She couldn't hear it, much less understand it, but it didn't matter. That one moment of silent communication with Aaron had given her the strength to excuse herself from the boorish gentleman and ask the woman nearest her about her fashion choices. They were, by standard definitions, rather eclectic.

And so the evening went with Lilah having mixed results when engaging in conversation, sometimes feeling flatly outclassed, sometimes feeling completely intrigued. And all the while keeping track of Aaron's activities, Aaron's discussions, and Aaron's gaze which frequently met hers even from across the room. It was like they were dancing with their eyes, and it lifted her heart every time they came together.

The only bad note the entire evening came from Clara as she resolutely ignored Lord Loughton. She refused to speak with him, refused to acknowledge him, and whenever he stepped near, she found some excuse to move to the opposite side of the room. He didn't seem to mind. Indeed, if Lilah had to guess, he seemed to find her reaction amusing though a dark glint sparked often in his eyes. Whatever was happening between him and Clara, he was clearly not put off by her behavior.

In time, the evening ended. It was early by the standards of the London elite. Lilah was certain that Lady Byrn was only now moving to her last ball of the night. At the height of the Season, she would attend two or three events in an evening. She would also not return home until shortly before dawn.

But these people were of a different class. The men had work to do in the morning and when they left, so too did the women. Lord Loughton departed near the end to act as escort to Miss Smithee, the lady of eccentric attire. The rest took their leave soon afterwards, and when Lilah turned to express her thanks to Clara, she was met with her friend's irritated huff.

"Well, that was unnecessary, don't you think?" Clara asked.

"What?"

"He needn't have escorted Miss Smithee home. Meredith has been travelling all over London by herself since she was sixteen."

"I thought it was kind of him," said Lilah.

"Very chivalrous," added Aaron.

To which Clara gave them both a huff and flounced off to bed. Lilah and Aaron shared a moment of amusement—silently, of course—but that was all before Lilah turned toward the parlor. "I should clean up some before bed."

"No, you shouldn't," he said as he gathered her arm. "I now have a well-run household thanks to you. The servants will care for that in the morning."

She knew it was true, and besides, she enjoyed the touch of his hand on hers and the warmth of his gaze on her face.

"You didn't enjoy tonight, did you?" he asked.

"Not true. I did," but her tone indicated how diffident she felt about the whole thing. "They are all old friends. It was hard to find my footing with them." At least it had been hard until he showed up.

"You will. Or you will find your own friends. I think you were beautiful tonight. Everyone felt at ease around you. And you got Mr. Sesay to explain about his favorite magistrate."

The boorish barrister? "I simply let him talk and talk and talk." She frowned. "Why is that important?"

"Because Mr. Sesay is normally close-mouthed, but he felt comfortable with you. And so he talked to you."

She couldn't fathom it. "He talked ceaselessly."

"About unimportant things. But eventually, he opened up to you. He told you about the case he is working and why it might succeed with one magistrate and not another."

"And that's important?"

He shrugged. "It shows you have a talent for making people comfortable." He touched her face and stroked across her jaw. "And comfortable people confide things. It's a valuable talent."

Maybe to him. To her, it felt like she was the repository of their thoughts with no one listening to her own.

"How was your day before the party?"

"Very good, actually."

He leaned against the balustrade. "Really? Tell me."

She wanted to. She wanted to ease back into a chair and share her life and her thoughts with him over a good glass of wine. But more than that, she wanted to kiss him. She wanted to feel his hands on her body as he showed her how much he wanted her.

"I'd rather..." Her voice trailed away. She couldn't say aloud what she wanted. She couldn't put in words how desperately she wanted to kiss him.

He must have understood. They'd played this dance every night for the last two weeks. His hand rose to her cheek as he stroked his finger down along her jaw.

"Clara picked her favorite single gentlemen tonight expressly for the purpose of interesting you in one of them. Did none of them catch your fancy?"

"How could they with you here?"

"I stayed away, Lilah. As long as I could stomach it. I gave you time to find one and fall desperately in love."

She arched her brows. "In three hours?"

He shrugged. "I spent the whole time pacing my office, counting the seconds."

She chuckled at the image. "It will take much longer than that to forget you."

His expression sobered. "I want you to have everything you deserve, Lilah."

"What about everything I want?"

He dipped his chin. "That, too."

She smiled, finally feeling the rightness of this decision. "I want you, Aaron. In my bed, in my life. If only for tonight."

His hand stilled on her cheek. His breath suspended. "And what about a respectable marriage? A family?"

"I will leave those for another day."

"But—"

"If ever I find someone who I want more than you, then he shall have to take all of me. Including my past."

She could see the desire in his eyes. She felt the hunger in his body or perhaps that was the need pounding in her own. She drew her hand to his face, mirroring the way he held her. He pulled it to his lips and pressed kisses against her fingers.

"I am trying to honor you, Lilah. I am trying to think about the proper order of things—"

"For once, Aaron, trust me to think about my needs. Trust me to know that you are worth it." And with that she stretched up on her toes and pressed her mouth to his. She felt his iron control crumble with every second they touched. Soon his mouth opened, his body seemed to swell around her, and suddenly she was lifted into the air.

He carried her straight up the stairs to his bedroom. And finally, gloriously, she got exactly what she wanted.

CHAPTER TWENTY-THREE

AARON DIDN'T KNOW the exact moment when he decided to marry Lilah. The idea had been growing on him for a while now. Every night when he left her side to sleep alone in his club had him staring into the darkness thinking about his choices. Had he indeed closed off his heart out of fear? Had his daily struggle to *not* repeat his father's mistakes turned him hard and mean? He didn't think so. At least not yet because whenever he looked at Lilah, everything in him softened. It felt like his pulverized heart sought comfort in her, and the rest of him wanted to comfort her.

He was dazzled by her, and so for good or for ill, he would marry her. He'd been trying to determine the best way to ask for her hand when she turned it all around on him. It befuddled his mind, and so he lost the proper order of things and saw, as usual, only her and what she wanted. He swooped her up in his arms and carried her upstairs. She twined her arms around his neck and kissed him while he was maneuvering his way down the hall to his bed. He had French letters there. Whatever happened between them tonight, he would protect her from pregnancy. He could do that much at least. Until after the vows were spoken.

He'd barely made it through his bedroom door when she captured his face with her hands and drew him down for a kiss. She demanded in a way that made his blood surge. His arms tightened around her and if he could have made love to her while standing right there, he would have. But even he had limits. He stumbled forward, grateful when his legs knocked against the edge of the bed. He broke the kiss and was gratified to hear how she gulped in breaths. He, too, was struggling. The scent of her made his head spin and yet he pressed his nose against the curve of her neck and inhaled her deep into his lungs.

"I can think of nothing but you. Day and night, I dream of you."

She lifted her chin such that they were eye to eye. "Are you turning poetic, my lord?"

"No," he said with complete honestly. "I'm stating a fact. You've consumed me."

She smiled, her expression mischievous. "Not yet, I haven't." She abruptly nipped the edge of his jaw. He felt the scrape of her teeth against his evening beard, and the hunger inside him surged to a maddening degree.

It took all his concentration to lower her gently onto his bed while she nibbled across his chin until she could claim his mouth again. Then she was gloriously settled, and he could finally use his hands for more than supporting her weight. He let them trail over her body, spanning the narrowness of her waist, cupping the wonder of her breasts, and then—most specifically—to the buttons that held her gown together. She was equally enthusiastic with the buttons of his waistcoat.

Very soon their hands were tangled together as they tugged and pushed at each other's clothing. She began to giggle as she tried to push off his jacket and waistcoat at the same moment. It didn't work, especially as he was just then trying to release the ties of her stays without removing her dress first. His chuckle came next as he tried to fondle her breasts that were somehow smashed between the sides of her dress and the press of whalebone.

"Good God," he huffed. "I want to tear this thing off you—"

"But I haven't the strength," she finished for him.

He had the strength, but not the willingness to destroy something of hers. He rocked back on his heels, forcing himself to stop touching her long enough to strip out of his clothing. She did the same, sitting up as she pushed aside her gown and unbound the ties of her stays. Then while he was pulling off his linen shirt, she wriggled out of her dress while he watched her breasts sway beneath her shift.

"Stop," he rasped.

She looked up. "What?"

He helped her toss aside her dress, but then he touched her face. Her skin was flushed rosy and her lips were a moist temptation, but he held back from tasting them. Instead, he let his hands flow upward into her hair, pulling out the pins one by one until her hair tumbled down her shoulders and back.

He felt her sigh as a shudder of relief flowed through her body. He pressed his fingers to her temple and then along her scalp as she arched into his touch.

"That feels so good," she murmured.

She looked good as her head dropped back into his supporting hands and her neck stretched out in beautiful display. He'd always thought a woman's neck as sensuous. Smooth skin, delicate arch, and the way she moved it told him if she was stressed or anxious or relaxing into something more. And she was definitely relaxing into his embrace.

"Don't stop," she murmured.

"I wouldn't dream of it."

She opened her eyes in a slow flutter. "I have wanted you since I first saw you as Lord Ares, but I don't think I fell in love with you until we went to the Lyon's Den."

He smiled at her. "It was your first quickening, Lilah. Of course—"

"Not then. Before. You took me to the den despite hating everything about it."

He frowned. "You would have gone without me anyway. It was safer—"

"With you. Yes, I know. Everything is safer with you." She lifted her head from his hands and stretched up on her knees until they were face to face. "You've always protected me." She arched her brows. "You threatened Reuben Bates, didn't you? If he mistreated me."

He winced. "I don't threaten. I merely—"

"You made your opinion known. And the consequences if he goes against your choices."

He cupped her face. "I will not have you mistreated."

She smiled. "Even when I don't see it, even when I'm not thinking of it, you make sure I am safe."

He dropped his forehead to hers. Did she not understand? "I would be devastated if you were harmed. Protecting you keeps me sane."

"Appreciating you makes me happy." And with that, she kissed him again. Her hands roved down his neck and chest as she pressed apart the sides of his shirt. He felt her hands, glorious on his body, but more than that, he felt her appreciation in the way she explored his body. She let her hands glide over his chest. She murmured a deep, throaty sound. And she smiled at him in a way that made him stronger.

She loved him. He could see it in every gaze, every caress, and every kiss. And he stared down at her in wonder. She. Loved. Him. She had said it before, but this time he felt it. This time he *knew* it.

He felt his heart crack with the realization. He felt his soul split from the feeling. And as his heart opened and his soul expanded, he became overwhelmed with gratitude.

She loved him.

He was loved.

Even though he had offered her nothing. Even though he had left her for a year. Even though he had chosen his career over her and even now had promised her nothing. She still gave him love.

She loved him.

So he worshipped her.

She loved the way he caressed her head, so he delved into her hair and felt her tension ease. Then he stroked down her neck because he couldn't resist touching something so gorgeous even as he stroked lower. He pushed her shift down her shoulders, then grinned as she abruptly stripped it away. Such beautiful breasts. He touched them because he couldn't stop himself. He continued to knead and stroke them because she gasped and sighed as he played. She threw back her head as he pinched her nipples, and she reached for him. He let her explore his chest as she willed, but he delighted more in teasing her nipples with his tongue. Sucking her into his mouth to hear her gasp. Scraping his teeth along her nub to hear her cry out. And then letting his free hand flow down her quivering belly until he pressed into her wet, intimate folds.

She whimpered then, a sort of stuttered cry that was both need and confusion. He looked up from her breasts to scan her face. He felt her legs spread to give him better access even as she gazed at him.

"I want more than pleasure," she said. "I want you."

He didn't understand her words, but he understood her body. Her legs were drawn wide as his fingers opened her further. He plunged one into her depths and rolled another over her clitoris. She writhed beneath him, arching and gasping. He watched as her neck stretched, her mouth widened, and her eyes took on the dazed look of rapture. Almost there… Almost…

"No!" she abruptly pulled away from him. Her breath was heaving as she scrambled backwards.

He froze, uncertain what he'd done.

Then she pointed a finger at him even as she struggled for breath. "Together, Aaron. Or not at all." Then she slammed her mouth against his. She tugged at his shoulders and tried to pull him fully onto the bed with her.

He held her back as he held himself back. "I'm a big man, Lilah."

"I'm a strong woman, Aaron."

She was. He knew it. And he wanted her so badly.

He watched her expression shift from need to confusion.

"Why don't you want me?" she whispered.

"I do," he rasped. "It's all I can do to stop."

She shook her head. "Any other man would have taken me a hundred times by now."

"I don't judge myself by other men," he said.

Her expression shifted as she studied him, clearly trying to understand something he didn't know either. Why was he holding himself back? Why couldn't he just take her as any man might when offered something so glorious? Why did he stand there, his cock pounding with hunger, when she lay before him so open to him?

She slowly leaned forward. Her glorious breasts bobbed before him, but his attention was on her hands as she gently tugged at the button on his falls. His buttocks tightened as bursts of sensations flooded his body. As she released his clothing, she pressed and bumped his organ. And when he thrust outward, she caught him and held him such that he pushed into her palms.

Need thrummed in his ears and he shuddered from her too tender grip. He wanted a tight hold, a wet channel, and her, her, her.

"Do you think I'll demand too much of you?"

She demanded too little of her life. She accepted rebukes and condemnation as if they were her due. They weren't. If ever a woman could forge her own destiny, it was her. By simply continuing to do exactly as she intended.

"I think you value yourself too little," he said as she tugged the last of his clothing down. He kicked it away out of habit, and soon he was naked before her. Naked in body and soul as she continued to press him with questions.

"Do you think you will hurt me?"

How could he not? He was a big man, she was small. He was an earl, she was a bastard. He had money, power, and respect. She had no home of her own, a job she was just learning, and no clear future beyond struggle. The differences between them were staggering. It would be all too easy to abuse her love, to take her for granted, to *take* when all he wanted was to *give*.

She tugged him close, and he couldn't refuse her. She pressed her mouth to his and he plundered her, thrusting his tongue deep inside. He climbed onto the bed because she pulled him. He pressed kisses into her mouth, her cheeks, her neck, because she wanted him to. At her urging, he climbed atop her.

"You're everything I've always wanted," he said. The words came out as a groan as she rubbed herself along his cock.

They could do this again, he thought. He could rub himself along her folds. They could fly together, and he would not take her virginity. He would save that for their wedding night. He began to thrust, feeling the wet slide of her body against his. Sensation shot up his spine. Heat and wet and *her*.

He fondled her breast and she cried out in pleasure. And when need clawed at him, he dropped his hand to the mattress and looked at her. So beautiful. So happy. She met his gaze as their bodies rolled together.

And then she caught his hips, her grip tight. Her feet were pressed into his calves, holding him in place. He didn't mind. He was strong and she was so sleight as she arched, and her weight came down on his legs.

"I love you," she said. "I want this."

Then she shifted her hips, she adjusted their bodies and she held him where she wanted to. Their rhythm had been steady, but this was a change. He could have stopped. He could have poised at her entrance, but in a flash of awareness, he finally comprehended the truth. Suddenly, he knew why he had held himself back from her.

If he did this, he was the one who would fall. Even now he'd been holding a little part of him back. Even though he planned to marry her, he held a piece of his heart back out of fear that it would all go bad as it had for his father.

The choice was so clear.

If he gave her his seed, he would give her all of himself. He would never give her up. No matter what the future held, she would always own a part of him. And he would never release her from his body, his heart, or his soul.

She would be his.

He would be hers.

He thrust.

She cried out in surprise, and he stilled. He was a big man. She'd been ready, but maybe not so ready.

"Lilah?" he rasped.

"It's… You're…" She swallowed then slowly she nodded, but he didn't know what that meant.

"Too much?"

She moved her bottom a little. Just enough to make his eyes roll in pleasure. Then she did it again, and he groaned. It was impossible to stay still while she did that, and yet he did. He would not… Unless she said…

"Lilah," he gasped.

"Yes," she said. Then she squeezed him.

A bolt of sensation shot through his spine, and he met her gaze and held it. "Yes," he said as he pushed all the way inside.

She cried out. She gripped his hips with her thighs and held herself completely impaled. "Do that again," she said.

He grinned as he slowly eased his way out.

"Yes," he said as he thrust.

"Yes!" she said, but this time there was laughter in the sound.

He echoed it. How could he not? This was the most joyous thing he had done in his entire life.

"Yes!" he said with her as he thrust again.

"Yes," she laughed as her body met him, matched him, and demanded more.

And more.

"*Yes!*" the cried together as they soared.

And then he fell.

CHAPTER TWENTY-FOUR

HOW WAS IT possible to be so blissfully happy and yet so furious with herself at the same time? Lilah had loved every intimate, glorious moment of her night with Aaron. She had felt such things that she'd never imagined before. Once he'd taken her, there had been no stopping them both from exploring one another so intimately. And then, she'd fallen asleep in his arms.

Nothing had ever felt so good, and she didn't regret it for a moment.

And yet she did regret one thing. They hadn't done a thing to prevent a baby. How could she be so stupid? How could she have risked dooming a child to the same half existence she lived? And yet the idea of bearing Aaron's child filled her with joy. She wanted that babe. She wanted it all and more. And yet she was furious with herself for forgetting it.

She knew better.

So, apparently did Aaron, because the knowledge had come to him during his morning ablutions. He'd been grinning as he rose from the bed, but then he returned a second later with his eyes wide and his hands shaking.

"I forgot," he said. "How could I forget?"

And when she understood what he meant, she stared at her own hands and cursed her idiocy. "How could *we* forget?" she corrected because she was as much to blame as he.

"You needn't worry," he said, but she held out her hand to stop him from speaking.

"I know," she said firmly. Because she was the daughter of an actress. Some things, she knew how to do. Or at least, she knew who to ask. "I'll handle it," she said.

"Wait!" he cried as she hastily pulled on her clothes.

She paused to look at him only to straighten to her full height when he looked chagrined. "Aaron? I promise you, I can—"

"No, no," he grumbled as he ran a hand down his face. "This isn't how I wanted to do this."

"What?" She finished buttoning up her gown and began searching for her shoes.

He grabbed her hands and pulled them up to his mouth. "You don't need to prevent a baby." He said as he pressed a kiss onto her wrist.

"I won't repeat my mother's mistake," she said.

"Yes…I mean no." He huffed out a breath. "I'm doing this all wrong."

She chuckled at how adorably flummoxed he looked. Aaron was definitely not at his best without his morning tea. "I need to get going if I'm to stop by—"

"I want to marry you, Lilah. I…Please, say you will make me the happiest of men and be my bride."

She gaped at him, her mind unable to comprehend his words. He couldn't possibly be proposing to her now. Now! When she was barely dressed and worried about being late for work. And then to her total shock, the man dropped to one knee before her. He pressed his lips to her knuckles as he studied her face with an unsettling intensity.

"Say yes," he urged. "Say yes and then you don't need to… to…"

"Are you offering because there might be a baby?"

"What? No. I mean, yes because you needn't rush away, but I planned to do this."

"When?"

"What?"

"When did you start planning to propose to me?" And why was she arguing with him? He had finally, gloriously offered her exactly what she wanted. Marriage! And yet she could not stop the questions. "When did you decide, Aaron? Was it last night when we… Is it your honor that is forcing you to propose? Because you bedded me?"

"No." He pulled back from her without rising from his knee. "I've been thinking of it for a while, but last night decided it."

"When we made love?"

"Before that."

"When you saw me with other men?"

He opened his mouth to speak but then snapped it shut with a frown. Then he cleared his throat like he was beginning a speech. "Lilah, those details don't matter. You've said you love me. I'm offering to marry you. Now you say, yes."

She bit her lip. She wanted to say yes. She wanted to throw her arms around him and give him exactly the answer he demanded. It was what she wanted! And yet, the words would not come. Instead of gleefully accepting him, she took an incomprehensible step back.

"Lilah?"

"Do you know that Mrs. Dove-Lyon has had several offers of marriage? She's refused them all."

Aaron blinked in confusion as she pulled her hands out of his.

"What use to me is a man? That's what she says. She makes her own money, she makes her own decisions, she runs a business—all without a husband."

Aaron's hand dropped down to his side. "What does Mrs. Dove-Lyon have to do with anything?"

She wasn't exactly sure. Not in a way that she could express right now. But it was important. Just as the way he had proposed to her was important. He hadn't said he loved her, and he'd ordered her to accept.

"I gave up the *ton*. I'm a shopkeeper now."

"But you don't have to be. You can be a countess. You can be *my* countess!"

He was getting angry. She knew so much of his body now and he had not even pulled on a shirt. He knelt before her wearing only his falls, and she still could not believe she stood apart from him. He was everything she'd ever wanted. She loved him. And yet, she could not say yes.

"What of your career?" she asked. "What of the damage to you for marrying beneath you?"

He winced, but he did not look away. "We can marry quietly. You need not be in the public eye. Certainly, I will not have the benefit of a political wife, but I have managed so far without that. I'll find a way to continue."

"You'll stash me away in the country, perhaps, like your father did with your mother?"

He nodded. "Yes, that will work. So long as I don't turn to bitterness and you don't get angry at me, we shall rub along well, don't you think? You're not like my mother, and I'm not my father. We won't turn out like them."

That will work? Good God, had he really just said that? "What of my registry office?"

He winced, his expression unhappy. "I know that's important to you. I know how hard you work there, and of course you can continue for a while." He pushed up to his feet, his brow tight as he continued to think out loud. "Yes, I can see allowing you to continue for a while, but you'll have to give it up eventually." He cast a besotted smile at her belly. "Once the babies begin, you'll need to care for them. You'll have help, of course, but you'll be a countess. You can't run a registry office and be a countess at the same time. And even if it were possible, what would we tell the children? That their mother was *working*?" He chuckled at the very idea. "No," she echoed softly. "I can't be both, can I?"

He smiled as he stepped forward, reaching again for her hands. "So it's decided? I'll have to travel home to get the ring from Mother." He rolled his eyes. "She'll be furious, of course, but I don't care. I'm a man who can choose his own bride."

She searched his face wondering what she was looking for. "You can't even admit that you love me."

His eyes widened before he exhaled in relief. "Is that what this is all about?" He smiled at her. "I love you, Lilah. I will marry you."

"No," she said. "No, you will not."

Her words landed like stones dropped between. He had been leaning in for a kiss, but at her words, he froze. And she took that second to slip away from him.

"I won't do it, Aaron. I've given up the *ton* and everything that goes with them."

"What?"

"I won't be hidden away with a mother-in-law who hates me."

He snorted. "We'll set her up in the dower property. She doesn't have to live with you."

"I'm going to live in London!" she snapped. "I'm going to run my registry office!"

He pulled up to his full height, his expression turning fierce. "I will marry you!" he said, as if that were the answer to everything.

"You will not!" she shot back. "I will not."

"But what about…" His gaze hopped back to the bed and he gestured at it with distinct motions. "We did…everything! You might right now be carrying my child!"

"Not for long," she said. Then she closed her eyes against the ripping pain that tore through her heart at those words. He, too, looked equally horrified, and she almost relented. She almost changed her mind and threw herself back into his arms. He was everything she wanted, and yet she'd refused him.

No, she realized with a horrified shock. He was everything she *had wanted*. And now she wanted something else.

"I will not hide away," she said. "I have found a purpose to my life, work that I enjoy, and respect for myself outside of the aristocracy."

He gaped at her. "I respect you."

"No," she said softly. "You love me. That is not the same thing as respect. And I suddenly find that I want both from my husband."

He stared at her, his mouth working but without sound. He clearly didn't understand her, and part of her was equally confused. She had spent the last year longing for this moment, and now that it was here, she discovered that she wanted something entirely different.

"I am sorry, Aaron. I should have realized earlier that I've changed."

Then she turned around and walked away.

"Lilah!" he cried.

She stopped long enough to grab her boots, then she bolted from the room.

CHAPTER TWENTY-FIVE

A N HOUR LATER Lilah knocked at the door of her mother's
theater. It was late enough for the performers to be awake,
but not so late that there would be no time to talk to Margarite.

Her old friend greeted her with warmth. The situation was
explained and just as quickly handled. As was the lecture on ways
to prevent pregnancy. It took a half hour at most. And when
Margarite was done, she patted Lilah's hands.

"Was it good?" she asked.

"It was wonderful," Lilah answered, though her heart broke
on the words. Her voice too because Margarite's expression
softened.

"You love him?"

"Yes."

"And he's a nob." It wasn't a question.

"Yes." It cut her to say it, and tears leaked from her eyes, but
she didn't sob. She was done with that. But she couldn't stop her
mind from spinning into useless questions. Why couldn't she
have fallen in love with a man who could claim her? Legally,
socially, and with no repercussions to his career? Meanwhile,
Margarite wrapped her in a full hug as if they were nine-year-old
girls again.

"So you've returned to us," she said.

"What?" Lilah asked when they separated.

"I don't blame you fer trying to become a nob. You got blood of yer father, and why not make the best of it?"

Lilah's gaze dropped to the floor. "I did."

"You did, but now you've remembered your mother."

"I never forgot her."

Margarite leaned forward. "You mean you never forgave her. You think I don't remember what you said when we were kids? How you wanted a real father, a real family. And you cozied up to your father and begged him to take you in."

"I didn't make him!" Lilah cried. "I wanted him to love me."

"And he did love you. And you got him and his family, right and tight." Margarite's expression sobered. "An' once you left, you never looked back. Not until today."

"My family loves me. Even Lady Byrn in her own way. They love me!"

"Of course, they do, but your mom loved you too. And we loved you here. And I loved you—"

"I wasn't allowed back here. You know that. Lady Byrn said I'd never get married if I associated with—" She cut off her words. She didn't mean to insult Margarite for her lifestyle. Her friend had had little choice in her upbringing or how her future played out.

"With the likes of me," Margarite finished for her. "But you didn't get married anyway, did you?"

Lilah looked down at her hands. "No, I didn't." She didn't explain that Aaron had asked her. How could she tell Margarite that she'd been offered everything a woman was supposed to want—marriage to a peer—and yet turned it down? But Margarite seemed to understand her unspoken thoughts.

"And now you see that you've a place in this world and it ain't such a bad one. Just like your mum. And you've got a trade you like, right?"

She did. She'd barely started to do what she wanted with the registry office, but it was still rewarding work that she enjoyed. "Yes," she said softly.

"An' now you have a man that you love, an' no harm done."

Did a broken heart count as harm? "What if I'm pregnant?" she whispered, her thoughts and her emotions spinning at the thought.

"Your mum didn't mean for you to happen either. These things don't always work." She gestured to the various methods they used to prevent babies. "But it came from love. Surely you remember that. If I can remember, you can too, yes?"

Yes, she remembered. Her mother and Lord Byrn had loved one another. And they'd created her out of that love. She knew it because her father had said so several times. Her mother too before she'd died.

"And now that you see how it happens, you can forgive her? Yes?" Margarite was pressing Lilah's hands as she spoke. There was something more to her words than asking for understanding about Lilah's mother.

"What are you trying to say?"

Margarite bit her lip and looked ashamed. But even as her cheeks turned ruddy and her gaze would not steady, her hands remained strong where she gripped Lilah's. "You understand about your mum now. About how she loved where she loved, and you're doing the same with your gent. You love where you love."

She did see that now. And with that realization came an easing. She hadn't even realized that she'd been angry with her own mother for birthing her. But how could she hate her mother when she might have made the same mistake? "I don't blame her for making me," she said softly. "I came from love." How freeing those words were.

"Then you understand about me," Margarite said.

"You?"

Her friend tsked and tilted her head. She was jerking it toward the dresser where her cosmetics sat. Her cosmetics and several knives. Lilah's gaze traveled the room then and picked up details she hadn't noticed before. She saw Margarite's costumes intermixed with a man's clothing. Her slippers with a man's boots. And not just any man.

"You're with Jamis?"

Margarite shrugged and released a nervous giggle. "He's not like we thought as kids. He can get mad sometimes, but he's never hurt me. And he's got a way of saying things that only I understand."

"You love Jamis." It was a statement, but Margarite acknowledged it with a grin. "Does he love you?"

"He says so. An' he treats me well."

Lilah leaned forward to search her friend's face. "Are you happy?"

She nodded, but there was a nervousness in her expression. "We're going to get married, Lilah. We're going to marry, and I'm going to help him run the troupe."

"You do that already."

"I know, but now it'll be official. I'll be his wife." She blushed such a pretty rose as she spoke, and Lilah could tell she was happy.

"That's wonderful, Margarite. That's better than wonderful. It's fan—"

"Would you come?"

"What?" Margarite's words had come out so rushed that Lilah wasn't sure she'd heard them properly.

Margarite took a deep breath and spoke again. "I want you to come. More, I want you stand with me. You're the closest thing I have to a sister, and you're the highest nob we know that would stand with me."

"You're asking me to be your bridesmaid?"

"I am. I want you there, but you've always been so proper. Even as kids, you knew which was the right fork and the like when I didn't even know there were different forks."

Her mother had made sure she knew these things. It made life easier when her father had visited. He liked his daughter to know how to act properly.

"I didn't know if you'd want to be seen with me," Margarite

continued. "It won't help you get your gent to the altar."

"I'm not worried about that." And how the words freed her even more. She'd spent so much time trying to cozy up to the *ton* that it was like finally catching her breath to say, no more. She would not cater to their whims ever again.

"I'd love to stand with you," she said.

"And you'll help me do it proper?" Margarite pressed.

"If you'll let me."

"Thank you!" Margarite threw her arms around Lilah, and they laughed in true delight. Then they spent a wonderful hour talking about weddings and lovemaking. Eventually, however, Lilah had to return to the registry and Margarite had to get ready for her performance. She wasn't just a rope dancer. She performed in smaller parts in the theater as did most of the troupe.

Lilah had taken one step out of the door when Margarite abruptly grabbed her hand. "I forgot to tell you!" she cried.

"What?"

"A Scottish gent came by asking about the letters."

"What letters?"

"The ones Jamis tore up. The ones to your mother."

"Whatever for?" And what Scottish gent? The only one she could think of was Lord Loughton.

"He had some idea who might be writing. I made sure Jamis said what he knew. He's not so mad at you now."

"Because I hired him to do the séance?"

Margarite nodded. "And because I told him to stop being an arse, and he listened."

Lilah laughed and kissed Margarite's cheek. "Thank you for helping."

"I don't know what good it will come to, but at least Jamis is helping now."

Lilah smiled. "You're going to be the most beautiful bride ever. And Jamis is very lucky to have you."

"An' I make sure he knows it!" Margarite answered with a laugh.

Lilah walked away smiling, her heart healing. How her life had changed in just a few weeks. She was running a registry office, she'd loved and lost the man of her dreams, and she was now planning Margarite's wedding. She didn't feel happy, exactly. But the sorrow was easier to bear. Until Clara burst into her office wringing her hands in distress.

"Whatever is the matter?" Lilah asked as she rose from her desk.

"It's all a mess," Clara declared. "What do I know about planning a ball? I've messed up the invitations, the food, and the musicians. Aaron will be so angry. And Liam has gone back to Scotland!"

That last was said on a wail. Which meant, of course, that in addition to running a registry office, getting over losing the man she loved, and planning Margarite's wedding, she was now also organizing the pomp and circumstance surrounding Aaron's full ascension to the earldom.

CHAPTER TWENTY-SIX

LILAH WASN'T PREGNANT. That shouldn't be Aaron's first thought as he greeted his mother on his front doorstep, but it was the pre-eminent one and there was nothing he could do to change the course of his thoughts. Lilah wasn't pregnant according to the missive she'd left on his desk.

"Good afternoon, Mother. You are looking well." He extended a kiss to the air above her cheek. His mother did not approve of her children smudging her cosmetics.

"I'm looking horribly done in. Really, Aaron, you're an earl now. You need to think of appearances, and your mother cannot be harrying about England in a ramshackle carriage."

The ramshackle carriage was barely a year old. It was huge, ornate, and it made him cringe every time he saw it. "I did offer to send my carriage."

"Your ugly thing? All black with a tiny crest. Really Aaron, you're going to ascend to the title tomorrow. I do hope you've paid attention to these details. Otherwise, everyone will think you're impoverished."

"I have left the details to Clara. I'm sure everything will be exactly as it ought."

His mother froze halfway up the house steps. She squeezed his arm as if in terror, then she squeaked his sister's name. "Clara? Clara!"

"Yes, Mother. She's—"

"But she'll make a disaster of everything!"

A month ago, he would have thought the same thing. Indeed, he did think exactly that. But thanks to Lilah's help, everything would be perfectly fine. "I've kept an eye on the planning," he said. It was the only way he could get any news about Lilah. "I am content with the results."

"Good God, men are such fools," his mother huffed. Then she rushed up the front steps with amazing verve. "Where is she? Clara! Clara, come here this instant and tell me everything. Don't leave out any detail. There may still be time to avoid complete disaster!"

Aaron winced, regretting the fact that he'd cleared his schedule for his mother's visit. Now he would have to stand with Clara while his mother chastised them both for nonsensical reasons and then tried to change every detail of his celebration. It was exhausting, but it was what a good man did. And it was the perfect cap on a day when he'd learned that Lilah wasn't pregnant.

"And why doesn't your butler have an arm? Everything about an earl must be perfect! Imagine opening the door and seeing that every day? Horrible!"

Three hours later, Aaron had a revelation. He wasn't sure if it was due to the brandy he'd drunk, his morose obsession with Lilah's empty womb, or the fact that his mother never, ever ceased criticizing everything around her. How had he lived the last year with her? How had he survived his entire childhood? Certainly, he'd known she was shrewish. Anyone could see that. But somehow it wasn't until right then that he finally saw the extent of her constant nitpicking. She even complained that the air in his home smelled like London. That's because the house was in London!

And that was nothing compared to what she said of Lilah. His mother hadn't even met the woman, but she made her opinion clear every five minutes.

"Really, Clara, I thought I taught you better than to rely on the advice of a by-blow. They have the worst taste, you know."

"Whatever gave you the idea that simple is elegant? Simple is for peasants like that by-blow."

"Did that by-blow tell you to wear that gown? And style your hair that way? Really, Clara, don't you have an ounce of sense of your own?"

Aaron grew exhausted correcting his mother. He must have said, "Her name is Miss Rees, and she has excellent taste," a hundred times. He also complimented Clara on her dress, her hairstyle, and the lack of cosmetics on her cheeks. Unfortunately, it only made his mother more irritable as she exclaimed that he never had the refined taste of an earl.

Normally he simply tuned out her comments, but he couldn't this time. This afternoon he was excruciatingly aware of how insidious his mother's attitude was. Especially when he learned that Lilah was spending the night at the home of one of Clara's friends rather than risk running afoul of his mother. That had been Clara's foresight. He had been hoping to catch a glimpse of her.

Which was the exact moment he had his revelation.

His mother was an impossible shrew. That much he already knew. What he hadn't realized until now was how much the rest of society was exactly like her. The political wives who advanced so many of his colleague's careers? Exactly like his mother. As judgmental, as impossible to please, and the kind of woman he despised. The ladies of the *ton* who sought to marry him? Cut from the same cloth. More than one debutante had taken pains to whisper damaging gossip about their competitors into his ear.

It infuriated him. Not just that such petty, ridiculous non-sense dominated the discourse among the *ton*, but that he had spent a great deal of his time playing into it. He had assumed—because his mother and everyone else said so—that an earl must set an example. He must marry the right woman, present himself in the right way, act as was appropriate to his station. And he had allowed them—most especially his mother—to color his thoughts on who was appropriate, what was respectable, and how he and everyone else ought to act.

What a fool he'd been! And he never would have seen it if he hadn't fallen in love with Lilah. Because she was *everything* he wanted and yet part of him had fought it—fought her—because she was so very different than anything he'd been taught to value. He'd even suggested that she couldn't do the work she loved because it would not fit the standard image of a countess.

No wonder she refused him!

So when his mother said for the hundredth time that evening, "Aaron, you're an earl now. You must lead by example," he had a new response.

"You're exactly right, Mother." He turned to his sister. "Clara, don't change a thing. I love every one of your choices for my celebration. And Mother, if you say one thing against her or my intended bride, I shall send you home to the dower house and never acknowledge you again."

Both women started, but it was his mother who responded first. "Your bride! What bride? Who is this—"

He held up his hand to silence her. Unfortunately, Clara was not so restrained. Her eyes sparkled with excitement.

"Is it who I think, Aaron? Is it really?"

He smiled at his sister. "If she'll have me." Which wasn't at all assured. "Not a word now. Either of you. I have to make plans."

"But who is this—"

"Mother, I suggest you find a way to curb your tongue or you will not have a fruitful relationship with me. And you'll never be allowed to see any of your grandchildren." The last thing he wanted was to allow her poison to damage another generation.

"What?" his mother screeched, but Clara stepped bodily in front of her.

"Never mind her. Go!" She pushed him toward the door. "Go make your plans. I'll keep Mama out of the way."

He didn't want to abandon her, but he could see she was adamant. And excited for him. If only he could be so assured.

Whatever he did now would have to be very public as he laid his heart out for all to see. And if Lilah refused him—again—the humiliation would dog him forever. For the rest of his life, every person would be treated to the tale. "That's the Earl of Kittrel," they'd say, "the man who once proposed to a by-blow in front of the whole *ton* and was refused. Can you believe it?"

But if that was what it took to win Lilah, then he would do it.

CHAPTER TWENTY-SEVEN

S HE WASN'T PREGNANT.

Ridiculous for that to be Lilah's chief concern on Aaron's big day. Today he was accepted into the House of Lords with all the honors of the title. He was feted by no less than the Prince Regent, and tonight he hosted a ball for all the elite in London. As this was also the end of this year's Season, all the ladies who had yet to capture a husband had turned out in force, making it the event of the year. Similarly, all the exquisite gentlemen were trying for one last night's lavish entertainment. Everyone who was anyone in the *ton* was here to add to the crush.

Thank God Lilah had learned from Lady Byrn how to throw a proper ball. Otherwise, she would never have managed it. Even better, Margarite and Jamis had been married four days ago on a glorious morning. Also, after careful direction from Lilah, Clara had risen to the challenge of the ball despite Lord Loughton's disappearance.

Best of all, her work had kept her so busy that she didn't have time to pine for Aaron. She had too much to do to miss his arms around her. Too many things on her plate to listen for his laughter or wonder about his day. And certainly too many tasks to double-think her decision to remain unwed.

She had made the right decision, but oh, late at night, she wished things had been different.

And in all that busy, wonderful work of life, what was she

doing as she stood surveying Aaron's ball? She mourned the fact of her barren state. How stupid of her! She didn't want an illegitimate child, and yet such were her thoughts as the crush of people began to file in. Because even if she couldn't have Aaron, she would have cherished his child beyond anything.

Naturally, she was not in the receiving line. That was reserved for Aaron and Clara. They both looked wonderful, of course, but Lilah had a special misty kind of reaction whenever she looked at him. She'd adored his raw power as Lord Ares, but tonight he was dressed in elegance. Black formal attire, crisp white linen, plus the broad swath of fabric across his chest that sported the seal of his earldom. It was all so impressive, and she couldn't help gazing at him with pride.

She was returning after settling a problem in the kitchen when Lord and Lady Byrn were announced. Elliott and Amber stood resplendent at the top of the stairs. She hadn't realized that her adoptive brother and his wife had returned to London after the birth of their first child, but here they were and looking for her, apparently. As soon as they passed through the receiving line, they headed straight for her with concern in their eyes.

She greeted them warmly, of course. And they in turn, pressed kisses to her cheeks while Amber squeezed her hands tightly.

"Did you think we would turn you away?" Amber said.

"We had no idea that Mama would cast you out," Elliot said. "I am furious with her, I can tell you that. And so I've told her."

"It took us forever to find out you were here. She didn't know where you'd gone."

"I insist you stay with us now that we've returned—"

"Diana is in confinement, you know," Amber continued. "The baby is due in a few months, but she wrote that she'd love to have you by her side. You mustn't think we'd ever abandon you."

Elliott nodded. "Even Gwen wrote, absolutely appalled with Mama. She and Sayres were due in this afternoon." He frowned as he looked about the room. "You've used their Lincolnshire daffodils, I see. That was kind of you."

"They'd take you in as well, of course," Amber said, "but you must stay with us. Say you will, please."

Lilah waited a moment to be sure they were done speaking. Neither of them were prone to talking over people, so the flurry of words was an indication of their distress. Lilah's heart warmed as much from that as from their earnest expressions. They truly did want her to live with them, and she was supremely grateful.

"You're so kind," she began, and her brother cut her off with a quick slash of his hand.

"Kind? Damnation, Lilah, you're my sister!" There was true pain in his eyes, and Lilah regretted that she hadn't called on her siblings for support. "I can't believe Mama would do that to you. Whyever didn't you write to me? I didn't hear of this until Amber learned from her father about that business at the Lyon's Den."

Amber's father ran the jewelry store beneath the Lyon's Den. She'd forgotten that he would be well aware of whatever happened in the gaming hell. And naturally he would share the news with his daughter.

"I am fine," she said. "Clara and I get along wonderfully, and she needed help with this ball."

"But we're your family," Amber said. "We'd never abandon you."

Lilah looked down at her hands where they were clasped one by Amber, the other by Elliott. So many feelings rushed over her, but most of it was relief. They hadn't abandoned her. They called her family. She was loved, and she had resources even if she'd gone to Clara first and not them.

"I am so grateful," she said, tears blurring her vision. "I hadn't wanted to burden you. Not so soon after your confinement." She released a soft laugh. "I cannot believe you're even here."

"We are. We came for you," Amber said.

"We can't stay long tonight. The baby gets fussy whenever Amber isn't around," Elliott said. "But I should like you to come 'round first thing tomorrow. I can send a carriage, and we'll discuss what's to be done." He sent a scowling look at Aaron. "I'm grateful that you found a place to stay, but it doesn't look good living here."

By which he meant that even with Aaron sleeping at his club, people would wonder if Lilah was Aaron's mistress. Which she had been—at least for one night—so she couldn't fault anyone for that assumption.

"I'll be working tomorrow," she said firmly. "But I would love to come by tomorrow night. I want to hold my nephew."

"So it's true," Elliott said, resignation in his tone.

"There's nothing wrong with a woman doing respectable work," Amber said in an undertone to her husband. "You let me work, too."

Lilah lifted her chin. "It is respectable, and I enjoy it. A very great deal, so if you mean to dissuade me from my job, we will have a difficult discussion indeed."

"You create art," Elliott said to his wife, but then he lifted a hand in surrender. "I want to see you happy, Lilah, no matter what you want to do. We can talk about it tomorrow."

Lilah smiled and pressed a fond kiss to her brother's cheek. He returned the embrace with his customary strength, but then he stiffened. And when Lilah pulled back, she saw why.

"Mother," he said coldly.

And sure enough, the dowager countess Byrn had joined their little group. Lilah hadn't even heard her announced, but here she was standing to the side. She had a death grip on her reticule and her gaze shifted nervously between them.

Ever kind, Amber greeted her mother-in-law, but didn't say much beyond hello. Which left Lilah to face her adoptive mother with uncertain emotions. On the one hand, the hurt from the woman's ultimatum still reverberated with pain. She'd thought she'd gotten past it but seeing the woman again brought all the fury back. On the other hand, she was mature enough to realize that if the lady hadn't tossed her out, then she would never have found her future. In a backwards way, she was grateful for what had happened.

Which left her tongue-tied. What could she say to the woman who had been her mother and yet had shut her out when she'd become disobedient? Nothing, apparently, because the lady herself spoke first.

"I was wrong and I'm sorry. Please come home."

Lilah stared at her adoptive mother, startled to hear her speak her apology so baldly. The lady never apologized like that. And while she was still reeling from that, Mama continued.

"I didn't think you'd really leave, and now you're *working!*" Her tone was so horrified, she might have said Lilah had become a bootblack or worse. "Your father would be ashamed of me, and I can't bear it."

"Ashamed because I'm working?"

"It's not the future he envisioned for you. We recognized you! He wanted—"

Lilah cut her off. "Father is gone. Whatever he wanted for me is gone."

"It's not just him. I tried to get you married. I tried—"

"I know." Because they'd both tried, but it wasn't to be. For all her faults, the woman had truly worked hard to see that Lilah got the future she wanted. Not the one Lilah wanted, but the one the dowager countess thought would be best for her. It was done from love, even if it was limited and short-sighted. "I know you tried," she said.

Tears slipped from the countess' eyes, and she surreptitiously dabbed them away. She was not a woman who cried in public and certainly not at an earl's ball. And yet here she was showing an excess of emotion. "I'm sorry I failed," she whispered. "I tried so hard to see you set up." She took a shuddering breath. "Please come back. I'll give you whatever allowance you want. We'll find a way to get you married. We'll—"

Lilah abruptly stepped forward and hugged her. The gesture was impulsive, but it was also heartfelt. They'd both tried to make it work, but it wasn't to be. And she found it easy now to forgive the woman's imperious ways. It was, after all, how the countess was made, and anger served no one. "Thank you, Mother," she said in the woman's ear. "Thank you for trying."

Her embrace was returned and then the woman pulled back with a shuddering breath. "So you'll come home?"

"No. But I would happily come visit, if that is acceptable."

"Visit? Of course, you can visit. But you can't mean to stay here. It doesn't look right. And there's no reason to… to…"

"Work?"

The lady nodded. "You don't need to."

"But I do. I want to, and I'm happy." That wasn't the exact truth, but the more she said it aloud, the more the Aaron-sized hole in her heart might heal.

"But you can't be!"

And here the woman's limitations showed. She could not understand that Lilah enjoyed helping others to learn their jobs, find good employment, and succeed in whatever life's work they chose. The countess didn't understand it.

"I have to check on the musicians," Lilah said. Aaron would be opening the ball soon. She had to see that everything was set to rights.

"No," the lady pressed. "Elliott tell her—"

"I think Lilah's made up her mind, Mama. As her family, we should support her choices."

"But she wants to *work*! Her father said she didn't need to. That she could marry respectably."

Her father was long gone as were the limits of her old life. So with a nod to all three of them, Lilah left to the life she wanted. And right now, that meant she had to make sure the musicians were in their place to begin the ball. It was a bit of a walk as they were on the upper floor, but she moved quickly through the growing throng. At first her thoughts were simply on performing her task, but as she maneuvered, she found her heart growing lighter and lighter.

Her family loved her. Even her adoptive mother loved her, and that was a wonderful feeling. They had their own ideas, of course, of how she should live her life. Didn't everyone? But now that Lilah had finally chosen her future, happiness had grown inside her. She wasn't letting anyone tell her how she should spend her days or nights, and that was liberating and delightful.

Silly of her to allow her thoughts to distract her, but they did. Which allowed a dark figure to step out in front of her to block her way. She recoiled in surprise, and he caught her elbow to steady her. They were beside the open doors to the garden and Mr. Reuben Bates looked very dapper as the breeze ruffled his curly locks.

"Miss Rees. I was looking for you."

"Mr. Bates! How nice to see you. Are you having a good time?"

"I am, I am," he said warmly. "Clever to bring entertainers to the garden. Keeps us all busy before the dancing begins." He gestured outside to where several of the acting troupe were performing. Margarite and Jamis were taking a holiday to celebrate their wedding, but several of the other performers were here doing acrobatics.

"They needed the work, and I was happy to use them. They're very good."

"Yes, they are," he said, his gaze never leaving her face. "You're proving to be an industrious woman, Miss Rees. The registry office is doing very well—"

"I've only begun the changes I want to make there."

He grinned. "Of course. And you've planned this ball and your friend's wedding."

"I had plenty of help, I assure you." Clara had done a great deal of the work once Lilah had shown her how. She'd even helped with Margarite's wedding. "I need to get upstairs to the musicians, Mr. Bates. Is there something you needed from me?"

He shook his head. "Nothing immediately, but I can see a bright future for you in my organization." He leaned forward. "If you were interested in more pay."

Her brows rose. She'd been running the numbers for a while now, trying to figure out how to live independently on her pay. Even if she shared a flat with Clara, her options did not look good. But she also wasn't sure she wanted to do more for Mr. Bates. He'd been unfailingly polite with her, but she'd heard a few rumors. He was powerful in the London underworld, and that was not something she understood at all.

"Just give it a thought," he said with a grin. "We'll talk tomorrow. And in the meantime, I believe there are several beautiful young ladies I could charm into giving me a dance."

"I'm sure there are," she said with a laugh. Then she ducked away. Her schedule for tomorrow was rapidly overflowing, but that was good. As opposed to the endless sameness of her life before, every day seemed filled with exciting new possibilities. It made her giddy. Apparently, one could have a wonderful life without marriage or children. And it appeared that was what was in store for her.

She made it to the upper deck and found that the musicians were already in their place. Lilah glanced down at the gallery below and saw that most of Aaron's guests were there and Aaron was just then looking at his pocket watch. He knew it was time to open the ball, and right on cue, he looked up to the upper gallery where she stood.

They were several yards and a floor apart, and yet her breath squeezed in her throat. How handsome he was, and when their eyes met, she felt as she always did in his arms. As if the world had narrowed down to the two of them.

Then he smiled at her, and her world brightened. She didn't care that they'd never wed, didn't care that she'd tumbled down from the elite world of the *ton* to the life of a working person. If only they had found a way.

Swallowing back her tears, she turned to the musicians. At her cue, they struck three loud notes. The guests obediently quieted as Aaron took Clara's hand and walked her out to the center of the ballroom. After the obligatory welcome speech, brother and sister would dance together for the opening number. Except as Aaron began to speak, Clara waved her hello, then drifted back into the crowd.

How odd.

It was hard for Lilah to hear from up here, though Aaron's voice carried relatively well. He thanked everyone for coming, said something about the drink a guest was imbibing that made everyone laugh, and then he turned toward the upper gallery. Obviously, he meant to direct the musicians to begin, but instead of doing that, he called out very loudly.

"There is someone especially whom I wish to bring to your attention. She has been invaluable in assisting my sister in the preparations for today's events, but more than that, she has been of special significance to me. Miss Rees, could you come down here please?"

What? *What?*

This was his night. He'd been fully settled with his title today and tonight was his celebration. Whyever would he want to taint that by publicly acknowledging her, a known bastard? But there was no help for it now. She had to come down from the upper deck. She had to maneuver her way through the entire crowd while he continued to speak.

"And while the lady comes down from her perch, I should like to enumerate some of the wonders I have learned of her. We first met when she became close friends with my sister Clara. In that time, I've noticed such wonderful things about her. Her beauty, of course, is clear to everyone. But she is also clever enough to match wits with me and my sister. No small feat when it comes to Clara."

Chuckles sounded from all around at that. Clara said, "Exactly right."

"Then I began to discover her many virtues."

It was fortunate she was out of hearing for much of what he said because she could not be called "virtuous" in any traditional sense. But she heard enough. He called her industrious, kind, and chaste. That last had her blushing to a bright red.

By the time she made it to his side, he had set her up to sound like the Madonna herself, and Lilah's face was burning with embarrassment. Such overwhelming admiration was unnecessary though she did appreciate his full-throated support of her character. That would help at the registry office and would certainly ease her family's concern about her staying in Aaron's household. But it was time for this speech to end. He was not at the House of Lords. She was not one of the veterans in need of government support. She was a woman who was unused to such focused attention. And so she said to him in an undertone.

"My lord, please stop. This is most unusual."

"Yes, it is," he said as he turned to look at her. "But I have not come to the most important part." He gazed at her with a warmth that made her toes curl. "I meant to do this earlier, but then I realized that my first act as an earl should be to claim my countess."

He sank down to one knee before her. She saw it happening, and her mind stuttered at the sight. He couldn't possibly be proposing to her. In public! And yet as she gaped at him, he continued speaking.

"Lilah, I have lately been reminded that an earl should be an example of the best. I have failed in that. I didn't see the good work you do at the registry office. I didn't value your character as equal to my own when you are really so much better than I. And most of all, I didn't understand that love means letting you choose your path in all things. Even after we're married. But I vow to give you everything you want, my love, including my respect. If only you will make me the happiest man on earth. Say you will be my bride."

This couldn't be happening. On the day when she had finally accepted that she had a full life without her greatest dream, here was Aaron offering her everything. She couldn't speak. She couldn't breathe. And yet her heart was bursting.

He loved and respected her! Finally, he had said it to her. And not just to her but to an entire ballroom of people of the *ton*!

"Aaron," she managed to whisper. He looked at her with love shining through his eyes, and she formed her answer, but she didn't give it breath. She couldn't. Not with a loud Scottish voice interrupting them.

"Wait! Wait! Miss Rees, you must hear me first."

She looked up just as Clara cried out. "Liam! You're back?"

"Loughton," Aaron snapped. "What the devil are you doing?"

The crowd parted just enough for Lord Loughton to push through. He was waving a piece of paper in front of him. "My apologies. My lord. Miss Rees. I came as quickly as I could."

"Can't it wait?" asked Aaron. He was still down on one knee and looking like he wanted to punch the Scotsman.

"Not really. Well, it could, but…" He took a deep breath. "Miss Rees, you should know that you have a sizable inheritance. It was given specifically to your mother and then to any child of hers."

"What?" she gasped.

He passed her the piece of paper. She glanced at it, but she could not understand one word of it. The words were clear enough, but her head was spinning. "Please explain," she said.

"Lord Kittrel mentioned to me about the letters from Scotland that were sent to your mother. He asked me to investigate from the Scottish side, if I could."

Aaron huffed out a breath. "But I didn't ask you to give us the results now. In the middle of my proposal!"

"Er, no. Of course not. But if she found out afterwards, she'd never know if you proposed out of love or because of—"

"Her money," finished Clara as she clapped her hands. "Of course. Very clever of you."

Lord Loughton flashed her a grateful smile. "In any event, Miss Rees, I daresay you're an heiress now. The money was your mother's and specifically for any child of hers." He made a vague gesture. "There was some scurvishness about it, to be sure, but the document never said anything about legitimate children. I made that point quite clearly." He grinned. "So the money is yours. You're an heiress."

From the side, she heard the dowager countess speak. "That's what her father meant. He said she had noble blood *and money*. That's what he meant!"

Lilah looked down at the paper in her hand then looked back at Lord Loughton. "I don't understand. How is this possible?"

"It was your grandfather. He reserved it for your mother upon her return to Scotland. Your mother and any of her children. The will stated it quite clearly. It was his way of trying to bring her back, I suppose. And now it's yours. You only have to go there and claim it."

Lilah stared at the man, her mind whirling. Why hadn't her mother said anything? But of course, she'd died when Lilah was nine years old. She must have said something to her father.

"Papa used to say he would take me to Scotland when I was old enough. He said that we would go on a special trip when it was time." But then he'd died before she'd been out of her teens.

"I knew he had a plan," her adoptive mother repeated.

"That means," continued Lord Loughton, "that you can choose your life however you want. You needn't work if you don't want to. You needn't marry if you don't want to. It's all available to you."

Yes, it was. But it had been before her inheritance had arrived. It was available because she'd worked for it, but also because Aaron was on his knee right now proposing to her.

"I didn't know, Lilah," Aaron said as he grabbed her hand. "I'm not proposing because of your money. I'm doing it because I love you. Because I respect you. Because I can't live without you—"

"Yes," she interrupted. "Yes, Aaron, I will marry you."

His eyes widened and his face lit up with joy. "Truly? Yes?"

She laughed. "Of course, yes! How could you doubt it? I love you!" And she was strong enough now to hold firm for what she wanted even against Lord Ares himself.

And then while all stood by and watched, he slid a ring onto her finger. It had a modern design of emeralds entwined together. "You're mine now, Lilah. I won't release you ever."

"And you're mine," she said happily.

"I love you," he said as he rose before her. Then he abruptly gripped her about the hips and spun her around. "I love you!" he shouted, as if it were a victory cry from Lord Ares himself. And she laughed because her heart was full, and all her wildest dreams had come true.

About the Author

A *USA Today* Bestseller, JADE LEE has been scripting love stories since she first picked up a set of paper dolls. Ball gowns and rakish lords caught her attention early (thank you Georgette Heyer), and her fascination with historical romance began. Author of more than 30 regency romances, Jade has a gift for creating a lively world, witty dialogue, and hot, sexy humor. Jade also writes contemporary and paranormal romance as Kathy Lyons. Together, they've won several industry awards, including the *Prism—Best of the Best, Romantic Times Reviewer's Choice,* and *Fresh Fiction's* Steamiest Read. Even though Kathy (and Jade) have written over 60 romance novels, she's just getting started. Check out her latest news at www.KathyLyons.com, Facebook: JadeLeeAuthor, and Twitter: JadeLeeAuthor. Instagram: KathyLyonsAuthor.